The challenge.

"The King desires to demonstrate to three human beings from this era of earth-time the glories of His Kingdom over yours. Therefore, He will select three people from North America who presently are in your grasp. These three will be exposed to life in the Kingdom as it will be in A.D. 2084.

"In the interest of fairness, the threesome will also be given into your custody so they may see the Kingdom of Darkness. After a few days, each will decide which kingdom he chooses. The choice each makes will be for eternity. Do you agree to the challenge, Zadock?"

The reply.

"Of course I do! So will Prince Lucifer. We'll see whose glory is enhanced by this fool idea of your king. By the end of this test we will have three more recruits for the Great War!"

The contest was <u>on</u>.

Also by Larry W. Poland

*How to Prepare for
The Coming Persecution*

2084

A NOVEL

Larry W. Poland, Ph.D.

Here's Life Publishers

First Printing, September 1991

Published by
HERE'S LIFE PUBLISHERS, INC.
P. O. Box 1576
San Bernardino, CA 92402

Library of Congress Cataloging-in-Publication Data
Poland, Larry W.
   2084 : a novel / Larry W. Poland
     p.   cm.
   ISBN 0-89840-310-3
   I. Title.
PS3566.0417A617   1991
813'.54—dc20   91-22306
                    CIP

Cover design and illustration by Garborg Design Works

For More Information, Write:

L.I.F.E.—P.O. Box A399, Sydney South 2000, Australia
Campus Crusade for Christ of Canada—Box 300, Vancouver, B.C., V6C 2X3, Canada
Campus Crusade for Christ—Pearl Assurance House, 4 Temple Row, Birmingham, B2 5HG, England
Lay Institute for Evangelism—P.O. Box 8786, Auckland 3, New Zealand
Campus Crusade for Christ—P.O. Box 240, Raffles City Post Office, Singapore 9117
Great Commission Movement of Nigeria—P.O. Box 500, Jos, Plateau State Nigeria, West Africa
Campus Crusade for Christ International—Arrowhead Springs, San Bernardino, CA 92414, U.S.A.

To
Frank J. Poland
whose unbroken faithfulness to The King
will surely earn him a governorship in the Kingdom
and to
Alta E. Poland
who is now with The King getting things ready
for her husband's and her son's arrival.

Acknowledgments

My thanks to Dan Benson and Les Stobbe of Here's Life Publishers, for believing in me enough to challenge me to stretch beyond the limits of my previous experience to the writing of my first book-length fiction.

My deepest appreciation to Donna Fletcher Crow, who not only believed in me and my ability to take on this project but who also believed in the vision of this book enough to spend countless hours editing, tutoring, proposing, correcting, and prayerfully interacting with the story and with me that this vision might be revealed.

Loving gratitude to my wife, Donna Lynn, who bore additional responsibilities to enable me to meet deadlines, cheered me on in the long days and nights of writing, and whose twenty-nine years of love and faithfulness have provided the foundational support for most of my adult life achievement.

Many thanks to the staff teams at Trinity Evangelical Free Church and Mastermedia International who—during the pressure to create this story—not only picked up the slack from their weary or distracted CEO but who also prayed for and cheered on the project.

Preface

The Time of This Story

Time on this planet is moving toward a climax, an end to life as we know it. A score of biblical prophets have declared it and have described this "end time." Jesus Christ announced it, confirmed the prophetic utterings of the past, and staked His deity on the reality of it. But God has kept to Himself the exact schedule of end-time events, making sure that no man knows the timetable.[1]

The year 2084 was chosen as a play on George Orwell's *1984*, not as a prediction of the timing of these predicted, future events. The date is useful in denoting some time in the future—some time the Bible assures us *will* come—whatever the date on earthly calendars when it actually does.

While the events of these last days are revealed in the Scriptures, they are frequently disclosed in veiled language or in symbolic representations. A general order of events is presented, but the specifics of the order are often confusing or seemingly contradictory. Therefore, biblical scholars differ widely on the sequence, timing, and even the literal reality of some events. Some have built whole systems of theology around their chronologies and interpretations. It is not my purpose in this book to enter this debate. It is enough for me and for you, the reader, to know that the end will come—the end to the present world order like the end to our earthly lives.

One biblical picture is clear and consistent. At death every person enters one of two settings. A person who has placed his faith in God goes to be with Him and with others who were trusting Him at death. This is a place of eternal bliss. A person who has not trusted God with his life goes to be with God's arch enemy, Satan, and with others who did not place their lives in God's hands during their earthly lives. This is a place of eternal discomfort. Even as you read these words, there are multitudes abiding in these two environments referred to in the New Testament as Paradise[2] and Hades.[3]

Our story—the Prologue—opens in Paradise in our time.

Jesus Christ promised that, after His return to earth with His believers, He will defeat the evil world structure, bind Satan and his cohorts, and set up a one-thousand-year, perfect world order on earth.[4]

This millennial kingdom of peace and righteousness is the setting for most of our story—chapters 1 through 14—in the year 2084.

In chapter 15 our characters are given a glimpse of events which take place after the end of the Kingdom reign and after a final Great War for which Satan and the demonic orders are released from their imprisonment. This war spells the ultimate and final defeat for all of the wicked, both human and angelic, and precedes the final personal reckoning of every man and woman before God at a Great White Throne.[5]

Chapters 15-17 take place at the time and in the vicinity of this final, judicial sentencing of all who have not made their peace with God. This is the point of entrance into eternal bliss for those who trust in God. Perhaps, for the sake of our eternal setting, it is the year A.D. 3010 or later, just after the Great War.

We hope that this story of three who visit these future sites and become part of these dramatic events will give you a hint of the beauty and glory which awaits those who trust in the true and living God. But one promise we are assured of in Scripture: that no earthly imagination can possibly conceive how magnificent the heavenly Kingdom will actually be. I am the first to admit to that limitation, and can only look forward to the real thing.

LARRY W. POLAND

2084

No eye has seen,
No ear has heard,
No mind has conceived,
What God has prepared for those
who love Him.

—1 Corinthians 2:9

Prologue

The Face-Off

In Our Time, In Paradise

An unsettling movement of forces was stirring the energy fields around Jireh Ben-David. Little shivers rippled his skin and the hair on the back of his neck bristled.

Something uncommon—against the natural laws—was about to happen. The delicate, spiritual harmony which marked the environs was agitated as it had never been before. But then, never before had a commander from the Kingdom of Darkness been granted entrance to the realm of Paradise.

The wind stopped its gentle caresses of the landscape. The cloudless sky seemed filled with eyes and ears watching and listening for what would happen. The King's people set aside their daily routines to pray for the success of the encounter, to pray that The King's will would be done "in Heaven as it is on earth"—as they knew it ultimately would be.

Jireh Ben-David sat atop the hill alone, a magnificent, dark-skinned man who had persevered in trusting his God amidst the religious hostility of his Moroccan homeland. This man, who had known nothing but poverty and servitude in his earth life, now enjoyed the riches and power of Paradise privilege. Now he was preparing to face the greatest challenge of his life, praying that he could stand up to the supernatural tasks the Savior had assigned him.

As Jireh waited, he reflected somewhat randomly. This was all so new and strange, this favor The King had granted him. The confidence He had placed in Jireh, choosing him for this crucial mission, was gratifying, but Ben-David's new name still had a strange ring to it. It was normal to want to return to the Moorish name he had used in earth life. His new name sounded so, well, Jewish. *But then,* he thought, *this name bears honor, the honor of a "governor designate" when The King establishes His kingdom. For that I will get used to it—joyfully!*

There was no sign of the evil commander yet, but many signs of the presence of the Kingdom of Darkness. Jireh struggled to avoid succumbing to *temptation*—a foreign experience since death had taken him from his earth life and brought him to live with his Lord. It was so strange once again to feel the inner gravitational pull, the spiritual down-draft on his soul. It had been so wonderful for these seven years to be free of the good-man/bad-man war within him. To sense it now—in ever-so-slight a degree—brought back unpleasant memories. They were memories of those times when he actually succumbed to the vile, self-exalting, law-breaking excesses of his earthly flesh. From immoderate indulgence in food to sexual lust, from ill-managed anger to self-righteous pride—the old vices crept back into his memory, a memory cleansed of them all since he had received his new body, mind and spirit upon entering Paradise. How great it had been living in Paradise! Every day a euphoric experience.

Jireh knew today would be different. He was no longer saddled with the nature he had carried with him during his earth life—the inner dissonance which had tormented him even after he met the Redeemer. That damnable defect had been removed in his transfiguration and no longer troubled him. Still, twinges of temptation—to be anxious, to doubt—picked at him.

The King's instructions had been clear: *Entertain the enemy commander only long enough to make the challenge. Execute the challenge with boldness, and interact only so long as is necessary to get a response. Then send the demon chief back to his nefarious world!*

It was so illuminating to interact with his Master. His motives were so totally pure, yet so very different from man's. Here He was, directing a plan to accomplish ten thousand—if not ten million—genius objectives in a single, three-person exercise. Like His testing of Job—the contest with the Prince of Darkness, the torment and restoration of a single man, the moral pressures on the man's wife and family, the philosophical and theological struggles of his earnest-but-misguided friends, and the resulting millennia of moral instruction for hundreds of millions. What infinite cleverness could result from the mission which was about to begin? Jireh could only wonder. But he was determined to do everything his Lord had asked of him—everything. He had been told to come to this hill and wait. He came. He waited.

The atmosphere around Jireh Ben-David darkened as the radiance of the heavens seemed to fade slightly. A spiritual chill fell over him, attempting to steal his joy and quench his power. The Dark Side commander was coming. He could sense it in his soul.

In an instant the demon chief appeared, about fifty yards down the slope. As agreed, he had come alone. Could it be that this physically unimpressive creature was really the Serpent General in Lucifer's forces, this stocky hulk with the dark, deep-set eyes, dressed in the slick, black uniform? Then Jireh reminded himself that this was just the "manifestation of the day," one of many external forms these heinous creatures don to suit their vile objectives. This was obviously his "intimidate the good guy" disguise! It wasn't working.

The commander swaggered arrogantly in deliberate steps up the slope, his arms swinging out from his body and his fist clenching and unclenching. As he drew closer, Jireh could see the burning embers in his eyes, the fire of Hell. His visage was etched with contempt for the Kingdom, for the realm of righteousness, for Jireh. A pronounced sneer crossed his face as if to say, *Why am I wasting my time with you, dog?*

"Commander Zadock?" Jireh asked boldly.

"Zadock *the Third*, if you don't mind." The visitor's sarcasm sliced the thick atmosphere.

Jireh did not rise. That was his directive. Rising would show respect, deference. No citizen of heavenly realms ever defers to servants of the Prince of Darkness. Power, authority, and respect all flow the other way.

"I'll get right to the point, commander. The King—"

"*Your* king!" Zadock bellowed.

"*The* King!" Jireh held firm.

Zadock muttered an obscenity.

Jireh continued. "The King desires to offer a challenge to you and your commander-in-chief. He desires to demonstrate the righteous power of the Kingdom which He soon will set up on earth—after He returns there for His bride, the Church of Jesus Christ."[6]

"*Whore* is a better description than bride!" The Serpent General stared bullets into Jireh Ben-David, then turned halfway away from him, crossed his arms arrogantly and lobbed sarcastic comments over his left shoulder like grenades.

"Commander, I think you would be wise to watch your mouth," Jireh said. "You've read The Book. You know the time I'm referring to is one when you and your cronies are given a one-thousand-year, all-expense-paid 'vacation' on bread and water."[7] Jireh was not unkind, just clearly in charge. Now that the protocol of rank had been observed, he stood to emphasize his point.

"Not a chance such imprisonment will happen!" Zadock snorted in derision. "That's a prophetic lie!"

Jireh ignored the mockery. "The King desires to demonstrate to three human beings from this era of earth-time the glories of His kingdom over yours, the contrast between life in our realm and life in yours. Therefore, He will select three people from North America who presently are in your grasp. These three will be exposed to life in the Kingdom as it will be in 2084, a time when I will have accepted The King's appointment as a provincial governor."

"So you're going to be a big cheese! No doubt a recipient of the Goody-Two-Shoes Award!" Zadock chortled. The visitor was intrigued now, listening intently, undoubtedly scheming how this offer might be twisted to the advantage of the powers of Hell.

"These three will be shown the Kingdom in all its glory. But—in the interest of fairness—The King has determined that the threesome also be given into your custody so that they may see the Kingdom of Darkness, hear a presentation of life in your domain. After a few days of this exposure, The King will ask each to decide which kingdom he chooses. The choice each makes will be confirmed for eternity. The ultimate kingdom citizenship of each will be secured and irrevocable." Jireh studied Zadock as the Serpent General turned to face him. Zadock looked as if his mind was racing in high gear, plotting, calculating. "Sound fair enough?" Jireh asked.

The defiant sneer returned to the Serpent General's face. "Sounds like a cake walk! If you start with people from the earth at this time, we can't lose. Commander

Lucifer has been firmly enthroned as the Prince of the
World for so many generations that every earthly culture
essentially socializes humans to our kingdom's values.
No matter who you choose—except those psychotic
born-againers of yours—they will already possess *our*
worldview. We will have an unbeatable edge!" Zadock
was enjoying his boast. His barrel chest swelled to full
capacity. "And if you pick *old* humans, you won't have a
snowball's chance in . . . you won't have a chance!" He
roared in laughter at his own half-joke.

Jireh didn't smile. "That's where you're wrong,
Zadock. We will capture the soul of at least one of the
three, even if each makes his own free choice. We are sure
of that." Jireh was confident, firm. "The capture of even
one who is so firmly in your grip, so thoroughly brain-
washed to your worldview, will demonstrate to the
universe the transcending greatness of The King and of
His kingdom and the power of the Truth over lies. The
story of these conversions will be told throughout the
ages as a point of glory for our King."

"I may vomit! If your god were not such an
egomaniac, he wouldn't be running around thinking up
schemes to bring glory to himself!"

When will they ever learn? Jireh breathed to himself.
His eyes locked onto the fiery pupils of his adversary.
"Do you agree to the challenge, Zadock?"

"Of course I do! So will Prince Lucifer!" Zadock the
Third was salivating at the prospect of victory. "We'll see
whose glory is enhanced by this damn-fool idea of your
king! By the end of this test we will have three more
recruits for the Great War!" The Serpent General glared
at Jireh and added, "You know about the Great War . . .
you've . . . *read the Book!*"[8] His words were dagger-edged.

"Yes, and I've read who wins that war," Jireh
replied, speaking more pleasantly than Zadock deserved.

"More lies!" the visitor bellowed. "Lies! Lies! Lies!" The ember eyes were now flame throwers.

Jireh ignored the theatrics. "Shortly The King will make His selection of the three individuals. After a time with us, they will be surrendered to your custody until we bring them back to hear their decisions. Agreed?"

"Agreed." Zadock snarled, peering out from under the awning of his bushy, black eyebrows.

"Then let's shake." Jireh extended his hand to Zadock. As if weighing whether he should lower himself to any social gesture with a low-life like Jireh Ben-David, Zadock studied Jireh's hand for moment. Finally, condescending, he extended his. As he did, a large, gold, diamond-studded band with a pentagram on its crown glistened from his ring finger.

Zadock muttered some indistinguishable curse under his breath and spun away from Jireh. With two swift strides he vanished in a small cloud of darkened atmosphere.

The Kingdom was fully aware that Zadock had left. Now that he was gone, the breezes stopped holding their breaths. The atmosphere relaxed. The invisible eyes and ears in the heavens focused once again on other parts of the business of the universe. The cold spiritual chill and psychic darkness lifted from Jireh Ben-David and fled the Kingdom as the Kingdom subjects wrapped up their special prayers with words of thanksgiving and returned to their daily involvements.

Jireh knew he'd see Zadock again. What a thrill it would be to see this sinister braggart feasting on his own mockery. One thing was sure, Jireh had to handle this royal mission with extreme diligence and care—to make sure it turned out a victory for the Kingdom and The King.

He relaxed. His first assignment had been carried

out. Then it hit him: This was not the end of the confrontation, but just the beginning. The contest was *on*.

1

Light Years Away

2084 in the Kingdom

An other-world glow filtered through the tall forest jungles around Karae, creating a pyramid of light beams around her from a focal point above. Not since her visit to the giant redwoods had she viewed such awe-inspiring towers of bark and branches. Not since she was a tyke had she felt so eclipsed by the grandeur of stately giants like the ones which now embraced her. *Never* had she sensed that light had personality, that sunbeams were messengers, that shadows were narrators poised to tell stories that would change her life forever.

Where was she? She didn't recognize this place. How did she get here? In spite of the beauty surrounding her, Karae felt alone in the midst of the towering forest. It was the aloneness of having gotten off the train at a rural stop in a foreign land and not seeing a soul who understood, who cared, who could guide.

Her mind struggled to reconstruct the events in her life just before finding herself here. She had been on the 210 freeway driving home from Burbank. She and her mother were driving back from the hospital where her mother had undergone a heart checkup. She remembered approaching the Lake Avenue Exit, negotiating onto the exit ramp.

Her mind stalled. *I can't remember anything after that. Why can't I remember what happened next? What happened to the car? What happened to Mom?* There were no answers, only a kind of sickening silence.

Like waking from a deep sleep and not knowing where you are, Karae surveyed this strange, primeval forest. She had not yet decided whether she was dreaming, or how she had gotten here, yet in her spirit she was not afraid. A peace possessed her—like having your daddy hold your hand in the dark or riding with a peace officer through a violent neighborhood, or being carried across the honeymoon threshold by one strong enough to conquer you but tender enough to kiss you.[9]

Peace in the atmosphere. Strange.

She looked at herself. Her tailored, pinstriped, $500 business suit was hardly jungle apparel, the expensive silk blouse hardly safari wear. She was grateful she had changed out of her pumps before taking her mom to the doctor after work. She brushed away some tiny wild flowers which clung to her skirt and stroked the wavy, jet-black hair away from her pretty face. Pulling a small compact from her pocket, she checked the mirror, more to see if this were really she than to evaluate the state of her eye shadow. It was Karae in the reflection, all right. She brushed a smudge from her coffee-tinted cheek and put the compact away. Her eyes once more drank in the strange loveliness of her surroundings.

You can't stand here entranced forever, she rebuked herself. *This isn't the Louvre!* Karae collected her thoughts as she stepped cautiously over the luxuriant carpet of green which hugged the bases of the regal monoliths around her. *I must find someone who can tell me where I am, someone who can get me home.* At the thought of home, a sickening sensation engulfed her. For a half second it occurred to her that if she didn't figure out what was happening, she might never see home again. Her ailing mother would die without her. A clearing . . . if only she could find a clearing. Somehow she had to get out of here. She had to find someone who could help. Somehow . . .

There were no clearings—nothing but dense, fern-like growth, draperies of Hunter green, and flowers. Flowers! Giant orchid-like blossoms two feet in diameter, leis of extravagant color necklacing branches and boughs thirty, fifty, maybe seventy-five feet up into the foliage. And at her feet zillions of minuscule blossoms in a full spectrum of colors, all growing *in the shade.*[10]

Then, as if a chamber ensemble had just begun to play, she heard the sounds. If they were the whistles and chirps of birds, she saw none. If they were the organ pipes and oboes of the wind in the leaves, she felt no breeze. If they were the blended voices of some *a cappella* choir, she saw no one. Yet she heard them all, a fugue, a sonata, a hymn, a lullaby in whole notes and eighth notes and rests. All sounds from Nature—but Nature like no Nature she had ever known.

Pausing occasionally to take in the stunning audile and visual beauty of this wonderland, she tiptoed, then sprinted, then plodded, then paced for hours with no real clearings, no direction, no people . . . not a single soul. Her heart kept pace with her feet, dancing, then trudging, then stopping . . . no other heart to beat with hers.

Home. Where was it? How could she ever find it? Would she ever see it again? She fought off the depressing feelings tied to those questions and sat down. This was no longer a dream. It was real. But every time she asked herself where she was, and how she had gotten to this other-world, the answer eluded her. Putting her face in her hands, she repeated, "There has to be a way out of here. There has to be . . . "

For a man who has lived on both sides of the Pacific, Won Kim thought to himself, I should be able to figure out this strange environment. Won's Ph.D. in microbiology with a minor in computer programming, his analytical skills, and his thorough, stoic approach were all failing him now. There was something—there were *lots* of some-things—in this place which didn't compute.

Won stood transfixed. The waist-length green lab coat hung loosely over his slight frame. His open-collared white dress shirt protruded a scientifically accurate one-half inch below both coat sleeves. The thick, rimless glasses obscured little of the lightly olive complexion of his boyish face. His blue-black hair was parted with the accuracy of an algebraic equation and slicked down nicely, except for sprouts on his double crown which had proved the nemesis of all his barbers. Won scratched his head more in puzzlement than in itch-relief.

The light in the sky—like none Won had ever seen—had the warm glow of twilight but the ample lumens of midday. It came from everywhere at the same time, not from the sun. Where *was* the sun?

There was no sun, no visible east or west, no sharp shadows all creating straight lines from their edges to the blazing ball somewhere above the horizon. It was, well, *indirect* light.[11] Shadows, soft ones, were cast in starburst patterns around every vertical object. And as one moved, the shadow stars rotated but didn't disappear or change in shape. Won pulled a note pad from his lab coat and jotted notes—like scientific observations—of the unusual things he saw.

From the foothills where he stood, Won could see a mountain "starburst" to the north of him, or whatever direction it was. And the mountain was different, very different. There was no timber line. Despite the height, maybe 20,000 feet, lush vegetation grew to the pinnacle which lacked the snowcap common to other mountains this size.[12] If he wasn't mistaken, he could see orchards growing on the mountain sides—unplanted, natural orchards at three-fourths the altitude of the peak. Fountains of sparkling, crystalline water flowed directly out of the largest masses of granite to splash and prance their way down through the crags and crevasses to the foothills where he stood in wonder.

"Impossible!" Won exclaimed, observing the water-from-the-rock phenomenon. But some stirring in his spirit shouted, *POSSIBLE!* And, as if soundly rebuked by some cosmic post-doctoral authority, Won set aside the matter "for further research." He had more pressing concerns, like finding out where he was, why he had suddenly found himself in this strange environment, and how to get back to the lab.

He trekked down the lush hillside, across water-colored meadows which lay like gargantuan Amish quilts with acre-sized patches of wild flowers stitched together with streams and hedgerows.

His mind did a scan of all the places in the world he had visited, all the places he'd seen in pictures, all the places he'd been told about. The discriminating attributes of this place fit none of them. *I came all the way to America from Korea to end up here? I earned a doctorate in science to perish in a lost wilderness? I invested all those years on research and am considered for a Nobel prize only to die in the wild? It doesn't make sense!* He shook his head from side to side as he traversed a tiny stream of gurgling, clear liquid.

Life had not been easy for Won. He was the oldest of seven children, the one chosen to emigrate to America from a suburb of Seoul with his father at age 13. He had handled most of the domestic chores for the two of them—washing, cooking, and scrubbing their tiny, rented room—while his dad worked day labor until he had saved enough to buy a tiny liquor store. Then Won was stock boy, janitor and part-time clerk until they had set aside enough money to bring the rest of the family to the U. S.

That was a long, hard, six years, but not so hard as pursuing college in his second language and then doing graduate work in another culture. His parents burned candles and offered sacrifices to the spirits at a tiny in-home shrine for success and prosperity. Won didn't buy those notions. He burned the candle at both ends and reached deep within his own spirit to succeed. He had made it by demonstrating the indomitable perseverance which seemed to be formed in the genetic structure of the Kim family. Now, at age thirty-five in an unfamiliar world, Won feared he would lose it all.

He had to get back to Austin. Harry, his teaching assistant, knew the "how" of their research but not the "why." He could never put the data into a form that would impress the Nobel evaluators. If that research didn't get finished right and get finished now, Won was in trouble. Further delay could risk all the efforts of the University of Texas to establish the leading microbiology research lab in the nation, threaten their federal funding, and cost them hundreds of thousands of dollars in lost time and wasted effort.

Won probed his memory gap, struggling to reconstruct the events between his working in his lab and arriving here. There were no events between! He and Harry had been working on an experiment, taking readings from a computer-driven measuring device. Two other researchers were working with nitroglycerine and volatile chemicals on the other side of the small laboratory. That is all he could remember. Questions.

Wherever in the world is this? Won thought again, this

time with more urgency. Again a rebuttal from his inner man seemed to answer, . . . *a new world, Won, one you've never visited before. Stop trying to analyze it, and enjoy it.* But since analysis was his stock-in-trade, this was an unacceptable answer.

As he bent down to examine the leaf structure of a collar-button-sized wild flower, he weighed options for getting himself out of his fix. If only he had a vehicle like Captain Kirk's *Enterprise.* Then he could get "beamed" out of here!

All riiiight, what a place!" exulted Arthur "Mac" McNeal aloud as he splashed merrily in the water of the river beach. "Eat your heart out, Club Med!" Now, if he could just find a happy hour somewhere, a place to grab a little liquid refreshment so he could wiggle his toes in the sand, down the bubbly, and soak in the scenes. Even his Viewmaster didn't have 3-Ds like these!

But there were no river bank watering holes, no bottled enjoyment, no leggy ladies hanging off bar stools. In fact, for the first time in his life, entertaining thoughts of these sensual pleasures made him feel a little uncomfortable, like he had just let an expletive slip in front of the minister. "But, what the hey," Mac recomposed himself. "I've got exploring to do."

Explore he did. Up from the banks of this sandwrapped tributary Mac cavorted over a pile of rocks that had been stacked as if by some giant stone mason a few yards from the water. Finding his way hand-over-foot to the top of this horizontal Stonehenge gave him a commanding 360-degree view of the area.

Mac's lizard-skin cowboy boots had come in handy, boots he wore to be hip. He'd seen few cows and no ranches growing up in urban Ohio. But the boots were the finishing touch on his Hollywood-casual image.

Tight, pre-washed, pre-faded designer jeans and a bold-ly-styled, powder-blue knit shirt with a polo player stitched into it contributed to the style. Mac's hard-body physique belied his lack of discipline, and his out-of-control locks of fashionably long, blonde hair made him an object of attraction for a continuous string of eligible and even ineligible ladies.

Mac wore blue a lot because he knew it accentuated the azure in his eyes. They were bright and impish, and seemed to emit some kind of electrical charges that intrigued, flirted, persuaded, or seduced as Mac altered their mysterious current. Ten thousand dollars' worth of orthodontics had given him an almost-too-perfect smile, but one he could vary to suit his objectives. His natural, fair complexion and baby's skin was the envy of the coterie of young women who had pressed their cheeks to his. The male and female consensus was that Mac was a lot more good looking than he was good.

He stuck his hands into the waist of his jeans as if to cover his flat tummy and surveyed the scene. "Awesome," he gasped as he pivoted slowly, taking in the circumference of natural wonders. The fast-moving river disappeared into a stand of trees taller than any he had ever seen back home, a dense forest rising maybe one hundred feet or more out of the flatlands on both sides of the river. Beyond the forest the foothills of a Fuji-like peak rolled into the mountain itself, which jutted thousands of feet into the air.

The air was clear, not like the air in the urban sprawl he called home. In fact, the air was so crystalline that even distant objects seemed to possess serrated edges, edges which made the scenery stand out like the standups in those kid's books which jump out at you from the book's binding when the pages are opened. And no clouds . . . why no clouds? The humidity was perfect and the temperature a consistent and comfortable 70ish, as if the whole planet were encased in a galactic greenhouse with a perfectly controlled climate.

Hardly a crowd around here, Mac reflected. *If anybody called this party, I must be here on the wrong day to catch the action.*

The last thing Mac remembered before opening his eyes in this new world was finishing a cocktail at the after-work happy hour down at the Kit Kat Lounge. He often stopped by on his way home from his office to flirt with the girls, spar with the bartender, and exchange jokes with the guys. "Something's great about drinkin' buddies," he would often say. "They may be lounge lizards, but they are what they are. They are authentic!" Often he would add, "A whole lot fewer hypocrites in saloons than in churches." That line usually drew affirmative nods down the bar.

He mused about where the action might be in this unspoiled wonderland. It occurred to him that bird watching, and chasing the giant butterflies that flip-flapped over the landscape around him, might be the only activities permitted in this calendar-art valley. That thought was a little unnerving! He missed the Kit Kat. He missed Wanda, his current lover. He missed the sales meetings. "Nothing like the high-octane hype of a sales meeting to get the juices flowing," he would often say.

Mac didn't miss Mass. Despite his Catholic upbringing, Mac had joined other Irish who had relegated their faith to the level of a rabbit's foot, a lucky charm, a four-leaf clover. The Church was a handy thing to have around to make you feel like you had the metaphysical bases covered when all else failed. Mass was reserved for the infrequent visits of his mother—she insisted they attend—and he hated going. Mac's view was that religion was near the bottom of the hierarchy of priorities. It definitely was not something you would let get in the way of doing your own thing or having a good time.

So far this new place was Dullsville. A nice place to visit, as the saying went, but . . . He mulled over the rest of the thought—living here—for a number of minutes, then snapped himself back and muttered "What the hey" and started down over the rock pile toward wherever.

Karae was still intermittently bouncing and dragging through her forest conclaves, stopping now and then to romanticize over the beauty in which she had somehow been placed. It seemed that everywhere was a perfectly framed picture, one that surely would have won first prize in the university Camera Club contest had she only had it to enter back then. The visual feast and symphonic sounds around her had lulled her into a trance-like state, one which covered much of her deepening concern over still not knowing where she was and still not finding even one other person.

Suddenly, a cracking sound. She froze in mid-step. Her mind suddenly jerked into a code-red alert while paralysis grabbed at her. That was not the crack of a falling branch. Come to think of it, there *were no* dead or dying branches. Every tree was pure and clean and healthy, as if laboratory-grown and in perfect fulfillment of the Creator's design.

There it was again! Unless something were crushing something, there would not have been two noises timed so closely. Only large animals or mortals made that kind of forest sound. But she had seen no animals, not even the ugly little creepy-crawlies that inhabited all the forests she had entered before.

More cracking, breaking sounds! Then there was movement in the tropical plant about twenty feet away— not *far enough* away! Karae glanced quickly around for the fastest escape route while keeping one eye fixed on the area where the sounds and movement originated. Her shoes weighed like concrete blocks on her feet and her arms felt like they were glued to her body.

A grunting, snorting noise.

Now her heart air-hammered her breast, and the veins seemed to swell in her neck. It had to be a *being*.

Then, like the stage curtain at a theater, the foliage parted, and standing before her—towering over her a good three feet—was a gigantic tiger, a beast of elephantine proportions with gorgeous stripes and a lithe tail which swished back and forth against the foliage. His piercing eyes were fixed on Karae, and his mouth opened to a grin as though dinner were about to be served. Suddenly, the monstrous feline sprang for her.

Splitting for her escape route, Karae dashed into the forest pathways, racing for all she was worth around and through the steeplechase course which lay before her. The powerful beast behind her had taken up the chase. How could she ever stay ahead of him? The tiger bounded in great leaps after her, deftly maneuvering his giant frame through the trees in pursuit. She stretched every stride, quickly focusing every step lest she fall.

Karae's breath was now coming in agonizingly short bursts. Sharp pains began to tug at her side. The muscles in her legs began to tighten. It was obvious that her mind was making contracts that her body could no longer fulfill. She didn't know how much longer she could last.

That didn't matter to the furry monster on her tail. He seemed hardly phased by the race, barely winded by the hunt. As he drew closer to her, she could hear the great wheezes of his lungs, hear the thunderous pounding of his paws on the earth. She knew it was only a matter of seconds before her body would refuse to cooperate any longer, only moments before he would have her in his grasp despite her painful efforts to drive on.

The gap closed between them as Karae faltered. The

tiger soared in marvelous springs which covered twenty to thirty of her paces in a single leap.

Then it happened. As her left ankle twisted on un-steady footing, Karae felt her body falling sideways into a bed of dense ground cover. She tumbled into the soft cushion of green, and rolled into a face-up position in time to see the behemoth land on all fours over her. As she stared helplessly into the saucer-sized eyes of the panting monster, her vocal chords tightened to scream. But then she was seized, not by the striped goliath peer-ing down at her, but by *peace*—that same, eerie, inner peace which had warmly wrapped her in her first hour in this strange world.

The hot breath of the animal rushed past her ears as the giant mouth drew closer and the cat lowered his body beside hers. Cocking his head a bit to the side, the tiger paused, opened his toothy orifice, then extended his tongue and took one loving swipe up the side of Karae's face.

"Yuck," she said, half in disgust at the sandpapery greeting and half in relief that the creature had not been pausing to say grace. She raised her hand to stay the follow-through of another wet kiss and heard a quiet, extended rumble coming from the beast. A feline purr at the lower end of the register came from deep inside the tiger, expressions of affection from the *basso profundo* of the forest.

Gaining confidence now, Karae raised up a bit, and the tiger courteously moved aside enough to let her stand erect. No fear—just peace. She extended her hand to his luxuriant mane and her hand sank into the furry collar. Drawing closer, the tiger nuzzled her hip and rubbed his ear on her side.

Unexpectedly, a tear trickled from Karae's eye and splashed on her cheek. The little girl in her quickly pushed aside all adult restraints, and she reached under the awesome neck with one arm and over it with the other. Her hands barely touched. She buried her head into his and squeezed the powerful neck in her arms. Her new friend rumbled back in his deep-breasted purr. She rested her head on the cushion of fur for a moment, then kissed the velour surface of his boney nose.

Images flashed in rapid multi-media in her mind: the stuffed tiger she received for Christmas when she was seven, the one which kept her safe night after night between the covers; the dream she had had of having a pet tiger all her own; the big picture which hung on the wall in Mrs. Washington's Sunday school classroom, the one with the lion lying down with the lamb;[13] the lioness-with-cubs poster which hung in her college dorm room.

What did all this mean? What kind of world was this in which nature was so extravagantly rich and the beasts of the jungle were tame enough to hug? Or was this a rare domesticated creature that somehow had wandered into the wilds? Wait, no tiger was *this* domesticated! She rubbed the Bengal's furry coat, stroked his velvety ears. He accompanied her with his rumble. Somewhere lay the secret to the mysteries of this strange new world—and the way out of it back home. She had to find both!

Reveling in this free travel package to a very different world, Mac eased from the top of the rock pile and began feeling his way down the boulders the thirty or thirty-five feet to the bottom. He stopped about half-way to observe a stunningly beautiful leaf on a vine which grew out between two of the immense stones. More intricate than anything he had ever seen, the leaf had three levels of leaves-within-leaves. The overall shape was conical, but upon closer inspection was made up of a complex network of leaves which were, in turn, made up of another network of leaves. Mac was no botanist—he'd barely

squeaked by Biology 101 in college—but there was something so unusual about this leaf, this vine, this rock pile,
this valley, this world, that it was beginning to spook him.
Where was he anyway? Was this earth? Had he been
transported by Leprechauns to a distant planet where
Irish go when they've been really good—or really bad?

Preoccupied with his musings about this idyllic
place, Mac unconsciously shifted his footing. His right
foot slipped on some fine grit and in a nanosecond he was
grappling at air handles, trying to stop the inevitable fall
to the rocks below.

"Help!" But no one was within hearing distance
and, if they were, they could not have reached him in time
to help. Terror seized him as he began his plunge. Flop-
ping his arms and legs like a rag doll, Mac made a
desperate stretch for a small sapling growing in the crack
of the rock only to have it brush by his hand.

This is it, he thought as the air rushed by him and he
neared the end of his plunge in a position guaranteed to
end in a crushed skull, broken neck or sure paralysis. But
suddenly, like a plummeting tightrope walker being
caught in a safety net, something slowed his speed and
brought him to a rest *feet down* on the rocks below.[14]

His heart was pounding—but not for long.

"Eagle has landed!" he exclaimed with a guffaw to
whomever might hear, and trekked off toward the river
bank with hardly a second thought as to what forces—or
unseen persons—had kept him from certain injury.

But that was Mac. Spoiled son of a wealthy,
workaholic industrialist. Street-wise and cynical, he was
the product of a big high school's pressure to "be there
or be square." Campus clown of John Hayes High
School's class of '87. Nominated "Most Likely to Be a
Jerk" by his Phi Delta fraternity brothers at Otterbein
College, winner of the homecoming Chug-a-Lug beer
drinking contest, and excelling in mediocrity in anything

that even *smelled* academic. With a wry smile, Mac would quote: "I serve one purpose in this school on which no man can frown; I quietly go to class each day and keep the average down!"

The short link between Mac's mind and his mouth had gotten him everywhere—into deep trouble with a host of authorities, into a street fight with the toughs from a rival, Black neighborhood, into shallow relationships with innumerable ladies, and to the top of the national performance charts in medical equipment sales. As a result he tended to despise rules, ethnics, gold-diggers, and people who couldn't sell, sell, sell! His credo was, "You're not really in trouble unless you can't talk your way out of it." He had talked his way out of most of his troubles and had the arrogance to prove it.

A little scrape with death wasn't going to slow him down. He'd had many such close shaves before, and would probably have more. Brushing off his good fortune as a payoff of some cosmic debt owed to him, Mac bounded down the river bank toward the tall forest, looking for more fun and games. Surely a place this great would offer wine and women if not song—at the end of the trail.

By now Won Kim's wristwatch told him it should be getting dark, but nothing in the heavens was confirming the message. The galactic glow was just as bright and warm as it had been earlier in the day, if a day can be "early" or "late" when there is no sun traversing the sky to define those concepts.

Won was hungry. He had been snacking on the wonderful assortment of wild berries he had found on his way down from the foothills. But now he wanted something more, well, substantial. Hardly had the thought crossed his mind when a gust of wind swept about him. Or at least it felt like wind. With it about a half-dozen pod-like objects floated to the earth within his view.

Reaching down to examine the objects, Won detected a wonderful aroma, something like the smell that used to fill the kitchen when his mother had baked rice cakes. *Do you suppose this is edible?* Won asked himself as the pod-cake became Object of Scientific Analysis Number 71 of his first day in the valley. The consistency was not unlike angel food cake. And the pillow shape was certainly unusual if this had blown in from one of the forest trees. No seeds, no leaves, no bark, no shell, no stem, no variation in consistency.

He broke open the small loaf which fit nicely in the palm of his hand. When he did so, the rich fragrance filled his nostrils. The hunger in his stomach and the aroma of his new discovery joined forces in his mind and sent coded messages to his salivary glands to open up. Won put the cake to his lips. It had barely touched his tongue when an alarm bell went off in his mind.

Could it be poisonous? He lowered the cake and re-examined it, his mind searching known data identifying poisonous plants.

I think the probabilities are less than 5 percent that this is harmful, he concluded. That risk was manageable.

Biting off a chunk of the stuff, Won Kim was awed. It had an incredibly sweet and delicate taste. Whatever its origin, a few of these would be filling and delicious. He would find out soon enough if they were nutritious too. He mentally double-checked the figures on his poison-probability scale and reconfirmed 5 percent or less. Half of the cakes were gone in short order.[15]

As he ate, his mind wandered back to days in Korea before he and his father had come to the States. He remembered the modest apartment in Seoul. It was nothing like his townhouse in Austin. It had small rooms exploding with siblings and bustling with activity. Extended family floated in and out of the tiny quarters like they owned the place. Everything was compressed in size compared to the bigness of America, especially of *Texas* America.

He thought of his American wife, Mary. He missed her now, really missed her. Where was she? Would he see her again? And his two-year-old, Justin. Just thinking of that bubbly little bundle of smiles and hugs made him want to cry. He didn't cry much. It wasn't the way he'd been brought up. But now, what he wouldn't pay to give Justin a couple of bear hugs, toss him in the air like a rocket and catch the little guy in delighted mid-scream. Would Justin grow up without a father, or was this strange world just a dream, a dream you couldn't pinch yourself out of? If only he had more answers and not so many questions.

I was just sitting on a stool in my laboratory processing data, Won tried once again to reconstruct the events which had brought him to this place. *I had just entered a command into the computer and was waiting for confirmation on the screen that the command had been executed.* At that point his mind shifted into overload. He couldn't remember doing anything, seeing anything, feeling anything. *Next thing I knew I was here—wherever here is!*

He pushed aside the hollow ache that was developing inside him and munched on another organic rice cake. Rice. That thought took him back home, too. One thing was a given in Korean homes—rice! Rice in the morning, rice in the evening and rice at noon.

He laughed to himself at the joke his Texas roommate used to share to explain Won's oriental eyes. "You Asians get those slanted eyes from holding your hands to the side of your face in horror every meal as you say, 'Oh, no, not rice again, not rice again!'" The laugh felt good. He realized that he had been awfully intense during this long day, not unlike he often felt at the end of a typical day in his research lab.

Satisfied after his strange-but-delectable meal of Whatever Cakes, Won resumed his hike across the meadows in the direction of the tall forest he had seen from the foothills. Maybe civilization was on the other side of that forest. Perhaps that was the way home from here.

He froze. A human being! About two hundred yards away, just on the edge of the trees, he could make out the form of an attractive, nicely dressed Black woman standing beside something gigantic. No, it couldn't be. But it was! Her arm was gently embracing the muzzle of an eight-foot-tall tiger!

2

Three's a Crowd

Hello," called Karae from the edge of the forest. Her call echoed across the valley. The man in the distance turned in her direction. Karae had spotted the stranger before he spotted her. He was easy to see in the open meadows.

He appeared reluctant to answer her call. Karae didn't know why. Maybe he thought she was some Tarzan's Jane—but she couldn't imagine that she looked the part. Or maybe it was the tiger. Seeing her new furry friend would slow anyone down!

"Hello," Won Kim yelled back.

He appeared harmless enough: all alone, about 5'6" tall, well groomed, straight black Asian hair, round-rimmed glasses, well-worn and out-of-fashion clothing.

"Don't worry about the tiger," she assured the man in a shout. "Can we talk?"

"Sure." Won hesitated for fear the tiger might be setting them both up for a double-decker lunch. But he found his way through the flowers and grass, closer to the forest edge and to the odd couple who watched his approach step by step, his eyes steadied on the animal until he got within twenty or thirty feet of Karae. The tiger had been nibbling on some long grass, but, upon seeing Won coming, turned away from them both and started back into the forest.

"Come back! Come back!" Karae called to the beast. But the jungle cat had other business to tend and couldn't be dissuaded from pursuing it even by a few swats on his backside by Karae.

"Oh, rats," she blurted as Won now came within handshake range. "I didn't want him to leave."

"Well, if he's your pet, won't he come back?"

"Oh, he's not mine. We just met a few hours ago. But I was already in love with him."

The newcomer looked confused. Karae smiled as she watched him try to collect his thoughts. Finally he appeared to relax and extended his hand.

"I'm Won Kim." His handshake was tentative, a bit shy.

"I'm Karae." She grasped the man's hand firmly.

"I like to know people's last names. I guess I'm just not a first-name kind of person."

"Johnson," Karae responded with an understanding smile.

"Pleased to meet you. I guess I usually say that, but this time I really am pleased. I have been here in this valley a whole day, and you are the first soul I've seen."

"You don't live here?" Karae was trying to read his eyes.

"This may sound strange, but I don't even know how I got here—or how to get out!"

"I guess we have more in common than I could have guessed." Karae relaxed a bit, stilled by the misery-loves-company dynamic in their new relationship.

"What do you mean?"

"Well, it just so happens that I have been in this valley a whole day too. And it also just so happens that I don't have a clue how I got here or how to get out."

"You must be kidding." Won sounded tentative, as though processing this new information. "Well, then, what about, er—Garfield? I mean, it's not every day you see an eight-foot cat with a woman in tow."

Karae laughed. It hadn't occurred to her what kind of picture the two of them must have made. She had been so caught up in fellowship with the domesticated beast that a lot of things had escaped her. When she thought about it, Garfield seemed a good name for him.

"Garfield, as you call him, is quite a story. While I was coming through this forest, I heard crackling noises, and he appeared out of the greenery just a few yards away. I took off running—"

Won cut her off. "You didn't need to be scared," he declared rather clinically with an air that indicated a fresh burst of insight. "Because Garfield is herbivorous."[16]

"What do you mean? Tigers are carnivores." Karae had gotten a decent grade in Zoology.

"Not that one. He nibbled on grass like a horse all the while I approached you. Was he eating green stuff the whole time you were with him?"

"I guess so."

"Strange place we are in, Ms. Johnson." Won began talking with a slight Ph.D. affectation, the kind subtly calculated to let non-Ph.Ds feel as if they are entering the battle of wits half-prepared. "There is no sun in the sky, just this high-pressure sodium-type glow; there are strange shadows, no clouds, rivers flowing out of rocks, fruit trees growing to the top of 20,000-foot mountain peaks, floating rice-cakes blowing in from nowhere when I begin to think of hunger—and now an herbivorous tiger! I give up."

"Floating rice cakes?"

"Another time, Ms. Johnson . . . "

"Call me Karae."

"Well, all right. Karae." He wasn't ready to call her

by her first name and when he did, he mispronounced it *Carry* instead of *Care-AY*. "I'll tell you about the rice cakes some other time."

"I admit this place is strange. There are two-foot orchids growing in the forest and strange music coming out of the air, but I kind of like it."

"I haven't heard any music, but I don't need anything else to motivate me to get out of this place. Is it presumptuous to think we might want to team up for survival?"

Karae hesitated, as if thinking of other options besides trusting this stranger. "From the friendliness of this environment, I'm not sure survival is the question. But if we are going to try to find our way back home, I suppose two heads are—"

"Excellent," Won broke in. "I've been thinking of alternative plans for escape. Want to hear them?"

"I'm not sure I do," she responded with a glimmer in her eye. This was going to be a very interesting adventure with this guy, she told herself.

"Well, let's go. I figure there are three reasons we need to get away from this forest and onto higher ground. One, we can see the lay of the land better. Two, we could signal anybody who might show up. And three, we could avoid any dangers the forest might hold for us."

The forest had been such a comfortable, wonderful place for Karae; not only was she unafraid of it, she was reluctant to leave it. She surely hoped she would meet Garfield again. Maybe she would be able to return and enjoy the rapturous beauty and music again. For now, though, it probably made sense to go with Won to higher ground.

The two started along the edge of the forest before heading away from it. They had just taken a few steps when a hideous scream brought both of them to a state of rigor mortis. It was a loud, screeching, unearthly sound, coming from directly above them. Then silence.

Won and Karae looked at each other in terror. *What now?* their eyes seemed to say to each other. Neither moved a muscle.

The sound came again from the same direction, but now only a few yards away.

Both were afraid to look. Slowly, cautiously, they turned in the direction of the noise. All at once, branches in a nearby tree moved a few feet up and a form burst from the shadows. Whatever it might be was swooping down on them like a bird, coming right at them. It was too fast for them to get out of the way, even if they had found release from their catalepsy.

"Tarrrrrrrzzzzzaaannnnn!" shouted the creature as it dropped at their feet. In terror, they sprang backward.

"How you doin' dudes?" the creature grinned at them.

Mac.

"What—who—who are you?" the two blubbered in panicked unison.

"Me Tarzan, can't you tell? I left my loin cloth back at the Hilton!"

Karae flushed with anger. "If this was a joke, it was decidedly unfunny," she barked. Won Kim was still trying to extricate his heart from his throat so he could speak.

"Hey, no offense, lady. I've been up in that tree eavesdropping on your get-acquainted party. You sounded harmless enough, so I thought I'd drop in on you. Things have been awfully dull around here anyway, don't you think?" Mac seemed pleased with his Tarzan act.

"This kind of dull we can live with. It's shrieking

idiots swinging on grapevines we could do without."
Karae was still steamed.

"Chill out, miss. I meant no harm. The name is Mac."
Tarzan extended his hand to Won. Won stared at it as if
he didn't know what to do with it.

"The name is Mac," the mid-sized Irishman
repeated, giving a slight additional thrust to his extended
arm.

"I'm Won Kim." Won extended a limp washrag of
a handshake. He wanted to add, "I'm not sure I'm pleased
to meet you," but didn't have the nerve. Emboldened by
his previous meeting with Karae, he did add, "I didn't
get your last name."

"I didn't give it, Chinaman. It's McNeal."

"Korean," Won reacted. He had long ago grown
weary of the abrasions Americans give Asians by assum-
ing they're all Chinese or Japanese.

"You live here?" Karae queried Mac.

"No, I live in Cleveland . . . if you call that *living*."
Mac threw his head back and laughed in deep appreciation of his humor. The appreciation was not mutual.
"And, since you asked, I just hit this turf early today. As
a matter of fact, I could be on Mars for all I know. Must've
blacked out or something . . . "

Karae and Won looked at each other. *Add a third
member to the Misery-Loves-Company Club*, their eyes
seemed to say.

Karae sized up the newcomer. Stocky, well-built, a
six-footer with blond hair, Paul Newman eyes, and a
sideways smile that smirked even when Mac wasn't. His
attire was rather hip, and the clothes, while casual, were
obviously designer-expensive.

Mac broke the silence. "Well Chinaman, I overheard
you say you had a list of alternatives for trying to get out
of this place. Let's hear 'em."

"Korean," Won said firmly. "And the name is Won Kim."

"Excuuuuse me, Mr. Kim," Mac replied, more with impishness than sarcasm.

Karae wasn't sure how she felt about this intruder. By now her frightened anger had subsided, and she was able to view him more objectively. His good looks she could handle. He was going to do more to liven the party than she would have bargained for, but maybe three heads were better than—no, better not assume too much.

Won gave a circular motion with his arms as if to gather the other two around him. "What do you say we have a forum on how we plan to get out of this place and back home, or at least how we survive until we do?"

"I'm game." Mac dropped to the grass and crossed his legs Indian-style. The other two followed his lead, though Karae knelt to keep her designer suit from being soiled.

Won assumed the role of moderator and began with the systematic approach of a researcher. "Do either of you have a clue where we are? Is there any place on earth you think this could be?"

"I haven't traveled that much, but I've never even seen a setting like this in pictures." Karae lifted her hands up and out in a gesture of helplessness.

"This may sound weird . . . " Won seemed reluctant to venture his idea. " . . . but I'm not sure we're on earth."

"What makes you say that, doc?" The idea was one Mac hadn't considered.

"The absence of a sun." Won removed his glasses and used them as a pointer. "The strange light, even with cloudless skies, is my best evidence. If the planet we are on doesn't revolve around the sun, it can't be earth . . . unless some pretty radical changes have suddenly occurred."

Karae appeared troubled at that thought. "But how

did we get off the earth, if we are not on it? How did we get here at all?"

"Beats me." Mac was more sober than the other two had seen him since his arrival. "Last thing I recall I was sitting in the Kit Kat Lounge having a couple of drinks. It was happy hour. This blonde was flirting with me and just when it seemed like maybe I might get somewhere . . . I guess I felt faint, but I can't remember anything after that."

"Interesting." Won stuck the ear piece of his glasses in his mouth. "I can't remember anything since my laboratory. My research assistant and I were analyzing data and . . . I vaguely recall a bright flash but nothing else."

"I was heading up the freeway off-ramp to go home," Karae offered. "I remember nothing after that."

Won scribbled some notes on his pad. "Well, I guess that line of questioning wasn't very helpful. Maybe we'd better figure out what to do now that we're here."

"Food's no problem." Karae pointed toward the forest. "Everywhere I went, the trees were drooping with lush fruit—the hugest, most beautiful produce I've ever seen."

"And the streams are so full of fish you could sweep them out with your bare hands," Mac added.

"If Karae's experience with Garfield is typical, wild animals are no threat. They aren't wild!" Won's deduction seemed to please him.

"I say we stick together so we can benefit from each other's experience at whatever we do face, and head for high ground where we might be able to see what lies in the distance around us. Maybe we'll see some sign of civilization." Karae's practical, good sense was showing.

"What are we waiting for?" Mac jumped to his feet, ending the council meeting abruptly.

Won helped Karae to her feet and the two followed

Mac up a slope. Eventually Won and Mac fell into step beside each other. Karae was captivated once again by the exotic flowers and trees which formed glorious scenes everywhere she looked. She walked a pace or two away, enjoying this wonderful new world while Mac and Won calculated aloud possible ways to escape from it. That strange peace she had felt in the forest and in her encounter with Garfield settled over her again. She wondered why Won hadn't felt it or heard the music.

It had been a long day and she was getting weary. Even though the sky showed no signs of proclaiming twilight, everything within her did—weariness from walking, fatigue from wondering, hunger from living on berries and tree fruit, and strain from struggling with two new relationships with men she would never have chosen as friends. She wondered about these two guys. Should she trust them? If so, why? If not, why not? Why should they be taking the lead, just because they were male? Who elected Tarzan their leader? What good was a Ph.D if the Korean had no clue as to where they were and how they had gotten here?

She was confused—and lonely. She missed her mother. She desperately wanted to know that Mom was all right, or even to know that she wasn't. She missed California. With all its problems—smog, traffic, crime—it was home. When you were there you at least knew where you were. She even missed Garfield. He was something big and warm and friendly to hug. Won and Mac weren't candidates for that!

About a mile more across the meadows and up the side of a foothill the trio trudged, their strides and tempers growing shorter with each step.

"Where do you two men think you're taking us?" Karae plopped down on a large, stool-like clump of grass. "This is getting us nowhere!"

She was accustomed to being in charge of her life.

Independent, self-sufficient, self-starting, she had achieved her present status without a whole lot of help. Her father had climbed out of the lower class by educating himself into a profession; this had put her in the Southern California suburbs. The you-can-do-anything-you-put-your-mind-to attitude of her parents had given her the confidence to carve out her own life and career path. It had gotten her through Cal State University in Northridge and had set her up in an executive position in the mortgage brokerage business. She hated being dependent, especially on a man—or men!

"Did you have your own alternatives you would like to propose, Ms. Johnson?" Won's voice carried an uncharacteristic bite.

"Maybe we should elect Ms. Johnson navigatrix," Mac said to Won.

"Knock if off, smart mouth." Karae's flat tone was calculated to be a verbal slap.

It was obvious that the wildly different backgrounds of the three, the frustration of being lost, and the diminishing hopes of finding a way out were grating on their nerves. Mac bristled and his Irish temper flared. "You'd probably find your way around the ghetto better than in a resort like this." Now he was playing dirty. But in a way it felt good to lift the lid off all the forced niceness of these new acquaintances.

"Look here, WASP, I never lived in the ghetto. I grew up in Pasadena, not far from the Rose Bowl. You're from Cleveland—*you* tell *me* about ghettos." She'd learned early that you had to come back strong when bigotry reared its ugly head.

Won had paled at this first conflict between the two. He hated direct confrontation. Maybe he could be peacemaker. "Uh, excuse me," he began, "but I don't think you two—"

"Stay out of this, Chinaman!" Mac cut him off.

"When we want a printout from you on what we should and should not do, we'll push your *PRINT* button!"

"KOREAN! KOREAN, KOREAN!" Won's high-control, intellectual manner was blown.

"Lay off Won—what did he do to you?" Karae's face burned in anger. "We were getting along just fine until you Tarzaned out of your tree house and spoiled the party. Why don't you go back into the jungle where your ancestors came from?" There was no stopping her now.

"*My* ancestors, African queen? Listen closely, the tribal chief is calling you back."

"Look, I'm trying to find a way out of this Never-Never Land, a way back home to my desperately ill mother, and *I don't need this!* I don't need the hassle! I don't need the ethnic slurs! I don't need two men to get me out of here! I don't need you two!" Karae bit back angry tears, spun on her heels, and strode resolutely to a spot a few yards away.

She was going to find a way out, a way to civilization, a way to Pasadena and home and Mom if she had to call down the gods to make it happen. The last thing she needed was two men with excessive testosterone levels telling *her* what to do.

While the argument raged on between the warring males, Karae became aware of something happening around the three of them. The atmosphere in their vicinity was growing darker and seemed charged, like that of an electrical storm. Yet the charges weren't electrical. They seemed intangible—almost *spiritual.*

Now she could feel it. It was like the oppressive blanket of gloom that settles over the casket at a burial service for one who has chosen to go to Hell. Or like the eerie weightiness at a seance. Finally it struck Karae and she froze. Since the gloom couldn't be perceived by sheer reason, Won hadn't picked it up. And since there was a personal war to be won with Won, Mac was preoccupied and clueless.

In a later instant, Won made a serious mistake. In his anger at Mac, he unloaded a Tae Kwon Do punch into Mac's midsection, one which sent him reeling.

"Why you . . ." Mac groaned as he toppled over backward. When he hit the ground, his hand landed near a rock the size of a grapefruit. He grabbed the stone and, lunging to his feet, hurled the projectile at Won. The rock grazed Won's head, opening a small cut. Then Mac threw himself at Won, taking a knee to the midsection as the two fell in a heap with Won on the bottom. Karae watched the struggling adolescents with contempt.

Suddenly the clear sky above them was split by an incredible crack of lightning, a blinding flash of light, and a nuclear-like blast of thunder. The two men stopped grappling, and all three of them, petrified, gazed at the point which the bolt of lightning had hit. There, standing among them, was a man—a glorious mountain of a man maybe seven and a half feet tall with handsome, angular features, long, golden hair, and . . . *presence.* His eyes burned like fire and his voice came from somewhere deep within his cavernous chest.

"I wish your welcome to the Kingdom could have been more cordial," he boomed. "But you three have been here only one day, and already you have brought discord to our realm. I was dispatched to deal with you and with this problem. Dissension is not permitted here. Disharmony is an ethic of the Dark Side. If you choose to practice it, you may join the disembodied spirits in the Place of the Imprisoned."

Karae couldn't form a response, much less a defense or a rebuttal. She hid her face. A deep spirit of remorse settled over her, a strange and heavy guilt far out of proportion to what she would have felt back home. She felt such shame, guilt far beyond the magnitude of the offense.

Won Kim was pale and drawn, his head turned away from the others. Mac was visibly stunned, struggling to emerge from the state of shock which had gripped him, trying not to show the terror he was experiencing.

"I have been ordered by the governor of this realm, the Honorable Jireh Ben-David, to bring you to him for accountability. Nothing must mar the joyful harmony of the Kingdom." While a clear rebuke, The Man's words had no malice, no cutting edge. They were pure and guileless and kindly. But there was also no mistaking that he meant exactly what he said.

"My guests, you will come with me." His tone rang like brass. The timbre cut like a knife. You knew in your soul there would be no question, no hesitancy, no resistance. Authority.

At that word the three began to feel a lightness lifting them. In a moment they had ascended above the earth and were moving at double the speed of light—they knew not where.[17]

3

Dynamic Encounter

An incredible jewel—a dazzling gem!" was all Karae could say about metropolitan Jehovah Jireh.

The city sprawled from horizon to horizon, glistening in the omnidirectional radiance of the sunless skies. Splashes of color adorned buildings in glorious friezes of precious metals inlaid with semi-precious stones. The streets were boulevards 150 feet wide divided by spectacular gardens, dancing fountains, terraced waterfalls and beautiful sculptures.

Karae drank in the aesthetic wonders of the metropolis as she walked along its streets with her three compatriots. The city center was an architecturally coordinated mosaic of high rises with colors, styles, sizes, shapes and building materials forming a work of art from any angle. Each building was set like a jewel in a crown among acres of ponds, flowers, trees and gardens.

How could there be no signs of wear, of deterioration, of needed maintenance, of damage, of graffiti, of stain from the elements?[18] No urban filth. Not a scrap of paper in the streets. No dirt or debris in the gutters. No pollution tainting the air, the water or the view. No billboards, commercial messages, telephone poles or antennae marred the artful beauty of the metropolis. The only man-made things were obviously planned and executed with omniscient forethought and artistic sensitivity.

And the aromas! Karae inhaled in delight as various scents danced by. They reminded her of the orange blossoms of Pasadena and of the rose garden behind her home. The fragrances changed as the trio moved along.

Then there was that same musical harmonic she had heard in the jungle—woodwinds and reeds all coming from Nature. They provided accompaniment for great choruses of wild fowl. The grass under their feet was so fine and weedless that it looked and felt like fur. The flowers were more velvety, more soft-petalled than she had ever felt before. The air was fresh and invigorating, more so than she had breathed even outside of the Los Angeles basin.

"What gives the climate here such a different feel?" Karae addressed their host. As long as they were going to be here awhile, she might as well learn as much as she could from The Man.

"The climate is controlled by a water vapor canopy above the earth,"[19] their guide answered. "It never rains here like it did on your earth. Heavy dew is on the ground each morning, and underground springs provide ample sources of water which naturally irrigate every square foot of earth that needs it."[20]

Won Kim was too overcome by the explanation to respond. He just stroked his chin pensively and scribbled some notes on his pad. The wonders were coming too fast for him to digest. Even Mac was temporarily distracted from his devil-may-care attitude.

Karae was beginning to form a perception of the city's master plan. The streets were laid out in a giant matrix spreading out from two major thoroughfares which ran perpendicular to each other, like a huge Christian cross throughout the city. Side streets took on the aura of the naves and flying buttresses of a great Gothic cathedral. The streets were polished white marble with variegated veins of pure gold through them. In earth's sunlight they would be blinding to look at, Karae realized, but with this indirect lighting the streets reflected the beauty of the surrounding gardens, fountains and structures without being too bright for the eyes.

No cars, trucks or busses filled the streets. They were lined with walking people, or people with strange, creatively designed vehicles ridden just for enjoyment. It seemed that each person could transport himself from place to place just as their guide had—by telekinesis—to any place in the galaxy, at any speed.[21]

As the three rambled along behind The Man, transfixed at what they were seeing, families strolled by them on the streets. The little bands of family members seemed so "together" in peace and tranquility. The scenes made Karae wish she had known that kind of home—a loving, bonded, unbroken one. Then she noticed the lovers who strolled hand-in-hand, enjoying romantic walks among the extravagant flora of the boulevards or in the 1200-acre parks that seemed to be within short walking distances for everyone.

The people of the Kingdom were as spectacular as the land itself. All were handsome—with clearly differing features—but very handsome. There was not a crippled, deformed, sickly, dull-eyed person among them.[22] All were exceptionally tall, strong, and well-developed by all standards known to the three visitors. Countenances were clear, radiant, and marked by the kind of innocence and purity seldom, if ever, found on the planet Karae, Mac and Won had come from.

As the foursome trekked along the streets toward the city's center, they could overhear conversations of those along the way—parents with children, peers, vocational associates. Even the conversations seemed melodious—like psalms, hymns and praise choruses Karae remembered from her church days.

"Greetings in the name of The King!" a passerby called with a wide, joyful smile.

"And may He prosper you," returned their guide with equal graciousness.

What a delightful interchange, Karae observed. Their manner of greeting and interacting was so free of prideful self-promotion. They seemed confident, yet humble. They demonstrated leadership qualities, yet preferred one another in honor. They were mutually strong in spirit, but gracious; of varying creative gifts and talents, yet mutually reasonable and cooperative. Tranquility and the deepest and broadest affection marked the demeanors of every citizen. A strange mix: incredible diversity merged into oneness of community spirit and mutual respect. Their character fit the grandeur—no, exceeded it—of the idyllic surroundings in which they lived.[23]

"We're not far from the provincial palace and the governor's mansion," The Man explained. "Stay close to me. We will be there shortly."

Down the long, broad ways far in the distance Karae could see spectacular silver arches stretching a thousand feet into the air and transgressing the four entrances to the city at each end of the two main streets. The Man stopped the delegation at a spot where they could see that they were at the intersection of the city's cross streets, near the geometric center.

"Here is the provincial palace, the Palace of Eternal Provision," their host explained as he pointed to it with obvious pride. "It is named so to commemorate the promise of The King to provide abundantly for all His subjects forever. Thus the Hebrew name *Jehovah Jireh*, which marks God as the one true and great Provider."

Even Mac seemed impressed with the grandeur, the magnitude of everything, even with some of the symbolism. "Wow," he whistled a long, low sigh. "That is some bungalow."

"Some bungalow, indeed." Karae found it hard to believe the palace that rose 1200 feet above the landscape with hanging gardens cascading over its terraces.

"The inside is equally awe-inspiring," The Man continued. "There are bigger-than-life pieces of art, sculpture, and dioramas. Elaborate holograms commemorate God's faithfulness to His children over time—His provision of a resting place for the ark of Noah, His provision of a lamb for sacrifice to spare the son of Abraham, His feeding of millions of Hebrew travelers for forty years with manna, Jesus' turning five loaves and two fish into a meal for more than 10,000 people . . . "

Their tutor seemed eager to expand on the glorious details of the palace. "Adjoining the grounds of the palace is the governor's residence, with 777 spacious rooms for the governor and his extended family." It was a regal, columned building. At the entrance an ornate gate fashioned from the alloys of exotic metals portrayed various types of foods which Jehovah had provided for mankind over the ages.

"Why no security, no guard house?" Mac's question may have revealed a slightly larcenous thought of his own.

"There is nothing against which to guard in the Kingdom, except occasional unintentional violations of privacy," their guide replied.[24] "The gates are always in the open position, welcoming visitors and guests into the presence of the man whose earthly life of love and devotion to his God has qualified him to govern in the Province of Divine Provision. This is only one of 144 regions across the world which completely express the grand character of The King."

"The world?" Won peered under wrinkled eyebrows at The Man. "What world?"

"Your world. Planet Earth."

"Uh-uh," Mac shook his head. "This can't be Planet Earth. Our world was never like this."

"Partly true, Mac." The Man raised an index finger as if to indicate that Mac had earned one point out of a possible two. "Your world isn't like this now. The human race has ravaged it. But it was much like this in Eden, before the Curse. What you are experiencing is the New Earth, one suited to the New Heavens—a radical renovation executed by The King after the end of the age you left."

"The age we were *taken from* . . . " Won was bent on scientific accuracy, even in small details, " . . . was the late twentieth century."

"You three have been thrust forward in time. You are visiting the same world—in dramatically remodeled form—in the late twenty-*first* century. When The King established His monarchy at the end of your age through military conquest, the devastation wrought by the three-and-a-half year conflict was scarcely believable. So He recreated the earth and the heavens as an abode for Himself and those who trust Him."[25]

The Man paused as if to let these concepts percolate into the understanding of the three. Their faces displayed various stages of puzzlement. No percolation. The perceptions were sitting on the surface.

"Now wait a minute," Karae held her hands up, trying hard to understand. "You mean to tell me you have brought us forward in time, but we are still on earth, only it's a *new* earth . . . "

"You've got it," The Man nodded. "You'll understand much better as time goes on." He turned and took the lead once again toward the palace.

Mac looked at Won and Karae, wide-eyed, and began humming the theme from *The Twilight Zone.*

Karae agreed with Mac's sentiment. This was too weird—too much to comprehend, more than all the science fiction movies she had ever seen rolled into one.

Now just outside the giant gates, Karae, Won, Mac and their host stood drinking in the artistry of the palace. Then The Man turned his back toward the gates to address the three guests.

"My friends, here in the Kingdom we honor and respect authority. No authority is ever abused. No official is less than a devoted servant, both of The King and of the people. No leader is anything but a model of virtuous attitudes and actions. Therefore, we joyfully surrender to those in privilege over us. I say this so that you can prepare yourself for your meeting with the governor. Need I say that it would be both offensive and risky to show anything but complete deference to this honorable man?"

The three looked at each other, a bit taken aback by such an unfamiliar sense of respect for authority. In quiet consent, they nodded to The Man.

"All right, then, we shall proceed into the palace. Follow me, please." Their magnificent host walked tall, straight; proud but not arrogant. Karae thought of John Wayne as she watched him, but then quickly realized that even the Duke in his cinematic prime did not come close to this magnificent Man in stature, handsomeness and confident demeanor.

As the three proceeded, Karae became aware of a growing conflict in her soul. She wanted so desperately to go home, but she also was very impressed with this place. Could she ever want to live here enough to ask to stay . . . ? It was an unsettling thought to her, one not easily answered and one she wasn't prepared to answer here and now. The vision of her mother's face floating through her consciousness made the conflict even greater.

The Man led them up the one-hundred-yard incline of inlaid jade to the entrance of the palace. On both sides of the ramp were perfectly manicured, flowering shrubs with a dozen or more colors of blossoms growing on each plant. Shaped into perfect spheres about six feet in diameter, the shrubs created, in the long view, two strings of colorful, botanic pearls which framed the translucent pastels of the ramp.

There were bridges over lovely ponds; moats which meandered through the palace grounds and bore exotic floating birds and enormous multicolored swans. Delicate trees like weeping willows, themselves ornamented with clusters of fragrant flowers, shed their tears over the banks of the watercourses on both sides of the ramp.

"Are you enjoying the sights of Jehovah Jireh?" their guide asked in what had to be the understatement of the day.

"Oh, yes, the city is beautiful!" Karae spoke for the delegation. It was obvious to her that her new friends were also transfixed by the spectacular beauty of the urban sprawl and awed by the material and spiritual ambiance of the palace. The sights had clearly over-shadowed the petty squabbles which had resulted in their being summoned to the provincial capital. Funny, she thought, how the things people think are big enough to spoil relationships over are so soon revealed to be so tiny! Their anger and unkind words had been eclipsed so quickly by the glories of this city and its people. She also noticed that the foreboding spiritual haze which had enveloped them during their conflict was now complete-ly gone.

Dwarfed among the grand marble columns of the palace, the company traversed the gold threshold of the edifice to arrive in a great hall which extended nearly a tenth of a mile into the heart of the structure. The ceilings of the great hall were marvelous ornate skylights in which thin panes of that same jade-like material in the entrance ramp had been fashioned into long, narrow, stained-glass windows with artistic portrayals of fruits, vegetables, legumes and grains. As if out of a cornucopia, the skylights flowed down the long corridor, projecting the colorful representations of God's bountiful provision onto the antique white walls of the great hall in lively splashes of color. At the end of the corridor, lovely music wafted along the walls from an open portal nearly twenty feet high with doors of thick, exotic hardwoods orna- mented with overlays of gold leaf.

"The music is like the music in the forest," Karae spoke in a whisper, not wanting to break the magic of the melodies. Inside the enormous doors was a retinue of strikingly uniformed male and female attendants tend- ing the needs of the governor who sat comfortably behind a massive cast-silver desk.

The Man whispered to one of the nearby attendants, and she turned to announce, "Your honor, the delegation of guests from Rural Province, Section 4." She turned again to the new arrivals. "Meet the Honorable Jireh Ben-David, governor of the Province of Divine Provision."

Their guide stepped a few paces ahead and mo- tioned to the trio to follow him more closely. As they approached the great silver desk, he raised his arm and extended a flat palm upward and outward toward the governor in a salute. Attendants quickly and smoothly slipped three chairs behind Karae, Won and Mac.

"Please, do sit down," the governor offered.

Karae was quite impressed with him. He was any- thing but what one might expect, considering the regal splendor which surrounded him. He had the same hand- someness of form and countenance which marked the rest of the citizenry, but he was neither officious nor arrogant. He was not trying to impress nor intimidate the three. Ben-David's eyes were kindly, compassionate and strong. When he looked at Karae, she felt that he could see inside her, but she didn't mind. He had a full head of hair which flowed in waves just to the top of his collar. It was very dark brown with strands of silver—indicating wisdom, not age. The governor was richly dark-skinned and, judging from the amount of torso which extended above the desk, he must have been more than seven feet tall, like The Man.

The Man vanished as the governor stood to speak.

Yes, Governor Ben-David was *at least* seven feet tall. He was dressed in a comfortable but elegant uniform. It was a rich, royal blue, cut precisely to fit his form, and had epaulets on the shoulders with gold buttons sculpted with a representation of loaves and fish.

"My friends, this must be a mysterious and uncomfortable experience for you to be thrust into our kingdom like this. First, to be dropped alone into our land from a past time with no explanation, no assurances of safety, has to be unsettling. Then, too, you must have encountered things that are drastically different from the cultures where you live."

"Yeah, gov, I've got a *lot* of questions for you," Mac jumped to his feet, only to be stared down by Karae and Won. Rebuked, Mac continued in a subdued manner, "Er, your honor, there *have* been a number of strange and, may I say, unsettling things about this visit so far."

"I'm sorry." The governor's kind eyes smiled as he spoke, indicating that he genuinely cared about even the slightest displeasure to his guests. "What can I do to settle things for you?"

What a nice man, Karae thought, noting the way the governor overlooked Mac's no-class approach and now sought a way to resolve the resulting tension. His balance of strength and kindliness was unlike any she had met before.

"You could start by getting us out of here and on our way back home." It was Mac again. Karae wondered what life must have been like for the mother of this problem child.

The governor shook his head. "You have been brought here for an unusual test at the orders of The King. Unless or until I have orders from The King himself, you will be our guests. We will endeavor to make your stay as comfortable and profitable as possible."

Won Kim spoke. "Your honor, we really would like to request permission to return to our homeland." He dropped his head slightly, suggesting a Korean-style bow.

His honor ignored the question, as if to reinforce that when he said a matter was settled, one or one thousand questions challenging his decision were equally out of order. "May I talk to you about the unfortunate scene you created in our realm? Of course, I refer to the acrimony which disturbed the peace of our land and for which cause you were summoned here."

The three grew even more still. Won dropped his head in a manner reflecting loss of face. Karae grew slightly edgy. Mac continued being Mac.

"Things are quite different where you come from, I know." The governor was forthright and serious. "But in the Kingdom the name calling, personal attacks and ethnic slurs we overheard have no place. And physical blows . . . " He shook his head in unbelief that it could happen in his realm.

How does he know what we said? Won wondered silently, glancing over his shoulder as if spies might be lurking nearby.

"Mr. Kim, let me answer your question." The governor directed his gaze at Won.

"Uh, I didn't say anything, your honor," Won blushed.

"Not verbally, Mr. Kim, but I read your spirit, and in that is the answer to your unspoken question.[26] In the Kingdom the spiritual part of man—at which level all true communication takes place—is unencumbered by the restraints of selfishness, ego exaltation, attitudes from the Dark Side, or preoccupation with the material world. Therefore, we have access at will to the thoughts of others. This is never a problem to us because the virtuous nature of our thoughts allows them to be read by others without ever being a source of embarrassment.

"When the spiritual character of our fair land and its inhabitants is disturbed by any spiritual force or person creating disharmony, we immediately feel it. It was quite simple for us to focus our powers of discernment on your threesome. In that manner we were able to hear both the spoken and—far worse—the unspoken contempt, prejudice and unkindness which you three projected."

Oh, my God, Mac thought. *Big Brother is alive and well!*

The governor dropped his head as if suddenly experiencing a pain in the heart. After an interminable silence he raised his head, stared laser-like at Mac, and addressed him with leaden tones. "Mr. McNeal, no one here may use the name of God in the loose manner you just did. And The King is no Big Brother. God is The King of our realm, His Son the Beloved Ruler of our world. Your use of His name as an expletive is most hurtful to Him and to me, His intimate and loyal friend."[27] He held his stare on Mac, waiting for a response. He didn't have to wait long.

"Look, gov, I've had it! This has been a long day for us. We got dropped into this plastic culture from nowhere, struggled to find our way out with no help from the likes of you, have a perfectly normal spat among tired, frustrated people, get snatched by Golden Boy and dragged here to Shangri-La, and now we get nailed for what we're *thinkin'*. I've had it, and I'm outta here!" Mac jumped to his feet and turned to leave.

Sensing impending judgment for Mac's outburst, Karae jumped in. "Your honor, Mr. McNeal does not speak for all of us."

"Oh thanks, sweetheart, turn on me when I'm the only one with the guts to speak the truth to the Grand Dragon here!" Mac completed his about-face and bolted toward the great hall. He had reached the giant hardwood doors when a flash of light shot from nowhere and struck him on the back of the neck.

There he remained, frozen in running position. The room grew deathly still.[28]

At the sight of it, terror overcame Won and Karae. Mac was quick-frozen in place, unable to speak or move. He stood like a statue of Mercury, rigidly balanced in mid-step. Won paled. Karae felt a tight knot grip her stomach. She fought to hold back frightful tears.

"Attendants, please bring Mr. McNeal back here with our other guests." The governor spoke as calmly as if he were asking for a drink of water.

Two attendants appeared from the shadows of the room and walked toward Mac. They picked him up as if he were a sporting-goods mannequin, his legs still locked in the position at which he had been zapped trying to escape. They carried him back to the empty chair, balanced him in front of it, and returned to the shadows.

"Now, Mr. McNeal," the governor gestured, palms up in a conciliatory manner. "It is important for you to realize that however uncomfortable it may be for you in our realm, you must adapt to our ways of doing things. Everything will be made clear to you in due time."

As the governor spoke this last sentence, Mac's locked muscles began to relax, as though thawing from a long winter's freeze. His feet joined each other at the floor, he regained his balance, and his arms dropped slowly to his sides.

"Do you understand, my friend?" The governor held him in a level-eyed gaze.

"Yes, sir." Mac's answer had considerably less fire than when he had announced his departure moments before.

The governor stepped around the desk and approached Karae. Without a word he put his sinewy arm gently around her shoulders. His embrace was strong, his body warm, his manner tender. He comforted her until she relaxed and regained her composure. Then, with a couple of delicate pats on her shoulder blade, he moved on and placed one hand on Mac's shoulder until he, too, had calmed. He returned to the other side of the desk. There was something special about his ability to console, to comfort, to encourage. Karae felt it at the deepest levels of her soul.

"I'm sure you must be hungry," Governor Ben-David said, breaking the tension. "Please join me in the banquet hall for dinner and accept my invitation to spend the night. I assure you, you will be well taken care of by my most gracious staff."

With the meeting adjourned, Karae's mind once again generated questions. Why did they have to stay here? What kind of "test" had brought them here? What chance did they have against people who read their thoughts, people who could call on unseen powers to transport them where they wanted them to go or quick-freeze them if they made a false move? She wasn't coming up with answers.

"Please step this way to the great hall." The governor stepped aside to let the guests enter.

They slipped into the cathedral-like banquet room, where great mahogany beams began at the floors and rose, curving inward, to meet at the peak of the ceiling.

Thousands of tiny lights, somehow imbedded in the beams, formed artistic designs on the walls, giving the room a fairyland appearance. Along the length of the hall, on both sides, were flags—144 of them—each with the colors and symbols of a Kingdom province. Four long tables stretched the length of the chamber, set with solid gold dinnerware and bedecked with grand crystal candelabras.

"I wish I had had time to dress for the occasion," Karae said. She meant it tongue-in-cheek, but she did feel a bit self-conscious in her business suit. Then it struck her: Somehow these people didn't seem to care what others were wearing. They seemed to look past one's clothing and external appearance and relate to the heart and soul. This notion seemed fresh and wonderful for a lady from Pasadena, where the society columns critiqued clothing more than they did character.

"What a magnificent feast, governor," she added. "Never have I seen so many delicacies at one banquet." The governor smiled acknowledgment. Karae reflected on the $1000-a-plate chicken and peas dinners she had attended at Beverly Hills hotels. What a joke they were compared to this, she thought. They might as well have been served in Styrofoam containers.

And there were gracious gentlemen and ladies at these tables. She wondered how so many people of every status could sit together without concern for social rank. Every person seemed so secure, so whole and mature in personality. Karae felt she could drop all her defenses and relate to any one of them honestly. What a relief from the self-glorifying, our-European-trip-was-better-than-your-European-trip patter at most dinners!

The talk at this dinner table was anything but boring. A natural beauty across the table from Karae radiated charm and wit as well as a genuine interest in her. "Have you had opportunity to attend the global worship celebration at Zion?"[29] she asked.

"No, I haven't." Karae selected a delicate pastry from the tray presented to her by an attendant. It held layers of creamy filling between paper-thin pastry, reminding her of Greek *baklava,* but enhanced with alternative layers of chocolate, strawberry, and vanilla-cream fillings. "Mmmmm," she groaned involuntarily as the dessert dissolved on her tongue.

The beautiful woman across from her smiled knowingly, then returned to the subject she had posed. "You must participate in it if you can. You will never be the same after seeing Zion and feeling the spiritual power of the festival of worship." The woman was very convincing. "No one can resist worshipping The King once he has shared in the global worship ceremony."

"Then I hope the governor will let us attend." The woman's description seemed to stir at the spiritual emptiness in Karae's own soul.

Changing the subject, she observed how physically attractive she found everyone in the Kingdom to be. "It seems that everybody here is gorgeous—in a unique way."

"It's because of the Kingdom bodies we have received," the woman explained. "In our past lives on earth we had deteriorating, degenerate bodies. But when one enters the Kingdom, he is given a perfect body. The new body is like his previous body *would have been* had it not inherited defects from generations of sick, broken, deformed, and disease-and-weakness-ridden ancestors."[30]

"And why does no one appear aged?" Karae asked.

"Oh, that's because of the Prime Factor Maturity that is built into our Kingdom bodies. You see, The King never aged beyond age thirty-three in His earth life, so now all the citizens of the Kingdom mature to a stage comparable to age thirty-three, the prime of life. Then the Prime Factor locks in physical strength and maturity, even though emotionally, spiritually, intellectually, and in other ways each person continues to grow and develop."[31]

"Can you really get to the place where you can read minds . . . or spirits? What is that like? Isn't it unnerving, embarrassing . . . even maddening?" Karae was on stride now. She was going to get as many questions answered as possible.

"Not really. It might seem that way to a person whose mind is filled with wrong thoughts. For instance, I will never be embarrassed to have a handsome man read my admiration of his physique. He and I both know my thoughts are not lust. My friends would never discover things I would not want them to know by discerning my spirit. Because of the new heart and mind we have all received from The King, no thoughts would enter my mind that I wouldn't be ready and willing to share with others."[32]

Karae wasn't so sure about this unearthly transparency. She vacillated between "weird," "incredible," "unreal," "intriguing," "attractive," and "wonderful." Was it really possible for any person to experience such a radical spiritual transformation that he could feel comfortable with others having access to his thoughts? Could anyone have such a dramatic change in inner motivation that he could keep his thoughts free from malice, lust, ill-motivation and selfishness even if nobody else could read them? There was something irresistible about the possibility, but how . . .

Karae's thoughts meandered off in another direction. She looked at Won. He had not heard a word of the table talk since the concept of Prime Factor Maturity had hit him. He was muttering half to himself and half to Karae, "How can a process be explained which enables a person to be locked into age thirty-three without physical degeneration, but still have all other areas of development and maturity continue? How can these powerful and attractive physical specimens live to the age of hundreds of years—without suffering the weakening effects of aging? How . . . "

The increasing list of unanswered questions was obviously getting to him. Karae chuckled to herself that Won's "For Further Reference" file must be occupying most of his mental file cabinet by now. It seemed he was thoroughly bewildered by the radical nature of his discoveries and the way they defied analysis by conventional scientific research techniques. This was a state no proud holder of a doctor of philosophy degree appreciates or tolerates for long.

Won had now turned to take notes on a conversation with an extremely eloquent man sitting near him. The man was describing his trip to the outer reaches of a galaxy while on an astronomy journey. Won was so enraptured by the first-person description of a galactic black hole that he didn't realize he had set his elbow in the icing on his pastry plate. Karae smiled. Won reminded her of the proverbial absent-minded professor who pours syrup down his back and scratches his pancakes.

A few chairs down, Mac was thoroughly consumed by consuming thoroughly. He devoured everything edible within reach and anything he could get others to pass, and had built his own dessert sampler and was systematically inhaling bite after bite. There was indeed one thing in the world that could distract Mac from women—at least for a while.

"Miss Johnson?" It was a quiet-spirited man sitting across from her, beside the beautiful woman who had spoken of Zion. He was a round-faced, bushy-eyebrowed man with a tousle of hair and a smile that divided his kindly face in two.

"Yes?" Karae liked him already.

"It is wonderful to have you join us as a guest." Karae perceived that he really meant his kind words. As the meal progressed, they chatted on a wide range of topics, exchanging the lead back and forth across the table. Now it was the man's turn.

"One of my most fascinating recent experiences came from a seminar I attended—one held by The King." Karae was rapt with attention. "The King described divine strategy and tactics from world events.[33] In one session He described the providential workings behind Napoleon at Waterloo and the effects they wrought in the lives of millions, including Napoleon and his mistress, Desiree. He illustrated His points by bringing actual visions of what happened out of the past so we could see for ourselves. Incredible to realize that God has a complicated and wonderful plan for everything that happens on earth!"

Dinner over, the three visitors were ushered to a grand parlor outside the great hall. It was filled with a variety of tastefully designed sofas and chairs, like a magnificent hotel lobby. Most of the furniture was arranged to provide a view of the dominant feature of the room, a massive, bronze fireplace which tapered from a width of twenty feet at the base to a column ten feet wide near the ceiling. The governor had excused himself from the banquet dais before his guests had finished and had returned to his office, so the conversation circle of large, uncommonly comfortable, overstuffed chairs held just the three.

Reflection time. If there had been windows into their minds one could have seen . . .

Karae was awed. She loved the people and conversation in this new fantasy world. Won studied every

detail of the hall's construction and decoration. Mac
loved the food, especially that one gooey fruit pie with
the heaps of rich, creamy vanilla sauce. Karae felt warm
thinking of the governor's kind embrace and tenderness.
Won went over mental lists of alternative approaches to
the governor which might convince him to secure the
group's release. Mac stewed over the humiliation of
being laser-zapped and lugged back to the starting line
of his would-be escape route. Karae thought how much
she really liked the Kingdom. Won rifled through his
mental file folders and dug out items for analysis. Mac
could not be more convinced; he wanted out of this
goody-goody place—out, out, out! Karae had an agonizing moment thinking about her mother. Won worried
briefly about the state of the research—whether Harry
was impairing the data collection—and wanted a hug
from his son Justin. Mac just wanted out—if he could find
a way to smuggle a truckload of the food with him.

In the governor's office, Jireh Ben-David sat behind his
silver desk. He had called an attendant who now stood
by the desk as he wrote out a short note. Folding the
document and inserting it into a large gold-foil envelope,
the governor handed it to the dutiful servant.

"This is for The King. It is urgent. Make sure it gets
to Him within the hour. I need a response from Him
before our guests awaken in the morning."

"Yes, your honor." The courier disappeared from
the room, and Jireh Ben-David headed out a side door
toward his personal residence. His countenance bore a
look of concern, grave concern.

4

Command Performance

A heavy dew signaled that the daily renewal had come to the Kingdom. One-tenth-karat jewels of moisture sparkled from every leaf, every frond, every blade. The starburst shadows intensified slightly around every vertical object, and the air, which was always clear, had a special potency all its own.

Karae took in deep, slow breaths of Kingdom atmosphere. As she did, her mind began to emerge from the plunge she had taken into deep, sweet sleep. She had no complaints about the rest time—elegant beds in cordial surroundings, a depth and quality of quiet that was calming to the soul as well as mind and body, and *peace.* Karae wasn't sure whether Won and Mac felt the Kingdom peace—or anything spiritual—as she did. Maybe it was because they were men. Maybe it was because they were not in touch with their feelings. Maybe it was because there were always so preoccupied with concrete realities.

While the three performed their daily ablutions in their private quarters, a lone figure dashed up the long incline into the entrance of the palace with a gold-foil diplomatic pouch under his arm. He raced down the long corridor to the governor's office and found it closed. He knocked quietly, lest he disturb an early meeting of Governor Ben-David's. No answer. He cracked the heavy doors a bit and peeked in.

There, kneeling by a long divan, was the governor. Tears were streaming down his face. He was praying. "Loving King, I need Your wisdom. These three aliens are not suited to life here in the Kingdom. I so much want them to be able to join us here, to share in the glories of the realm, but Lord, I fear the worst. There seems to be a hardness of heart or a spiritual blindness in them. They not only are missing the true spirit of the Kingdom, they seem to be resistant to any loving approach. Help me know what to tell them, how to relate to them, how to win them."

The governor continued speaking quietly and reverently, then listening for long periods of time before speaking again. After a number of cycles of this deep communication, he hummed a hymn to The King, rose to his feet, and headed toward the desk.

"Excuse me, your honor." The governor started at the unexpected voice in the room. "I have a message from The King for you in response to your inquiry of Him before sleep time. Forgive me for breaking into your prayers."

"Not at all, my brother," responded the governor. "I heard nothing, so there was no distraction or offense. Please bring me the message."

The governor took the gold pouch, gave his faithful courier an affectionate hug, and sent him on his way with a special blessing: "May Jehovah Jireh provide His bounty in every area of your life." The messenger thanked him and left.

The governor slipped into the chair behind his desk

and opened the pouch. As he read the message, his eyes moistened again. He dropped his head on the desk for a moment, then raised it to the skies, then put the message back into the pouch with a heavy sigh.

"Attendant!" Jireh Ben-David quickly recovered the gracious and decisive manner which usually marked his demeanor. An attendant was at his desk in a moment, as if beamed through space to the spot before him. He stood, like The Man, more than seven feet tall. He was stunning in a spotless white uniform that mixed comfort with style. Genuine gold trim set off the seams of the one-piece heavenly jumpsuit. His wavy locks of long, dark hair cascaded to his shoulders and framed his dark-skinned face.

"Yes, your honor." The attendant gave the same flat-palm-upward, straight-arm salute The Man had given when the three had first entered the presence of the governor. It was like an appeal to the Higher Power.

"We will have to act with haste. It is of the utmost importance that the three aliens be brought to me as quickly as they can be mustered. Will you see to it that they are in my office directly?"

"I will indeed, your honor, in the name of The King."

"Take your leave, then, and please see to it." There was urgency in the governor's voice.

The attendant turned, took a few hasty steps, and disappeared from the room. The governor walked to the window and looked out over the palace gardens. The cloudless sky reflected a deep blue in the mirror-like ponds. Only the wake left by the swans rippled the surface. The flowering shrubs and trees moved gently in the subtle breeze. In the distance the bustling, peaceful city was now fully at work and play. His gaze narrowed in on a lovely orange cluster of blossoms in the suspended floral window box below him. But as he stared at the miracle of form and design, his eyes focused somewhere beyond the delicate inner parts of the flower, as if losing the objects in his depth of field.

The governor was deep in thought. He had to devise a plan that would accomplish The King's objective with these three. There must be a sure way of doing it. He wondered about a galaxy tour . . . No, too impersonal. What about . . . His thoughts trailed off as they often did when he was in prayer, listening.

The solitude was shattered by a ruckus in the long corridor outside his office.

"Not so fast, White Tornado! This is as fast as I go at this time of day!"

The attendant tugged at Mac like a mother towing a child through a supermarket. Won kept pace a step behind in his deferring Asian fashion, and Karae followed the contingent.

"Mac, will you shut up and cooperate for a change?" Karae scolded.

"Look, miss priss, Mr. Clean here drags me away from breakfast before I'm finished and announces an appointment with the governor as if he is the voice of God. Then he wants me to keep up with him when he has a stride like an NBA center. I don't get it. What's the rush?"

"Mr. McNeal," the attendant's voice held studied patience, "when the governor requests your presence, he isn't to be delayed."

"Governor, shmovernor! It's time the Big Cheese mellows out. He'll go to an early grave with ulcers."

The attendant took a deep breath. "The governor, like all of us in the Kingdom, has no physical defects, nor do we go to early graves. In the Kingdom a person who dies at age 100 is considered a mere child.[34] I can also assure you the governor has no ulcers."

"Then he's a carrier. He's sure giving them to me!"

Won kept his eyes straight ahead on the end of the

long hall, his countenance pained by the boisterous outbursts from his unchosen colleague. He evidenced lack of sleep. He had spent the night making notations of his experiences which might give some clues as to a way to escape from the realm. In exchange for the sleep loss he had a lot of notes . . . but no plan.

As the delegation reached the portal to the governor's office, a strong spirit of quiet fell over them all. Karae grew somber and Won attentive. Even Mac seemed to turn into a pumpkin when he reached the spot where he had been iceboxed in mid-stride the day before. Just passing the spot seemed to effect an attitude adjustment on the rogue.

The attendant led them to the official meeting spot in front of the desk. The governor rose to greet them as the attendant removed himself to the shadow.

"A blessed day to you all," greeted Governor Ben-David. "May Jehovah Jireh provide His bounty for you today." The governor's unshakable grace and poise were awe-inspiring. Though he could not have failed to overhear the cacophony coming from the hall prior to the group's entry, he acted as if nothing out of the ordinary had happened. All three knew by now that even the slightest irreverence or tension was out of the ordinary for the Kingdom.

Other attendants appeared and seated the guests.

"I trust you all rested well?" They nodded assent. Mac started to say something, but a deathly glare from Karae caused him to think better of it.

"You will need an extra measure of energy today," the governor's voice rang with excitement. "You will be going to the capital city of the Kingdom—to Zion, the most magnificent city on earth. There you will witness the global worship of The King with millions of pilgrims from all over the world.[35] It is my hope that this will be an unforgettable experience for you, and that you will find it in your heart to begin worshipping The King."

All of Won's waking hours had been building up a burden of thoughts. He felt he could bear the burden no longer. "Your honor, speaking for myself, I really appreciate your kindness and hospitality. Who could fail to enjoy the lovely accommodations, splendid meals, most cordial company, and breathtaking sights. But your honor, you must understand that we are away from our homes. This world, whatever and wherever it is, is not comfortable for us. We wish to return home. May I humbly implore you to grant us leave and provide us guidance that we may return to our homes and families?"

The governor appeared reflective, as if seriously considering the request.

"Your honor, I agree with Mr. Kim."

It was Mac. He was uncharacteristically polite, as if not to spoil the chances of the leader's saying yes. "We have a saying where we come from that 'There's no place like home.' After a full day and night here, I, too, would like to be packin' it in for the old U. S. of A. Wha-da-ya-say?"

The governor didn't respond. He just studied them with a kind of Saint Bernard look—loving, impassioned, but pained.

Karae was silent.

"I think it is time for me to talk with you about some deeper things which are involved in your stay here."

The shoulders of the trio drooped an inch or two at the negative reply. In resignation, they slouched further back in their chairs.

"You are here at the orders of The King. From time to time over the ages He has been known to create such tests in which mortals are involved. These moral experiments are designed to result in greater good for those involved, for those who observe and hear of the tests, for the Kingdom, and for The King Himself.

"One such test was His contest with the Prince of Darkness over the fortunes of Job. As you may recall, it was God who challenged the Evil One to give attention to His faithful servant."[36]

Mac and Won surely didn't recall. The Holy Bible was definitely not high on their reading lists while they were growing up. Their biblical illiteracy was such that they studiously avoided categories like "Old Testament Heroes" even when playing TV game shows or Trivial Pursuit.

The governor went on. "The suffering of Job was most unpleasant, as were the weeks of abuse he endured at the words of his well-meaning and judgmental friends. But the test served a long-term, divine purpose. And in the end, the test created lasting good."

"I wish you'd get to the point," Mac muttered under his breath, only to receive another stern look from Karae.

The governor ignored Mac and continued. "There is more at stake here than your comfort, far more at stake." He grew deadly serious. "The destiny of your eternal souls is at stake."

"I can't believe my ears," Mac erupted. "I suppose it's turn-or-burn time for us. Why don't you just have the organist crank out five verses of *Just as I Am Without One Plea* so we can hit the sawdust trail and head for home?"

Karae and Won Kim noticed the atmosphere surrounding the delegation begin to turn heavy and dark. Mac's sarcasm had become bitter, to say nothing of high-risk. Was his memory so short that he had forgotten his instant journey into freeze-dried living the day before? Did he want instant *rigor mortis* again today? They both held their breaths for the governor's response. To their relief, it was both reasoned and gracious.

"Mr. McNeal, I know that situations you cannot

control are maddening to you. I will make just two statements to you, and I expect no rebuttals, spoken or unspoken. First, The King is in control here. I have no latitude to make decisions contrary to His perfect will. But you may all rest assured that The King does all things—*all*—with your best interest in mind. Secondly, your insolence has been so pronounced that I find myself repeatedly tempted not only to accept your request to return home but to personally give you an extra-large blast of telekinetic thrust to propel you there. But The King has decreed that you be given more experiences which, it is His deepest desire, can result in fundamental and far-reaching changes in your life, happiness, and eternal destiny.

"When the test is finished, everything you are experiencing will become perfectly clear to you. Until then, I will hear no more debate. Is that thoroughly understood?" On those last two words, the governor raised his voice and strengthened it so that the words echoed outside the door and down the long hall. The three not-so-happy campers recoiled in their seats and went silent.

After a long pause to assure that there was no remaining resistance to his words or his agenda, the governor continued. "In a message I received from The King today, I was given authority to grant you the highest privilege given to any man, to attend the global worship celebration for The King in Zion.[37] I will assign an angelic guide to you, and you will attend the ceremonies which begin tomorrow. In moments, you will depart on your journey. Since you have no baggage I assume you will be ready."

Governor Ben-David snapped his fingers. Out of the atmosphere in the room came The Man.

An angel! So that's what he is. With a burst of insight like the solution of an equation, Won checked off one of the "For Further Reference" questions in his mind.

Karae glanced at The Man and then back to the governor. When her eyes turned toward Jireh, he met her gaze straight on. For a brief moment their eyes stayed locked onto each other's. Karae couldn't read precisely what the governor was expressing. It certainly was warm, inclusive, even affectionate. In her spirit she almost felt as if he were expressing grief at her departure. She found herself wishing she could read thoughts like the citizens of the Kingdom.

Her thoughts were interrupted by The Man's booming voice. "Well, my friends, we meet again. As you can see, I have been appointed as your guide for this part of your journey. I certainly trust that we can conduct this visit to Zion without the hideous black cloud of broken trust and fellowship which surrounded you when we first met."

Karae felt numb, as if in a state of suspended emotional animation. Her mind ricocheted between curiosity about what they were about to experience, weariness of exposure to so many things which they couldn't comprehend, and longing to get home.

The Man quickly took charge. He gave a smart salute to the governor, did an about-face, and directed, "Come with me."

Once again, as they had at their first meeting with The Man, the reluctant tourists felt themselves becoming lighter, as if the authority of gravity had been overruled on the spot where they stood. As they ascended into the atmosphere, Karae could hear The Man praying in a whisper, "Oh King, enable them to see beyond the wonders of Your realm—enable them to see *You!*" She weighed that concept—seeing beyond the seen to the unseen Author of Everything. Had this been a failing in her life—focusing merely on the seen?

Before the members of The Man's First Airborne Squadron really knew what was happening, they were descending over an incredible scene as if in an airplane making its final approach. Below them lay a breathtakingly beautiful panorama. The shore of a great sea lay on the west which, in the omnidirectional light of the heavens, sparkled like a sea of cut diamonds. Matched in brilliance was the eastern border of the area, a crystal river flowing north to south and emptying into a tranquil lake of similar luminescence.[38] The hundreds of square miles between the two glistening boundaries were extravagantly verdant lands, blending hundreds of brilliant shades of green into a stunning rainbow of flora. Terraced orchards etched across the rolling hills like elevation lines on a topographic map. Sprawling meadows stretched across the plains and glowed with the brilliant colors of wild flowers. Fields of grain and vegetables quilted the landscape. Neat, unwalled villages and modest towns hid away in the greenery, slipped unnoticed into the valleys, and lined the shores of the great sea on the west and the sparkling river on the east.

As the flight party settled closer to the earth, Won was struck by the spectacular symmetry of Zion, a perfect square approximately eight and one-half miles on each side with three clear east-west dividing lines.[39] A gleaming, walled city, it lay on a point precisely equidistant between the sea and the river. *What engineering!* the scientist thought. The perfectly planned metropolis was tied to both the sea and river by a ribbon of sparkling water flowing east and west from its walls.[40] Three massive entry gates, evenly spaced on each wall, granted entrance to the throngs that flowed in and out.[41]

On the north side, a wide boulevard paved with gold emerged from the central gate of the city and led straight as an arrow northward for three or four miles.[42] Dividing the lanes of the pedestrian highway was a spectacular tree-lined aqueduct filled with glistening liquid which, while crystalline like water, seemed somehow more alive. Each reflected ray from its surface divided the spectrum of the heavenly light like a prism into the colors of the rainbow. The resulting vision was like a rippling kaleidoscope flowing from the north into the city.[43]

"It's like a collage of travel posters," Karae gasped. "It's the Notre Dame on the Seine and the cathedral at Cologne and a Bavarian castle all in one!" Her eyes had traced the north-south thoroughfare to its beginning, to the Temple of Jehovah.

There it was, at the source of the aqueduct and the terminus of the highway on the north, the crown jewel of the vast scene: a stunning, walled temple with inner and outer courts Won guessed to be 850 feet square.[44] Rising far above the height of the outer walls was a pure-white, marbled sanctuary embellished with red precious stones and gold overlay that contrasted sharply with the royal purple of the marble walls and courtyard pavements. Set, as the Temple was, on a high hill, the sanctuary could be seen for hundreds of miles in every direction in the perfectly clear atmosphere of the Kingdom.

Karae could now see the sparkling stream flowing from under the threshold of the sanctuary and through the eastern wall of the Temple compound. It grew broader as it moved southward, bending around the southeastern corner of the Temple to spill its waters into the aqueduct of the great white way.[45]

Zion. The City of God. The new capital of the new Planet Earth. The royal city of The King. The political and religious epicenter of unified world rule.

The Man and the trio were suddenly positioned just outside the south wall of the city, directly in front of the central gate. Above its massive entrance, they saw chiseled in great letters *ISSACHAR GATE.*[46] A throng of people filled the street outside the gate and poured in and out of the strikingly beautiful portal with its carved stone relief and multi-colored banners.

Karae looked at Won. His eyes were glazed. Roboti-
cally, he removed his glasses, wiped them with his hand-
kerchief, and placed them back on his nose. He fumbled
for his note pad, then, as if he realized it was no use—infinitely more data than he could ever log in—he stuffed
the notepad back into his lab coat.

Mac looked ecstatic, like he'd just stepped off the
world's greatest roller coaster. "Whoa," he sighed. "What
a rush!"

This time, Karae's feelings were more like Mac's.
There are moments in life when a glimpse of extravagant
beauty strikes a person with such impact that no emotion
can respond to it. The flood of feelings ebbs and flows
between laughter and tears and ends up a mix of both.
This was one of those moments—except that she could
not recall ever feeling exactly this way before. She
laughed out loud, moisture forming at the corners of her
eyes.

As the bustle of Kingdom citizens stepped politely
around them on their way in and out of the gate, the three
stood motionless, their heads craning skyward with eyes
wide and mouths agape, like country folk do when visiting the big city for the first time.

"My friends," The Man smiled. "What you are
seeing is barely a taste of what is to come. Welcome to
Zion at festival time! We will be entering the city here,
exiting on the north side, and walking up the Holy Highway toward the Temple. This is a trek of a number of
miles, so pace yourself. Let me know if I am going too fast
for you. Also, it is important that we stay together. With
all the festival pilgrims here, it would be easy to get
separated or lost. Any questions?"

"Yeah, when can we go home?" Mac tossed his head
to the side in a manner that dismissed in that instant all
the splendor and rich images around them.

"Mac McNeal!" Karae slapped him on the arm.

"How *could* you?" She didn't want to be brought back—not just yet. Her romantic vision at what she had just seen had been shattered by Mac's irreverent blast. Leave it to Mac to spoil a perfect world! He'd probably scream *Fire* during a love scene at the movies, light a firecracker in the middle of Mass, or blow his car horn outside a wedding ceremony! Karae didn't like being reminded of Mac's question which, she had to admit, had been gnawing at her as well.

"Look, friends, I have nothing more to say on that subject other than what Governor Ben-David has already expressed. Need I reinforce that until The King has determined that this experiment is finished you will remain our guests?" The Man's own thoughts went back to the governor's orders, to Jireh's story of the confrontation with Zadock and of The King's desire to bring glory to His name through this three-way contest. "I'll say it again: *The King has spoken.*"

Mac exploded, making a cutting motion with his hand across his throat. "I've had it up to here with *The King* business. *The King* this, *The King* that—what about us? What about what *we* want? Has nobody here heard of the Bill of Rights? Who gave *The King* the Almighty authority to tell us what to do? Doesn't anybody get a vote around here?" It was feeling good to Mac to ventilate his spleen. "Maybe it's about time some of *The King's* wimpy subjects begin telling him a thing or two!"

Though uncomfortable at his latest outburst, this time Won and Karae were clearly identifying with what Mac was expressing. Despite the beauty of this new world, they both were sensing a building—almost screaming—discomfort with their surroundings. It was an irritating, growing frustration with the "other" nature of everything, the empty, nameless ache of dealing with people and situations in which none of the old rules work. Homesickness. That's what it was, homesickness.

And it had developed in days rather than months. Yes, it was a magnificent new world, but they didn't belong.

"Please, sir," Won ducked his head in a respectful bow. "Please intercede with The King to let us go home. Mac is speaking for all of us." This time even Karae nodded a half-hearted assent.

"Mr. McNeal." The Man was passionate but gracious as he addressed Mac's protests. "I can answer some of your questions. Yes, The King does care about your desires. No, nobody here has heard of the Bill of Rights— we have all surrendered our rights to The King and then He has returned them to us as privileges. What The King did to get His Almighty authority was give it up in a sacrifice of love for people like you who didn't care one whit for Him.[47] And finally, no, nobody gets a vote around here. While democracy was the best form of rule mankind could envision in your world, it is woefully inadequate in the Kingdom. For when you really think about it, democracy merely reduces the character of society to the lowest common denominator of the evil of the masses. Surely your own experience could have told you that."

"But sir," Won didn't want his question left unanswered. "All arguments aside, and as nice as this kingdom is, we are uncomfortable here. We want to go home! Will you or will you not intercede for us with The King to get permission for us to leave?" Won didn't want his question left unanswered.

"I will not." The question was answered. "I fully support the decision of The King and the motivation of The King and the objectives of The King."

"Well, well, well—here's the wooden dummy on the ventriloquist's knee mouthing someone else's words." Mac's caustic manner cut like a knife. The atmosphere around them grew darker. Sensing the tension in the air, bypassers cut a wider swath around the foursome, interrupting conversations as they did so.

The Man stared at Mac. Mac stared back, his gaze icy, contemptuous, even cruel. The Man's gaze was compassionate, empathetic, but resolute. Without one more word, he turned and started into the Issachar Gate. The three looked at each other and, not wishing to be abandoned, fell reluctantly in line behind him.

"Won," Mac put an arm on his Asian comrade's shoulder and whispered in his ear, "we're going to find a way out of here and back home if we have to turn this whole stupid dream world upside down."

The Man turned once more and looked at Mac with an expression of grief.

Overhearing Mac's words, Karae sensed a feeling of grief herself, but she didn't know why. The Man's expression was similar to the one Governor Ben-David had shown before their departure from the palace, she remembered. Except his expression had had even more love in it.

5

No Way Out
But Down

Pilgrims from every part of the globe pressed through the streets of Zion. Setting aside their ordinary Kingdom dress for the occasion, the festival-goers had bedecked themselves in apparel that reflected their origins in the previous world. Men, women and children of every nation, tribe, culture and ethnic origin, from every era of human history, bustled through the marketplaces of the Holy City.

As if attending a grand costume ball, the righteous revelers danced in the streets, enjoyed concerts by myriads of street musicians, dallied at the galleries of art and handiwork, and relaxed in the great parks and pools of the world capital. As they sampled foods from various times and cultures in stalls erected along the streets, the global believers shared joyful, open interaction with those they had never before met.

Amazingly, no security forces were necessary to patrol such a huge gathering, for there was not a single threat to the wayfarers. No threat of physical harm. No threat of thievery. No threat of angry arguments or fisticuffs. No fear of evil or destructive influences to their children. No fear of loss of innocence at the expense of any of the forms of entertainment widely shared. Not even the threat that they might be exploited in the shops and inns.

Every citizen of the Kingdom knew the moral Law of the Lawgiver. Each person had had the Law written on his heart when he received his Kingdom body and the new heart that came with it. Should anyone break the Law of The King or even violate its spirit, he would experience swift and strong discipline. While no one could remember that having happened, it was clear that such would be the consequence. This benevolent tyranny created an environment of mutual relaxation and trust that was incredible to experience.

Most had come to the festival by telekinesis, but had they come by vehicle they would have feared neither congestion nor accident. Collective goodwill motivated people to accommodate the needs of others, even at the expense of self-interest. No one had to worry about keys left in vehicles, for most means of transport had no keys or locks. Who would show so little respect for another as to violate his property? That would not be the Kingdom way.

Despite their discomfort in this new world, the threesome could hardly keep from being swept up in the joy and abandon which marked the festival-goers. The spirit which pervaded the city and the relationships among the visitors was infectious, more like a family reunion than a gathering of strangers.

Karae and Won had joined a circle of street dancers and were learning the steps of a Jewish-style dance. At a distance, The Man kept an eye on each of his charges. He smiled broadly as he observed the way the pure spirit of wholesome enjoyment had begun to capture the imaginations of his guests. Their American garb fit right in.

Others with North American dress from the late twentieth century could be seen throughout the streets, even though they were a distinct minority.

While Karae and Won mastered some new dance steps and made new friends, Mac was drawn to a beautiful young lady at a booth presenting foods from what formerly was South America. She could have been Northern European. Great swells of strawberry-blond hair cascaded around her delicate features, past her shoulders to the mid-point of her back. Her eyes were big and round and hazel. She was tall like the rest of the Kingdom race with long, slender legs like stems on a rose. She had long, long natural lashes which made her eyes burst like a flower when she directed them his way. Mac didn't miss a feature.

"What's a nice girl like you doing in a place like this?" he asked with a raised eyebrow and his patented, salacious grin.

"I'm sorry?" The young lady seemed puzzled by the meaning of the question.

Mac decided to try another approach. "What's your sign?"

The woman smiled, but still appeared caught off guard. "I'm not sure I understand . . . "

"Oh, nothing." Mac was tempted to try *Do you come here often?* but he could tell that his favorite lines were not going to work here. He had it figured that by the time he explained their meaning, he would be in a deeper hole with her than he was now. "It's just a conversation-starter we use where I come from."

"And where is that?" The lady seemed to like Mac, regarding him with open-eyed interest.

"Cleveland. Cleveland, Ohio."

"I don't think I've ever heard of Cleveland or Ohio. In what Kingdom province is it found?"

"Oh, it's in a *very Christian* province called the United States of America."

Her innocent stare told Mac he had just swung and missed—strike three. "I mean, you could hardly find a more Christian province than the USA. We have evangelists on television, churches on every corner, Bibles in every bookstore. We even have *In God We Trust* on our money!" Surely this would dazzle her.

"Why would you need to put that on your money? Wouldn't everyone *assume* that you trusted in God? Wouldn't the currency already have the likeness of Jesus, like Kingdom currency does?"

"Well, not exactly. It would be more likely to have George Washington or Abraham Lincoln."

"Are those pagan gods?"

Hello? Anybody home? Mac thought. How had he ever gotten into this? "Well, I think it would be a little harsh to call them pagan gods, even though they probably have been deified to some extent."

"Well, your provincial governor must not know about this or he would certainly have brought those responsible for such idolatry to justice. I had no idea such a situation could exist in the Kingdom."

"Well, that's the difference. I really don't live in the Kingdom. I live in a democracy."

"Oh, I have heard about that form of government in seminars by Kingdom teachers. They showed us that while democracy is well-intentioned, if people are not careful the Enemy can erode the entire system by gradually undermining the spiritual character of the voting majority until they will vote in the most heinous and vile laws."

"I would say that analysis is a bit exaggerated." Mac was back-pedaling now, about as fast as he could.

"Why, I remember one illustration of a past government like that in the previous world—I *think* it was a democracy—where the laws became so perverse that they protected sexual perversion, child destruction and greed, and oppressed the righteous people, the pure believers."

"Yeah, well, I suppose that could happen." Mac was on the ropes, and this babe was preparing to land an uppercut to the jaw. He could feel it coming.

"Do you stand up for King Jesus in Cleveland against the idolaters and democraticians?"

"Well, I suppose I could do better at that than I do." Where, oh where was The Man when Mac needed him? It was time to move on and leave this weird chick to her South American cuisine.

"Then perhaps you would like to leave the festival and get alone and pray to The King, asking His forgiveness for not serving Him more faithfully in Ohio, wherever that is."

"That certainly is a suggestion I should consider, I'm sure." Mac almost choked getting the words out.

"Well, be assured of my prayers for you and for Cleveland."

"Thanks much. Say, I hate to leave, but I have an appointment to keep. I really have to go."

The woman gave him an intense look as her countenance fell. "You do not hate to leave." She seemed grieved. "You just lied to me. And you have no appointment to keep. I'm concerned for you."

"Yeah, well, you probably should be," Mac was desperate now. "I'll be going." *That was close,* he thought. *I almost said, "Nice meeting you!"* He hastened away from the booth wondering what had hit him. Talk about not getting to first base—he hadn't even gotten into the same ball park. And she was so beautiful, too. What a waste!

He felt a tap on the shoulder. "Well, Mac, did you get anywhere with the lady?" It was Won, smiling broadly.

"Won, where in the world have you been? Where were you when I needed you?"

"What happened?"

"I got nailed! She's a Jesus freak, and I thought any minute she was gonna have me on my knees, repenting for not saving Cleveland."

Won burst into laughter. "It couldn't have happened to a more deserving guy. How could she have known you were least likely of our whole delegation to be a born-againer?"

That line stung a little, even to a calloused guy like Mac. "Listen, Won, I'm as religious as the next guy. I just don't think a guy has to go to church to get in touch with God. I can commune with my higher power in the woods just as well."

"Get serious, McNeal. That's the oldest subterfuge in the world. If all the people who defend their religiosity with that line practiced what they preach, every forest on earth would be trampled into the ground by the masses by now."

"Look, Chinaman, I—I'm sorry, Won. I know you don't like that."

"No problem, Mac." The two dropped the matter and headed down the street looking for Karae and The Man.

T here they are." Won pointed to a spectacular fountain gushing a kaleidoscopic liquid. Karae and The Man were sitting on stone blocks around its edge, dangling their feet in the fluid like scores of others around them. The fountain had been constructed seventy or seventy-five feet in the air in a pyramidal shape, and the water rippled and splashed down over free-form structures into a pool at the base. Pedestals had been placed around the edges of the bowl-shaped pool as seats for the waders and foot-danglers.

"Having fun?" Mac asked the pair.

"Definitely!" They answered at the same time, then looked at each other and laughed—their voices like a joyful chord from an organ to accompany the splashing of the fountain. "Take off your shoes and join us. It's great!"

Mac had one shoe off by the time Won asked, "What is this stuff? Is it water?"

The Man replied, "*Living* water."

"Isn't all water living?" Won always had one more question, no matter how many were answered.

"Not like this. You see, this water has supernatural properties. Only God knows its true source. It flows from under the sanctuary a few miles to the north, descends off Zion Hill around the Temple walls and enters the aqueduct which divides the Holy Highway.[48] We'll see more of it as we go northward toward the Temple at procession time."

"What kind of supernatural properties?" Won's empirical mind was in high gear now—as was his skepticism.

"Spectacular healing and life-generating properties. Just leave your feet in the water for a few minutes, and you will begin to feel added strength and vitality entering your body. It is so powerfully life-giving that the sea it flows into is filled with fish and wonderful creatures— the same body of water you used to call the Dead Sea.[49] Even the trees watered by the stream between the Temple and the city grow far taller and healthier than plants watered from other sources.[50] The fruit trees bear fruit in monthly cycles—trees that generally bore fruit only once or twice a year in the old world."[51]

"C'mon, you can't be serious—monthly?" Won

blinked hard, incredulous. He had taken too many graduate level courses to believe this.

"Monthly. And, Mr. Kim, when I make statements of fact, I am *always* serious. When I am joking, I make sure that you are clearly able to tell that I am, lest I snare you unwittingly."

Well excuuuse me, Mac thought. He had been listening to the scientific dialogue through his own filter of skepticism. At the same time, his wet feet sure did feel good.

"Time to move on," The Man announced as he stood to his feet and stepped out of the water. "The procession will begin in an hour and we have to get through the city to the Holy Highway by then."

Reluctantly the waders and splashers stepped out of the pool, pausing one more time to admire the architectural beauty of the fountain. With shoes back on and feet and bodies refreshed, they traversed the streets of the marvelous city. The rest had given them a chance to digest the foods they had picked up along the way at the Booths of the Nations.

Glistening clusters of high rises rose in masterful symmetry throughout the city's walled enclosure. The walls themselves were integrated into the designs of the city plans. At some points terraced fountains cascaded down from the walls or from taller turrets spaced along them. In other spots flower gardens atop the walls overflowed with flowering vines, making it difficult to tell there were structures underneath them at all. Glorious trees landscaped the streets, buildings, and even the high rises. Some trees stretched ten to fifteen stories in the air.

As the four approached the north wall of the city, it became clear to them that increasing numbers of people had concentrated in the vicinity. Grassy areas in city parks and landscaped lawns near government buildings had become rendezvous spots for well-ordered contingents of similarly dressed nationals. Each contingent had large, beautifully fashioned banners, some twenty to thirty feet high, which they were preparing to carry.

"Up ahead is Judah Gate," announced their guide. "Directly through that gate lies the Holy Highway, the processional route to the Temple.[52] Make haste, we need to get to the starting point soon. Only a few minutes and the procession will begin."

The four picked up the pace. Karae and The Man led the way, while Mac and Won hung back a few paces.

Mac walked along in uncharacteristic silence, thinking back over the experiences of the last day and a half. Sure, it was a great place to visit, but now there was no question about it; he did *not* want to live here! Okay, so the place was spectacular. So was Disneyland! But Disneyland was phony happiness, too. This planet or world or land—whatever it was—was a Disneyland for Jehovah's Witnesses. The women were so straight it was sickening, and they tried to convert you to Jesus. The system was wired so tight you couldn't raise a finger or you got zapped by a king or a governor or an angel. *I am so sick of all these super-happy people,* Mac thought. *If Jesus is The King, Pollyanna has to be the queen!* They needed a little reality, a little excitement—a little *sin* to liven up this place! The longer Mac stayed here, the better Wanda looked to him. The better *Cleveland* looked.

Mac had worked himself into a state of passion, passion for getting out of this place pronto. He weighed the risks of various approaches. He could feign loyalty to The King and gain sufficient favor to earn a good-behavior pass out. Not a chance—the big wheels could spot deception anywhere in the galaxy. He could lie low for a while until he saw a chance to make a break for it. If he didn't get out of here soon, he'd be ready for the funny farm. Even worse, he may even get to like it here and become a fundamentalist like the rest! His mind was made up—he would make a break for it today, whether anybody went with him or not.

Suddenly an idea bonked him on the head. "Won," Mac nudged Won and whispered. "I think this could be our chance. We may never have a better shot at getting away than right now. This crowd must number half to three-quarters of a million, maybe more. With their attention riveted on the processional, what stops us from tipping off Karae and, on cue, grabbing her and slipping off into the crowd? Nobody will notice."

"Easier said than done, Mac." Won pulled a wad of folded papers out of his coat pocket. "There are a few items such a plan would have to deal with." He fumbled for his list of obstacles to escape. "First, there's the mind-reading capability of The Man. If he focuses on us, and we are thinking of escape, we're dead."

"That's the point, Won. If we make our move at a time when his concentration is on the procession, he may never know. Until then, we concentrate on something else every time he seems to be giving attention to us."

"Well, maybe. But what if we do get away? Where do we go? Who will help us? Everybody is so Big Brother when it comes to supporting the system."

"Hey, Won, we'll talk somebody into helping us. They are all so compassionate and eager to serve, one good sob story and they'll climb all over themselves to help!"

"Don't lag too far behind, men," The Man called.

"Okay, sir." Won closed a pace or two toward The Man and dropped his voice even lower as Mac followed. "Oh yeah? A sob story with one untrue ingredient in it will warn them in a second. You know they can recognize a lie at a hundred paces."

"Then we'll tell 'em the truth! We're lost. We don't know how we got here. We have family and friends back home worried sick about us: We don't know our way back. We don't have a place to stay. We don't have any money. You show 'em pictures of your little kids and portray the pitiful little urchins crying, 'Where's Daddy?' Now I didn't tell one lie, did I?"

"No . . . " Won was still skeptical.

Mac persisted. "Look, Kim, what are our alternatives? Wait until we get out of this mob, until The Man has his full attention on us like he—or somebody—has done nearly every second since we got here? Then what chance will we have?"

"Mac, they have their ways of finding us. That's how we got intercepted in the first place. They felt some disturbance in the force or something and dispatched this guy—" he pointed to The Man— "to capture us."

"That was because we were having an argument. This place can't handle confrontation. So long as we are in one accord and cooperating, peace and harmony will be our cover! We'll have 'harmonious convergence.' With one mind we can converge on the exit and be outta here!"

"Where is 'outta here'?"

"I don't know, but we have to try, Won! We have to try!"

The Man turned and looked at the two. They quickly shifted their attention to a massive corp of buglers which was gathering in formation just outside Judah Gate. The Man looked back at the musicians.

"A crooked smile, Won. That will be the cue. If I give you a crooked smile, that means head back into the city through this gate, Judah or whatever it is."

"Okay . . . " Won was unenthusiastic. "I'll get the word to Karae if we can catch a moment when Big Brother isn't reading our minds."

"Deal! You're a champ, Chinam—er, Won."

Won gave Mac a you-know-better-than-that look.

Now in close proximity to Karae and The Man, Mac kept Won at his elbow as they took in the beginning of the processional. Coming from the west on a street which ran parallel to the city wall was the parade's first contingent, the vast corp of male buglers in stunning red and gold uniforms. As each carried a long, straight, slender horn six to eight feet in length, they marched in formation and held the bugles over the right shoulder of the person in front of them, creating a glimmering sea of gold bugle bells. There must have been five hundred of them—all playing a coronation march with a blend and subtlety of sounds unimaginable for bugles.

Following the buglers came massive floats decorated with a selection of natural flowers like none they had ever seen before. They made the Rose Parade look like an afterthought. Great, gilded carriages bore priests from the Aaronic priesthood. A turquoise-robed *a cappella* choir of perhaps 1200 voices sang praises to The King as the singers paraded through the street, along the wall and around the corner onto the golden pavement of the Holy Highway. Light reflected on the processional participants from the living water which flowed down the center of the boulevard. Despite the dazzling sights before him, Mac kept looking for a chance to make a break, for a way to escape the gaze of their angelic chaperon.

"You still with me, buddy?" Mac wanted reassurance from Won.

"Still with you." Won was showing more confidence now. The idea of escape seemed to be settling in.

Now they could see banners of intricate tapestry on poles thirty to fifty feet above the procession, borne by strong men with specially braced flag standards. The banners bore the insignias of the various tribes of Israel, of the divine provinces from around the world, and of the major provincial capitals. Following each banner were delegations of people in ethnic, national, racial, and historic subgroups. A delegation of French Huguenot believers in eighteenth century dress followed the banner for El Shaddai province. Approximately four hundred Ninevite believers from 800 B. C. marched in formation following the banner of Jehovah Sabbaoth province, which featured a portrayal of a great sea creature with a man inside it. A band of fifteenth century Spaniards in colorful costumes marched under a banner with Christian symbols of Roman Catholic origin. They were from Jehovah Shalom province.

The procession was so spectacular that even Mac had become transfixed, so preoccupied that he had temporarily forgotten he was supposed to be looking for the right moment to make a break. Won, too, was thinking of other things—especially the structure of the massive floats and the delegations of Asians from various divine provinces. Karae seemed to be especially engrossed in the delegation from the Jehovah Jireh province.

"Will Governor Ben-David be attending the worship?" she asked their guide.

"I don't think so," The Man replied. Karae was disappointed. "The governor has meetings with his cabinet this week. Besides, I think he comes to the Tenth Month celebration. Even though harvest comes to the Kingdom monthly, the Tenth Month continues to be considered a time of special significance in Jehovah Jireh province."

"Why is that?" Won was becoming too predictable. Question Number 1372.

"Since *Jehovah Jireh* is the name for The King which denotes that 'God provides,' divine provision is tied to the fall harvest remembrance from the old world."

"Hmmmm," Won made another note on the folded

papers which had replaced the overflowing note pad he'd been carrying.

As the last of the delegations filed past, Mac could see that the procession was nearing its end. The final entry was a Promethean float with a gigantic sphere representing the renovated earth under The King. The globe must have been seventy feet in diameter with the divine provinces indicated on its surface in magnificent floral arrangements. It rotated on an axis that was not near the North Pole; instead, the axis penetrated the earth at the point of the Temple of God. Protruding out of the point on the globe was a ten-foot silver cross studded with a phenomenal array of precious stones which caught the light and projected laser-like reflections of color onto the viewing masses. Most breathtaking of all, the gargantuan globe had no visible means of support.

The crowds of onlookers *oohed* and *aahed* as the final feature of the procession passed. Then the broad thoroughfare disappeared as a sea of people pressed onto the Holy Highway to make the trek to the Temple.

Mac seized the moment. This was it! The focus of the masses was on the globe as people pressed into the streets to get a better look at it and begin their journey to the Temple. The Man still seemed to be transfixed by the procession's visual impact. Mac reached through the sea of humanity, tapped Won on the shoulder, and flashed him a crooked smile. Won's face whitened in a moment of terror. Then, instinctively, he tugged on Karae's sleeve—this was her signal. Karae glanced over her shoulder to see Mac already beginning to move away, against the flow of people.

"Are you—" she broke off her question to Won as she saw the back of Mac's head disappearing in the crowd. Won answered by spinning around to follow Mac. Karae's heart raced. She didn't want to miss what lay ahead, and she was afraid. But seeing the other two moving away, she realized she did not want to be left alone. Again, that faint homesick feeling swept over her and she felt her legs propelling her in the direction Mac and Won had taken.

Mac weaved his way through the people, running interference for Won and Karae. The gracious crowd parted like the Red Sea before them. They must have assumed that the three had pressing, royal business to tend to. It couldn't have been an emergency, for emergencies never occurred in the Kingdom.

Quickly, the escaping trio slipped among the thousands and darted back through the streets of Zion. Soon they reached an area of the city where the crowds were lighter. "Keep thinking unity. Keep thinking peace," Mac barked to his breathless sidekicks. "He can read our minds when we're negative. Think positive!"

They dashed in and out among the buildings, darted around and behind the lavish trees, shrubs and flowers, and skipped through small openings onto side streets.

"Mac, Karae—over there!" Won pointed to a building which somehow did not fit the style and architecture of the surrounding metropolis. Mac noticed a large gargoyle protruding from under the arch of the building over the front entrance. Enormous double doors with attractive carvings caught his eye. There was a shiny engraved plaque on the keystone above the door. *His Majesty's Department of Repatriation*, declared the gold plate.

"Let's go in here," Won said. "Could be our best chance."

Mac pulled open one of the great doors. The other two followed him, checking over their shoulders to see if anyone was in close pursuit. No one. All three inside, the large door closed behind them. They were in total darkness.

"I don't feel right about this," Karae shuddered. "There's something eerie about this place."

She had no sooner said these words when it felt as if the floor were dropping out from under them.

Mac emitted a long, terrorized moan. Won was silent as his body fell like a rag doll head-over-heels into the pitch-black, atmospheric darkness. Karae let out an ear-splitting scream as the threesome fell ever more rapidly into the blackness. Now Mac, too, was yelling in stark terror as they hurtled through the inky space. Karae caught a breath for the end of the fall, but they just kept falling. She had to gasp for another breath, and another, between screams. She braced herself against the terrible impact she expected at any second, one which would smash all their bodies to pieces against some immovable object. The collision didn't come.

As they continued their meteoric descent, Karae felt the atmosphere getting heavier and the temperature rising. A panicked thought flashed through her mind: *Is this the beginning of the end, or the end of the beginning?*

Just as quickly, a voice from somewhere inside her, an inner voice that sounded like that of Governor Ben-David, replied, *That depends on you, Karae!*

6

Sweet Seduction

Welcome, my dear friends."

The man standing before the three was absolutely radiant. He was handsome, impressive, and dressed in stark, tight-fitting black clothes which showed the muscular build beneath them. His countenance exuded an aura of subliminal magnetism—powerful magnetism, animal magnetism. His manner was refined, smooth.

The aliens found themselves in a cavernous room with twenty-foot ceilings covered with Renaissance paintings. Gem-like, Austrian crystal chandeliers hung in pairs about twenty feet apart down the length of the long, narrow chamber. Expensive, European, seventeenth century antique sofas, desks and tables were arranged in conversation areas throughout the room. It was large enough to serve as a hotel ballroom but obviously was a palatial parlor. Original oils by the masters—Reubens, Rembrandt, Renoir—hung on the walls, the larger surfaces covered with royal Bavarian tapestries.

"I'm so sorry to alarm you with the ride you just received! I won't even charge you for the ticket," the man said smoothly, with a slight chuckle. His deep voice seemed to ooze words rather than speak them. "My name is Zadock the Third. Let me welcome you to a new and much more wonderful land than the one from which you've come."

Won, Karae and Mac were speechless. Karae felt like a cosmic roller coaster had just dropped her unharmed into the new environment she now surveyed. As the horror of their terrible free-fall subsided, she struggled to emerge from her catatonic state. Apparently Won and Mac were in psychological decompression as well. No one spoke.

A stream-of-consciousness patter ran through Karae's stunned mind. *I can't stand it anymore. These last two days have seemed like months—months of being jerked around by unknown people, dazzled by unreal sights, terrorized, feted, stimulated, disappointed. An emotional Tilt-a-Whirl, that's what it's been.* Would she ever see Pasadena again? Her dear, helpless mother must be desperate by now. A few more days without her heart medicine and she would be dead. *Much more of this and I'LL be dead!* Karae thought. The people all seemed so nice, but not one of them had fulfilled her most urgent request—to go home!

Won was not whipped, just numb. He had been born to adversity. Life in Seoul had been a low-level Purgatory: poverty, overcrowding, lousy medical care, back-breaking labor since age ten. He hadn't been coddled like his American-born comrades. He grew up with pain, weariness, opposition, dog-eat-dog competition. He'd had to fight for rice in his own home, scrounge for survival on his own street. He hadn't known what comfort was until he hit the Lone Star State.

Now he coped with these other-world circumstances in the Asian way: by entering an altered state of consciousness. His curious mind turned to mush. No searching questions, no copious notes, no intellectual sparring.

I've got to get myself together. It was all Won could think. He had known so little affirmation in life that in tough situations like this he had always blamed himself. It was instinctive to do so by now; he'd always been blamed! If all through life the people who count are on your case, you soon learn to get on your own case when they aren't around. He could hear his angry father yelling at him to stop crying. He could still feel the slap on the side of the head his father often administered as reinforcement to ignore the pain of living. *Snap out of it, Won!* He barked the order to himself as if he were now his own unfeeling father. Then he lied to himself. *Maybe this is a way back to Mary and Justin and Texas. I'm going to find out.*

The way you could tell Mac was sobered was that he turned from outright hellion to imp. On the mischief scale he had plummeted from 9.5 to about 5.9. His feistiness had no more feist. His boisterousness had lost its boist. Somehow that terrorizing fall had sucked the air from his balloon. *It hasn't been that bad until now,* he thought. *Now it's BAD.* Mac was experiencing a rare moment of reality.

He was mystified at the downness he felt. There was something heavy about this place! He felt weighed down, depressed. Maybe if he could figure out this new character, he could work him for a favor, a get-me-out-of-here-and-home type of favor. The thought of a client to sell revived him.

"There, there, my friends." Zadock flashed a smile under a brow furrowed with unconvincing wrinkles of concern. "You look weary and confused. Let me assure you that things are not so bad as they may seem. You are among friends, and . . . " he paused for obvious, dramatic effect, " . . . you are going home."

"What? We can, really?" Karae's face illuminated.

"You're serious?" Won topped Karae's question. He

looked at Karae and Mac to see if they believed the words he had just heard.

"You'd better not be putting us on, whoever you are," Mac warned.

"I beg your pardon, my friend. I don't know what the people were like where you came from, but you will find that here we tell the truth! You can bank on that. When I tell you you are going home, that is exactly what I mean." Zadock's declaration of integrity had a slight tinge of over-sell to it, like a shoe salesman who assures you that a tight pair of leather boots will stretch over time.

"Fine. Where's the bus, the plane, the train, the zap gun, the time machine—whatever it is you are going to use to get us back?" Mac had impatience in his voice and a cynical look on his face.

"Sir, we didn't need a vehicle to get you here. We won't need a vehicle to get you home. Just trust me."

"Look, Drydock—" Mac was on the attack.

"Zadock, if you please." Their host's response was controlled, saccharine, syrupy.

"Whatever your name is, no games. We've had it with games."

"Oh, did the people of the Kingdom play games with you?"

"Yeah, we got zapped around the planet by an angel, lied to by a regional governor—"

"Wait a minute," Karae broke in, "Governor Ben-David did not lie to us."

"He most assuredly did," Mac pressed on. "He made noises like he cared about us, as if he sympathized with our desires to return home, but you notice nothing happened." An empty-handed gesture emphasized his point. "He talked out of both sides of his mouth. He had the power to make it happen, too."

"But he was following orders from The King!" Karae protested.

"The King, my foot. We never saw this mythical monarch. For all we know he is a figment of somebody's imagination, a handy rationalization for whatever the boys down the chain of command want to decide."

"Please, friends," Zadock held up his hands like a referee in a prize fight trying to separate the sluggers. "There is no need to quarrel. You are in good hands now that you are no longer in the Kingdom. You can relax. I am sure you will find the environment here much more to your liking.

"You must be so weary, and famished." Zadock's tone was dramatically sympathetic. "Before a leisurely dinner and a good night's rest, would anyone like a drink? We can talk about your struggles in the Kingdom and plans for your return home tomorrow morning. Please be seated."

"Tomorrow morning?" Won sought confirmation.

"Tomorrow morning," Zadock nodded. The room relaxed a bit. All four took seats in the nearest conversation circle. "Here is a key to a suite for each of you—down the hall through those draperies. I think you'll find your accommodations adequate. Now let me ask again. Would anyone like a drink?"

"A glass of rice wine would surely hit the spot." Won thought his request had near-zero probability of being fulfilled.

"Fine," Zadock responded. "When the young lady comes to take your order, name any drink, any brand, any vintage, and it will be provided. It's part of our hospitality."

Mac's eyes got really big really fast. "A gin and tonic for me, please."

"Just pass the order to the girl, Mr. . . . . "

"McNeal."

" . . . Mr. McNeal. Anything for the lady?" Zadock was solicitous.

"Nothing alcoholic, thank you."

"Fine. Name your favorite soft drink, fruit juice, coffee or tea—whatever your palate desires." Zadock was scoring points, and he knew it.

"I'd like a chilled glass of cranberry juice—is that possible?"

"Consider your desire fulfilled. Here in Wonderland no desire is left unsatisfied." Zadock snapped his fingers and a woman stepped out from between heavy velvet draperies at the end of the room. Dust floated from the closing drapes and settled toward the floor behind her.

She was a sensational beauty. Perfect facial features. Long, auburn hair to the shoulders. A Miss Universe figure. As she strode the length of the parlor, all six eyes were riveted to her. She wore an ankle-length gown of a material so delicate that it revealed instead of concealed the form beneath it. A long side slit revealed her shapely legs as she moved. Like a showgirl on a Las Vegas runway, she flowed rather than walked. Her ears, neck and wrists seemed to drip with mesmerizing diamond and emerald jewelry.

Mac let out an audible sigh as the young woman reached mid-room. Won was more discrete, but he wasn't exactly studying the great masters on the wall while the woman drew closer. Karae portrayed the kind of silent admiration one woman reserves for the exceptional beauty of another.

"Did Zadock get your requests?" Her voice seemed an octave lower and more resonant than the usual female voice. She was now within a few feet.

"Well, not exactly," Mac rose from his seat, grinning, strangely energized. "But seeing you has just changed my request."

"I'm handling requests for *drinks* at this time, sir." Her demeanor indicated that the question wasn't closed.

"Rats." Mac slapped his thigh in mock disgust and looked at Won and Karae for response.

"Mac, have you no class?" Karae rebuked the Irishman.

"Yeah. But when it comes to a beautiful woman, I can rise above it."

Karae shook her head in disgust. Won gave the woman his drink order while trying his best—and failing—to act nonchalant. Karae made her cranberry juice request and the charmer pivoted and slinked the distance of the room again, to the unbroken stare of four male eyes.

Zadock studied the two men. Karae studied Zadock. There was something unsettling about this man. For one so strikingly handsome and flawless, the unsettling part of him had to be more spiritual than physical. Physically, Karae thought, he was a real hunk. But his eyes seemed to peer beneath the surface of the person, to probe in areas where there are *No Trespassing* signs. And another thing . . . she noticed that his eyes never smiled! His face smiled, but his eyes never did—no sparkle, no light. Karae decided that she had better not trust him. At least, not until she got to know him better.

Miss Sensuality returned with the refreshments accompanied by another exquisite woman, an Asian lady, probably the runner-up in the same beauty contest which gave Miss Sensuality her crown. She was carrying a lovely tray of the most artfully prepared and delectable *hors d'oerves* the three had ever seen.

With gradual subtlety the ambiance of the room changed. There was music—first at a tolerable volume, but gradually it became louder, as heavy-metal blasts blared from unseen tweeters and woofers. Room lighting shifted almost imperceptibly into lower-candle-power, high-scandal-power illumination. Colored hues of red, blue and purple highlighted the walls from hidden spotlights. A ten-foot-square, holographic screen appeared in one corner of the room and projected a blinding sequence of sensual, wildly colored, masturbatory images. Incense-like fragrances floated through the room in waves. Soon the senses were overloaded with stimuli—stimuli calculated to elicit powerful animal responses.

The men were behaving with frightening predictability. Mac was doing his best to make time with the auburn-haired beauty. Won, the married man, was playing coy and uninterested with the Asian lady, but in a manner that was calculated to let her read the opposite. She was reading it like a book.

Karae folded her arms tightly as she analyzed the goings on. A cold chill gripped her and she heard her mind scream, *Wait a minute. We still don't know where we are! Wonderland? Is that what Zadock said? We know less about where we are now than we did when we were in the Kingdom!*

The multidimensional assault on the senses continued around her as she forced herself to think rationally. They had not been outside this room since they were dropped here at the end of a frightful sky dive. What was going on? Who was this Zadock? What was his angle? Karae got the feeling that this was all too good to be true . . . like the perfect crime. She had to figure this character out, find out what made him tick.

She didn't have to wait long to start. Zadock, his gaze now locked in on her, approached from across the circle and slipped next to her on the sofa. "How's your juice? To your liking?" She could smell the powerful, musk-like scent of his cologne.

"It was wonderful. So refreshing, thank you."

"Well, we want you to have every desire fulfilled here in Wonderland. You are my guests. I like to have my guests enjoy themselves." Zadock was silver-tongued, and right now the silver was well-polished.

But Karae's skin was beginning to crawl. This guy

had another agenda going, and she didn't like it. Was she imagining all this? Was this an unfair projection on an undeserving person? Her head was saying yes. Her soul was screaming no.

She glanced across the circle. The two women had clearly set aside their waitress duties and were most obviously engaged in deep two-on-two dialogue with Won and Mac. Somebody was baiting the hook. Somebody was nibbling at it. Karae wasn't quite sure who was doing which.

"It's a lovely evening, Karae." Zadock peered out from under his eyebrows suggestively. "Would you like to step outside on the balcony? There is a lovely view and fresh air. The blossoms in the orchard are in bloom and the aroma is wonderful."

What do I do now? she asked herself in a state of low-level panic. And how did this guy know her name? She hadn't mentioned it, nor had Won or Mac. What should she do? The guys were paired off. By now they didn't even know she was on the same planet, if this was a planet they were on.

"I—I guess that would be nice." Karae's voice betrayed a telling lack of enthusiasm.

Zadock extended his hand to help her from the sofa. Reluctantly she grasped it and rose. Gently, he directed their steps toward velvet draperies at the end of the room opposite from where the two women had come. Upon reaching them, he held aside one drape to allow Karae to pass. One step onto the balcony and she was overcome.

"No—I can't believe it!"

"What, my love?" Zadock's words were flowing like honey.

"It's Pasadena! My home!" She saw the lights of the city sprawling across the valley from the foothills . . . inhaled the fragrance of orange blossoms from the private orchards . . . felt the warm, dry California air just beginning to cool with the setting sun. Could it really be her home?

"I thought you'd like the view." He had a pleased look.

"Zadock . . . " She surprised herself by using his name. "Am I home? Is this Pasadena? May I go to be with my mother?"

"In the morning, dear." He slipped his hand around her waist. She was so totally transfixed by the sights, sounds and smells of what *had* to be California's City of Roses that his touch didn't register with her. She could see the lights lining Colorado Boulevard. There was a bustle of activity at the convention center. Then she caught a glimpse of Zadock's face in the moonlight. He was strikingly handsome. At that point, she realized that his arm encircled her waist. It had been a while since an attractive man had held her. She did nothing to discourage him.

"Karae, you are a very attractive lady—and very poised. I like a confident, self-assured woman."

"Thank you." Even if this was a line, it was pleasing to the ear. Another whiff of his cologne stirred funny tingles inside her.

"Do you enjoy the mortgage brokerage business?"

How did he know *that?* "Every job has its down sides, I suppose. But yes, I like it a lot."

"Have you ever thought of marriage, of family?"

"Sure. Most women do." Karae felt increasingly torn by a powerful approach-avoidance motivation. Something was drawing her irresistibly to Zadock. Something else within her wanted to push him away.

He was pulling her closer now. "Would it be attractive to you to have all the financial resources you need so that you would not have to work, would not have to care for your infirm mother, so you could travel to romantic places and enjoy the good life?"

This was spooky. This guy knew everything about her—her dreams, her insecurities. "Well, sure, I suppose everybody would like to be independently wealthy and have love and family to boot."

"I can arrange all of the above." Zadock's voice was firm, like he was going to press for some kind of decision.

"Nobody can arrange those things for somebody else," Karae protested mildly, pulling away from him. "You have to get those things for yourself."

"Karae, you don't understand. I can arrange *anything* your heart desires. How do you think I put Pasadena at the edge of the balcony and knew your name and your vocation and your mother's condition? There is not one dream of yours I cannot fulfill, little or great."

They were face to face now. He had slipped both hands onto her waist.

"Look, Zadock, I didn't just fall off the turnip truck. What's the gimmick? There is no free lunch." What was it that kept her interested in this guy's line? She wouldn't have given a guy like this the time of day before. What was it that let him draw her close?

"There *is* a free lunch, Karae! It's secured through the spiritual world. God lives in you as He does in all of Nature. All the power of the universe is no farther away than your skin! For ages eastern mystics and Tibetan holy men have known the secrets of both serenity and prosperity, of the most extravagant love and personal success. I know these secrets."

"Zadock, you sound like you're trying to get me into your Amway downline. I'm not buying it." She pulled away again.

"Oh yes you *are*, Karae. You *are* buying it. You are innately spiritual. I could tell the first moment I saw you. Your aura communicates a powerful inner spirit. It is the secret to your success in college, in business, in relationships. It is what makes you beautiful to me." He pulled her even closer than before. He was strong and his muscles well toned.

Suddenly Karae could not speak. A fire of passion was flaming within her. It circled her head and kept her mind from communicating to her heart. Zadock leaned forward to kiss her. She went limp, trembling slightly in inner torment. His lips were near hers.

And then she saw it.

Suddenly, in a single motion, she pushed Zadock away from her and screamed in horror. "Help! Somebody help me! Mac, Won, somebody!" Still screaming, she ran terrified from the balcony, through the draperies, into the great hall.

It was empty.

She dashed across the parlor and out through the draperies where their rooms were supposed to be. She found her room, fumbled with the key in the lock until the door opened, then slammed it shut behind her. Bolting the lock, she threw herself on the bed and sobbed.

Zadock remained on the balcony, grinning.

Mac and Won had long since disappeared with their dates into two different rooms.

7

The Dawning of the Darkness

A pair of gold earrings lay on the bedstand beside Mac's bed. Mac turned on the mattress like a rotisserie. He had been writhing there since the auburn-haired beauty had left the room sometime in the early hours of the morning.

His conscience was grinding him to powder. What he thought would be sweet had turned bitter—bitter as gall.

As usual, Mac loathed himself. "Mornings after" were among the few times in his life when he had serious thoughts. Maybe that was why he had so few on other occasions—the thoughts he entertained on these empty mornings were so devastating and lethal that he had to fill the rest of his life with variant forms of activity to compensate.

Sunlight poured through the window onto the bed. He burrowed more deeply into the covers, as if to hide from the searching beams of light. For some reason, sunlight was disquieting to him now. If only there were a television set or a radio, a CD player with some heavy metal music—anything in which to drown the searchings of his psyche, any anesthetic medium to dull his inner pain.

Why was the guilt especially heavy this morning? This was not his first time. He did, after all, have Wanda, his live-in lover back in Cleveland Heights. And there had been many others over the years. Why this searing misery today?

In tiny increments, he pulled the bed covers aside, taking momentary peeks at the world about him. Over a period of time he exposed one leg, then the next. He stumbled from the bed and began to do his daily duties, slowed by the ruinous hangover. This was not a hangover from alcohol. Far worse, it was the consequence of a binge of depravity. And it wouldn't go away.

Why did this always happen? Mac wondered angrily. Why did he feel so rotten afterwards when sex was supposed to feel so good? He reviewed his usual litany of rationalizations:

- "Intimacy is just physical, like scratching an itch. I don't feel guilt after a good scratch!"
- "I'm not married. I have no contractual relationship I'm breaking by having another woman. Wanda's and my relationship is 'open' by mutual agreement."
- "I'm not under some puritanical, moral code. That thinking is just oppressive cultural conditioning."
- "There is no cosmic legislator in the sky who set forth planetary rules for sexual behavior. We're here by evolution, not creation."

But for some reason, this morning he couldn't get his inner man to agree with the code he had carried with him for years.

As his mind and conscience fenced with reciprocating parries and thrusts, Mac gazed at the countenance in the bathroom mirror. He looked older this morning. Harder. Uglier. His mind wandered back to Miss Innocence at the fruit juice stand in Zion. He wondered if she ever felt guilt, if she ever had hangover of the soul. He pondered whether she ever looked older, harder, or uglier the morning after whatever innocent people like her did on the nights before.

"I have to shake off this remorse. It makes no sense." He slapped himself on the cheeks with both hands as he talked aloud to his reflection. "If you go on any more guilt trips, you'll have to join a frequent flyer program. Mac, old boy, you're not such a bad guy. You just like to have a little fun. Now get out there and close a deal with Drydock. You remember the credo: 'Everybody's a prospect! Sell! Sell! Sell!' "

Won Kim closed the door to his room behind him and stepped into the long hall. He was up early because of his sleepless night. His female guest had left him before midnight, right after their intimacies, but the iron-heavy weight of his adultery had been crushing him for the nine hours since. As he traversed the long corridor, he thought of his dear wife, Mary, and the weight became greater, reaching a critical mass which threatened to pulverize his soul.

"But she will never know," he rationalized aloud.

But you will! came an inner voice. The debate was on.

"But this is the only time I've ever been unfaithful."

One time too many, was the rebuttal. *It takes only one injury to scar the human spirit. Each additional scar just produces thicker callouses, more and more proud flesh to dull the spirit's sensitivity and power.*

"I'm not into spiritual stuff! I'm into the intellect. Mind is the power of man."

Mind without spirit is battery without charge, software without hardware, microchip without power, body without life.

"You sound like my animistic ancestors. I don't buy it."

You sound like a phony scientist who manipulates data to reach his own predetermined conclusions. You are rejecting the data from your own inner voice. That voice is screaming at you, "You have sinned!"

Sin. Now there was a word that wasn't in Won's working vocabulary. It was a word he didn't much like, either.

He thought of facing Mary. It wasn't a comfortable thought. Would it affect their long-term relationship even if she never found out? He admitted that it probably would because the memory would linger in his mind. Would she be able to tell something was different? He hoped not, even though Mary had that unusual ability to intuit things unspoken, to divine things unrevealed. Would the guilt be cleansed by time or just covered over with another layer of more current sins? There was that word again! He'd used it himself. He didn't know anything about how to cleanse sin. He didn't even believe in sin. So why should all this be troubling him now?

Suddenly a wave of remorse swept over Won. Tears welled up in his eyes, in the eyes of a guy who didn't cry. He felt so sorry for what he had done. He had betrayed poor Mary, who had always been so faithful to him. Maybe he could get rid of the horrible guilt by telling her everything. No, he couldn't do that! She would never be able to forgive and forget. Besides, there was no need for both of them to carry this psychological load through life. He was the one who had blown it. *Blown it* sounded better to him than *sinned.*

Suddenly he wanted to be by Mary's side, *close* by

her side. He wanted to hold her tight and make up for his unconfessed failing. He wanted to kiss her passionately to let her know in some non-verbal way that he was sorry for hurting her, for betraying their commitment. He wanted to hug Justin more tightly than ever before to let the little guy know that his dad was still worthy of respect, that he would not let anything like this happen again.

But inside him, in his solar plexis, it felt as if a tumor were growing—a cancerous growth, eating away at his peace, stealing his Asian tranquility until he could get home to Mary and to Justin. Would this be the day that the reunion took place?

Zadock had promised it would be. What was there about Zadock which made him question whether what he said was true? How could Won know? Aha! Submit Zadock's statements to content analysis! Subject his words to scientific scrutiny. The scientific method had never failed before.

Still aching inside, but fired with a new scientific inquiry, Won neared the end of the hallway where the draperies marked the entrance to the great hall. He parted the curtain to step through.

Karae had slept well after an hour or two of allowing the overwhelming flood of emotions within her to recede. Now she lay on her back in the firm bed, fully awake in the morning light, reflecting on the events of the past score of hours. She again felt the ambivalence that had bothered her when Mac and Won had tugged at her to leave the processional in Zion. She had come along only because she thought the effort might really get her home.

Then there had been the innocent step through the doors of His Majesty's Department of Repatriation—only to be siphoned down an infinitely long drainpipe to this weird other-world.

And then there was Zadock. What a bizarre and terrorizing experience that had been on the balcony with him! Karae did a slow-motion replay of the encounter in her mind. There was the stunning view of the night lights of Pasadena, the very same vista she had seen so many times from her home in the foothills above the city, only smog-free this time. There was the starry heaven above them, the fragrance of the orange blossoms, the fresh evening air, the aroma of Zadock's cologne, the tenderness of his touch, the handsomeness of his features, the piercing nature of his eyes. And there was the firestorm of passion which had overcome her as he pulled her close.

Then came the vision. In the split-second before her eyes would close and their lips would meet, Karae had seen the apparition in Zadock's face. It was Governor Ben-David—his loving gaze; his pure, compassionate, caring look. Without a word his countenance had seemed to emit a desperate warning, a reaching out to rescue. As she stared, Jireh's face had then faded from view and merged into the features of Zadock. Suddenly, the alluring, angular features which had attracted her to him changed and his deep, unsmiling eyes burst into flames of fire. His ivory complexion turned to hideous gnarled flesh splotched with open sores . . . his pearl-like teeth into ghoulish fangs, stained and decaying . . . his smooth, honey-covered words to gutteral, gear-grinding sounds. And his touch—his hands on her waist—had burned into her body like branding irons. HE WAS A MONSTER AND NOT A MAN, A FIEND AND NOT A FRIEND!

Karae replayed the explosion of revulsion she had felt, the scream of terror that had wrenched her throat, the adrenalin rush of strength which had freed her from Zadock's ghastly grasp, the heart-pounding race to the safety of her room, and the sobs of fear, anger and disgust which finally subsided into . . . peace. It was the same Kingdom peace she had known alone in the great forest and in the presence of the governor of the realm. It was indefinable, non-rational, overcoming, inner peace.

She felt that same peace now as she raced through a long list of unanswered questions. Was the vision of Zadock real or an hallucination? Where had it come from? Was Jireh able to communicate with her here in Wonderland? Was Jireh's appearance a warning of what might happen if she surrendered to Zadock? What might *this* day bring forth? Would this be the day she could go home, as Zadock had assured the three yesterday?

The question of going home triggered more nagging thoughts. This was the third day—or so it seemed. Had anyone been able to help her mom? Had she received her medicine? If not, she would probably be so weak by now that she could barely stand up. Karae pictured her mother lying on the floor of their home weeping, wondering why her precious daughter did not come to help her, crying out to God. Karae had never been unfaithful like this before.

With mixed emotions, as if watching her worst enemy drive her new BMW off a three-hundred-foot cliff, Karae stepped out of bed to face the new day.

Then she did something out of the ordinary. She prayed. She prayed to The King: "Dear King Jesus, I've never seen You, but I believe You exist. Would You please help me make it through this day?" She felt a quiet assurance in her spirit. "And may I please have Your help in getting me home?" She felt only noncommittal silence inside. "Please. Amen." Praying was a foreign experience, but it felt good.

As she readied herself for the new day, she could not help wondering what lay on the other side of that locked door. Which Zadock would greet her?

T op of the morning to you!" Zadock spoke cheerfully as Karae joined him and the other two guests in the great hall. It was the good-looking Zadock—with a smile that was overly toothsome.

"Good morning." She was unenthusiastic in her greeting. "'Morning, Won and Mac." The two guys muttered perfunctory greetings.

"Are you all ready for a hearty breakfast?" Zadock seemed unusually chipper. He didn't ask what kind of night they had had. Karae sensed that he probably knew.

"I could eat a brontosaurus," Mac rubbed his empty stomach.

"Then let's move to the dining room. The preparations are ready." Zadock led them through the draperies into a large foyer which was ornately decorated with medieval arms, shields, suits of armor and such. It was a dark, fortress-like area with no windows. The only light came from wall-mounted brass lanterns which cast flickering shadows.

Karae winced at the heavy atmosphere of the area. It was gloomy, not the kind of place you want to go at 10 A.M. It could have passed for the entry to a military history museum.

"Excuse the rather bleak decorations in this area." Zadock led the group toward a pair of large wooden doors which lay straight ahead.

It was as if he read my thoughts, thought Karae. *I wonder if he can read spirits like the citizens of the Kingdom.* She surely was in no state of mind to engage in deep questionings to find out.

"Wait a minute," Mac raised his hands like a policeman halting traffic. "Those doors . . . "

"What about them?" Zadock asked, feigning innocence.

"They are exactly like the doors that got us into this place, just like the doors on His Majesty's Department of Repatriation. Look, buddy, I'm not going though doors like that again. No more wild rides down the chute for me!" Mac was adamant, unmovable.

"Oh, I think you are mistaken. Or there must be a strange coincidence."

"He's not mistaken, Mr. Zadock." Won stepped forward and adjusted his glasses for a better look. "These doors are identical—even to the gargoyle mounted above them." He was visibly disturbed by the "coincidence" and by Zadock's obvious attempt at a cover-up.

Karae hadn't really noticed the doors in the rush to escape from the crowds of Zion.

"All right, if you must have an explanation," Zadock seemed resigned to telling the whole story, "I will explain everything over breakfast. But please, please, have no fear. The only thing behind these doors, Mac, is a glorious breakfast buffet. See?" Zadock opened one of the doors to reveal a large-but-intimate, octagonal dining room with gigantic oval windows on each wall. A sumptuous breakfast feast was laid out on tables on one side. Through the windows one could see a lovely pond surrounded by weeping willow trees and formal gardens.

"How beautiful!" Karae opened her arms as if she would embrace the scene.

"How yummy!" Mac smacked his lips, obviously targeting the food rather than the scenery. Nothing was going to keep him in the foyer now. He burst through the doorway without any thought of "ladies first." The others followed.

A coterie of male waiters stood at attention in black tuxedoes, waiting to serve the delegation. There was no sign of Miss Sensuality and the runner-up; in fact, no other guests were in the dining room. The waiters seated the four at a large, round, linen-covered table set with delicate gold-toned flatware and a lovely flower center-piece which looked convincingly real. An appetizer of fresh fruit waited to be eaten prior to the trek to the buffet.

Karae made a conscious effort not to allow her gaze to meet Zadock's. Small talk dominated the conversation over fruit. She studied him when he was looking else-where and looked away when his eyes moved in her direction. Zadock was at the three o'clock position at the table and Karae at six o'clock, making this eye dance pretty easy to execute.

The trip to the buffet tables was a tantalizing ex-perience, with sufficient food to serve a national conven-tion of teenagers. Karae hoped there were other guests in this hotel or palace or whatever it was who could keep the food from being wasted.

The grandeur of the food selection, the artistry with which it was presented, and the tastiness of the chosen items was the talk of the table for some time once the four returned from the buffet. The sumptuous provisions tasted great, but Karae noticed that they tended to sit like putty once inside the system.

Mac was inhaling enormous quantities of the feast, making repeated trips to the buffet only to lug overflow-ing plateloads of food back each time. Won, on the other hand, picked at his food, selected in modest quantities and with typical fussiness. Karae had difficulty working up a big appetite with Zadock at the table. Flashbacks to the night before kept her from concentrating on the lavish repast. Only periodic glimpses at the beauty of the pond and gardens outside the windows stilled her enough to enjoy the breakfast. Then, too, she sensed a strong after-taste developing in her mouth.

To wrap up the meal, the waiters presented choices of exotic coffees. As the guests sipped their coffee, and while Mac consumed yet another plate of food, Zadock assumed bigger-than-life stature in his chair and called the table to attention.

"Well, friends, you've asked me for some explanations, which I promised. Let's chat about a few things that I know have troubled you." Zadock was obviously set to pontificate. The wondrous breakfast had created a positive atmosphere for his guests, disarming them much like the last meal for a condemned member of the Mafia. Karae, though, wondered if their host was moving in for some kind of kill.

Zadock cleared his throat to speak and was just about to launch his first statement when Mac broke in.

"Hey, Drydock, when do we go home? This is the big day, remember?" The mouthful of pancakes did little to muffle his usual cynicism.

"I remember, friend." Zadock tried to brush off the question, and his annoyance at Mac's manner, so he could return to his prepared script.

Mac wasn't buying it. "Don't give me the 'friend' bit until you have told me *when today* we head home and *how today* we catch the bus." Mac could be obnoxiously pushy, but at this point the others were glad he was. After two days of getting nowhere, they all felt terminally desperate. Waves of eagerness and hope on one side and disappointment on the other had washed in and out of them like tides on a beach.

"We will deal with the timing of your return later, but now—"

"No, Z-man, not later! NOW!" Mac shouted, bringing both fists down hard on the table for emphasis. "We demand to know the whens and hows of our return NOW!"

Zadock's eyes burned an eery red—the flames Karae had seen in her vision the night before. He held his peace, but you could see the veins on his neck enlarge and his muscles tense. Mac had gotten to him.

"I'm sorry, Mac, but you'll just have to wait until—"

"I'M NOT WAITING ANOTHER SECOND, ZORRO!" Mac picked up his plate of partially consumed food and hurled it across the table at Zadock.

The food scored a direct hit in Zadock's face. Scrambled eggs splattered into his hair and slithered off his chin. A strip of bacon dangled precariously from his ear, then dropped onto the collar of his shirt. A half-eaten pancake adhered with syrup to his lapel like a mutant campaign button. Melon balls bobbed in his orange juice. A little green stem from one of Mac's vanquished strawberries sprouted like a spring bulb from his forehead.

Zadock's nose reddened quickly from the blow of the plate, which had landed upside down in his lap after painting his chest with garbage on its slide to its ultimate resting place.

The sight which had so quickly developed before their eyes—the transformation of Zadock from a picture of neatness into a waste disposal site—was more than Karae could handle. She burst into a roar of laughter. This was better than a *Three Stooges* movie! Shortly after Karae lost it, Won also went to pieces.

Zadock now breathed fire through his redecorated visage. Abruptly—out of nowhere—came an energy force like a rushing wind. It swept across the table in Mac's direction and seemed to punch him in the midsection. He doubled over with a violent gasp as the force launched him backwards, over his careening chair and onto the floor about fifteen feet from the table.

The table went stone silent. Any trace of humor vanished from the faces of the other two. Mac lay on the floor, barely conscious. A trickle of blood traced his cheek from a grazing with the fork that had been in his hand.

Without a word Zadock rose from the table and exited. Won and Karae rushed to aid Mac. All the while the tuxedoed waiters stood at their designated stations like statues—unmoving, unflinching, unsmiling.

Karae was seized by an uneasy sensation. What had Mac done? He hadn't seen Zadock as she had seen him. She had a forboding feeling that this was just a taste of the violence inside him, one more glimpse of the monster underneath the suave host. Someone had to cool him off or he could cancel their return tickets in a minute.

She thought of ways she might work on Zadock.

N ow, where were we?"

Zadock, back in his seat at the table, was the picture of composure and control. Nary a trace of food residue was on either his body or his apparel. Mac, considerably subdued, was back in his seat blotting his cut cheek with a facial tissue. The waiters had finally come to life sufficiently to clean off the table, chair and floor, so that only damp spots on the linens remained—spots covered with clean, dry napkins.

"As I remember, I was about to explain the mystery of the identical doors."

Considering what she had just witnessed, Karae was finding it quite difficult to concentrate on Zadock's explanation. Won appeared distracted, disturbed. Once again they had witnessed powers in operation which were unknown to them. But unlike Mac's freeze-dried encounter with Governor Ben-David, this energy had been delivered with viciousness, without restraint, with intent to injure.

"You see, my friends," Zadock was pompous, affected, "the doors to His Majesty's Department of Repatriation were either similar or dissimilar to the doors to this dining room depending on your perceptions. Neither of them is real anyway. Most perceived reality is

in the minds of the beholders and created by the spirit
force of other personalities.

"Once you all had made your decision to escape
from the Kingdom, I had tacit permission to communicate with you in any way I chose. So I created the false
reality of the building and doors of 'His Majesty's Department of Repatriation.' Pretty clever, don't you think? I
knew 'repatriation' was on your minds—finding a way
to get back to your home country. So I figured you would
be intrigued by such a department of the Kingdom."

Zadock was wallowing in self-praise. "You bought
the whole ruse and got the ride of your lives once you
stepped through those doors, doors which really existed
only in your perceptions!" Zadock laughed at his own
practical joke while the three stunned onlookers looked
at each other in disbelief.

"But those doors were heavy. We could hardly open
them." Won remembered how hard he had to push to get
them to move at all.

"Of course they were heavy—*in your perceptions!*
Have you never seen a hypnotist tell his subject a lemon
is chocolate? The subject eats the lemon with no sense of
sourness. The hypnotist tells the subject the temperature
is 120 degrees, and he pants desperately, sweats profuse-
ly and starts to remove his clothing in a 70-degree room.
This happens because someone has manipulated the
subjects' *perceptions* of reality.

"Forgive the deception, but not one thing you have
observed since you arrived here in Wonderland has been
real. The buildings, the furniture, the drinks, the
bedrooms, the food—yes, even the lovely ladies—all are
illusions. I have controlled your perceptions. There is no
ultimate objective reality. All reality is in the mind. So
when I created the dining room doors, I absent-mindedly
created the same doors I had created on the facade I
projected onto a side street of the Kingdom to lure you

here. You discovered my mistake and caught me in my error."

Mac, a bit sore from his violent landing a few moments before, savored in his mind the intimacies of the previous night. Had Miss Sensuality been a mirage?

Won questioned whether Zadock's message meant he was, or was not, an adulterer.

Karae struggled with the vision of the kindly Governor Ben-David and the terrorizing revelation of Zadock. Would Zadock himself have created *that* perception? Unlikely, she thought.

"But my dear friends, I don't want you to miss the point of all this. This is Wonderland because I can create any reality you desire. You are going to enjoy the way we live here, for if you follow me and join with the Wonderland subjects, then the whole world—no, the whole universe—is yours. If you want riches, I can create the perception of riches. If you want beauty, I can produce it. If you want pleasure, I can create any reality you can imagine. You certainly had no offer like this in the Kingdom, now, did you?"

The three shook their heads.

"I did not lie to you when I told you you could go home today. If you want to go home and leave Wonderland with all its potential to have and be and experience anything your mind can imagine, be my guest. If you choose, I can even create the perception of your going home, so you can enjoy all of the joys of being reunited with your loved ones. The perceptions will be as real as the pleasures you have experienced during your short stay here.

"I am going to give you one hour to make your decision. If you desire to stay and become a part of Wonderland, I only require that you swear your undying allegiance to me and to the Prince of Wonderland. Naturally, if I am going to vouchsafe these eternal secrets to you, I will need assurance that they will be in safe, loyal custody. A simple ceremony of allegiance will seal this irrevocable decision forever."

Zadock stood to his feet. The massive gold ring which he wore on his ring finger seemed to be more brilliant. The diamond-studded pentagram on the crown sent out beams of reflected light which danced off the table and the faces of his three guests.

"My friends, it is now 11:13 A.M. I will return at 12:13 P.M. to hear your decisions. I trust you will not turn your back on this opportunity of a lifetime." He turned sharply and strode from the room, signaling the waiters to do the same. They filed out to leave the three alone.

What a conundrum, Karae thought. Here, at an illusory table in an illusory dining room in a possibly illusory Wonderland, three bewildered aliens from another time and place were supposed to decide their destinies on information provided by a possibly psychopathic liar—in one hour's time? Unbelievable, absolutely unbelievable!

Fifty-eight minutes and twenty-one seconds of decision time left.

8

No Business Like Snow Business

Fifteen minutes and forty-five seconds left.

"Look, gang, I'm getting out of here." Mac was resolute. "I am going home no matter what Big Z offers. There was something nasty in that sucker punch he laid on me. This dude plays dirty, and I've seen enough of it. My vote is set in concrete."

"Now, Mac," Won looked at him with his characteristic, perplexed frown. "I don't think it would be wise to make a decision which would result in a short-term gain and a long-term loss. You heard Zadock say that we could have anything we wanted. He could arrange for us to go home and experience all the benefits of home and family along with being let in on the secrets of the universe, secrets which will enable us to have anything we desire—*forever!*"

The clock on the wall of the dining hall struck noon.

"Guys, Zadock is not what he appears." Karae looked at them with a sober, almost frightened look. "I had an experience last night which stripped the mask off this creature, and he is a monster—an attractive, cunning,

highly intelligent monster. He has impressive supernatural powers, but he is still a monster! I don't trust him
as far as I can throw his imaginary palace. I'm with Mac.
I say we go home."

"Wait a minute, you two . . . " Won thought the
others weren't considering the big picture here. He
would have to sell them hard if he was to change their
resolve.

"It better be *just* a minute. Zorro's gonna be back
here in no time." Mac couldn't have been less eager to
hear Won's pitch.

"We have been together in all we have experienced
these three days," Won continued. "Karae wasn't excited
about escaping from Zion, but she came along. Mac, your
big mouth has gotten all three of us into a heap of trouble,
more than once, but I've hung in there with you. I've had
my doubts about a lot of things we have done, but I've
gone along. We are a team. I feel that we have to hang
together or we may hang separately."

Karae wasn't sold. "If I hang, I want it to be because
it was my decision to hang. I don't want to hang because
I was pressured into some decision I didn't feel right
about at the time. I still say this guy is a monster. I don't
want any part of swearing 'undying allegiance' to him!
For my money, I don't ever want to *see* the creep again!"

"Okay, you two," Won persisted. "We have only a
couple of minutes left until we have to give our decisions.
Look around you. This palace, this hall, this food, the
lovely ladies—and I'm sure there are just as many
gentlemen, Karae—the promise of all this and the
benefits of home as well. I'm not into feelings and intui-
tions and visions. I am a scientist. I go with what I can
observe, what I can measure. I'll commit to anyone who
can deliver what I have seen with my own eyes."

"I suppose you've figured out scientifically how

some invisible fist used my stomach as a punching bag?" Mac rubbed his midsection, as if still feeling the pain.

"There are always things to be learned and studied. All I am saying is that I've seen enough to impress me, and I like what I see."

"Yeah, and you don't have aching ribs from a mystical blow to the gut."

"And," Karae joined in, "you don't have the vision of a ghoul behind that pretty face to give you a shot of reality therapy." She folded her arms tightly as if to dare Won to get through her defenses. "You make your decision, Won, I'll make mine. And mine is *no!* Read my lips: *No!*" She dropped her voice on the last word or two. She heard footsteps.

"Well, my friends," Zadock stood in the portal to the dining room. "I trust you have come to the right decisions." He strutted across the room wearing a dramatic red and black outfit, a tight-fitting, uniform-like suit with gold military buttons and epaulets on the shoulders. Red trim edged the lapels and trimmed the collar of the suit. Fine gold braid edged the epaulets. The suit was stunning. *He* was stunning. Even Karae was struck once again by his good looks and, well, class.

"What do you say we walk in the gardens beside the pond as I hear your decisions." Zadock pointed to an exit. "Some fresh air will do us all good. It should clear our minds." He showed no doubt that the decisions would go his way.

The three filed through the doorway and down a few steps to the flower-lined pathway which wound through the trees and gardens and along the bank of the pond. Peacocks and peahens nibbled and screeched. Manicured hedges and weedless rose gardens were laid out in artistic patterns across the landscape. The setting seemed to be a hollow ringed by low hills, which prohibited one's seeing far toward the horizon. "Let's go up to the gazebo." Zadock pointed to an ornate, pagoda-like structure which sat atop a small hill right on the edge of the water.

A strange and pervasive silence settled over the three. They filed along like criminals walking down death row. Inevitably—and soon—Zadock would ask for their decisions. Karae was struggling against ill-defined spiritual forces within her, which now, inexplicably, seemed to be drawing her to commit to Zadock. Mac was feeling the same inner conflict.

"Have a seat, my friends." Zadock pointed toward the wooden seats which surrounded the octagonal structure. "Well, who wants to go first?"

The three looked back and forth at each other.

"I guess I'll go first." Won was only slightly hesitant. "I think I'll go with you, Mr. Zadock. I've been very impressed by the things I have seen and intrigued by the things I do not understand. I like the promise of understanding the secrets of the universe. As a scientist, this is a major part of my search anyway. I see your offer as providing a shortcut to this knowledge. Also, I like the idea of having both the benefits of home and family and the potential of limitless, eternal dream fulfillment and prosperity."

Karae's heart sank. *You're selling your soul!* she cried out silently. What Won was doing was so wrong. Why couldn't he see through Zadock's veneer? Won was so intelligent, so analytical, so rational. How could he be so duped? An ache formed in her chest as she watched a self-satisfied smile cross Zadock's face.

"Well, congratulations, Mr. Kim. You have made a wise choice. I will schedule you into the induction ceremony this evening at 10 P.M. I know you will be pleased with the decision you have made." Zadock's countenance glowed. His pentagram ring glowed similarly in the light reflected off the pond. The ring seemed to possess a spirit of its own—one which reflected its powers in the radiance of its facets.

"Miss Johnson." Zadock's piercing eyes turned toward her like a roving searchlight. "Have you made your decision, my dear?" His speech was oily, crude oily. It oozed like it had on the balcony the night before.

Karae swallowed hard and spoke. "Yes, I have. I have chosen to leave your Wonderland, to go home."

"Miss Johnson," Zadock's tone was condescending, patronizing, "I am quite shocked and distressed." His visage darkened, turned slightly sinister. "I have wonderful plans for you, plans for good and not for evil, for prosperity and not for harm. How could you turn your back on the lavish opportunities I have offered? Certainly you have not fully understood the nature of my proposition."

"I think I understand it sufficiently." Karae's jaw was set, her gaze steady.

"Well, I am very, very disappointed over your decision. I'll tell you what. The induction ceremony isn't until ten this evening. I will hold the offer open until then. Perhaps we will have a chance to talk about this some more before then."

Karae didn't want to talk about it any more. She did not want to talk to Zadock any more. She just wanted to go home.

"And Mr. McNeal." Zadock's gaze now fell on Mac. "Have you made your decision?"

"No, sir." A line of tension showed around Mac's mouth as if he were going through inner torment. "I need more time to decide."

Karae's mouth dropped open as she looked at Mac in unbelief. How could he do this? He was so resolute just a few minutes ago! She couldn't believe what she had just heard.

Zadock smiled faintly. "I can arrange that. After all,

I've given Miss Johnson until 10 P.M. to change her mind on the very ill-informed decision she has made. I certainly could extend to you the same courtesy. After I have had a talk with Miss Johnson regarding her decision, I will be happy to chat with you about yours."

Oh, no, thought Karae. *He wants to "have a talk." How am I going to get out of this one?*

"Let me shake your hand, Mr. Kim, and extend to you a hand of greeting from the leadership of Wonderland. I know that you will find the induction ceremony this evening a high point of your life and an inspirational experience. And I trust that by this evening I can induct all three of you."

Won displayed a pleased look. He had made the wisest decision, he was sure. He found it a bit bewildering that the other two couldn't see the marvelous advantages which lay in store for him—and for them, too—in choosing Wonderland. He reveled at the thought of having the best of both worlds. He envisioned himself having it all—the Nobel prize for his research, status and wealth, and reunification with his family. He felt warm just thinking of holding Mary and Justin in his arms again. It seemed like it had been so long . . .

Zadock stood to exit the gazebo, then stopped outside the entrance and turned back. "Dinner is at eight in the dining room. The time is yours until then, Mr. Kim. Mr. McNeal and Miss Johnson, I'd like to have some time with you before then. Miss Johnson, I'll see you now." Zadock's tone indicated this was not a request; it was a demand.

Tentatively, Karae stood to join Zadock. He obviously was not going to have it any other way. Tension swelled within her at the idea of having a talk with the one who had held her close on the balcony, the one whose first kiss had been aborted by her screaming exit. *This is not going to be fun,* she thought.

"And could I see you in an hour or so, Mr. McNeal?" Zadock asked Mac.

"I suppose."

"Fine. Meet me here at the gazebo. Miss Johnson and I are going to be in the gardens until then."

A whole hour! Karae breathed a panicky sigh as Zadock walked away from the pagoda. They fell in step on the path which led down the little hill, away from the lake and into the garden.

"You've broken my heart, Karae," Zadock began. "I was so much hoping that we could have the time to develop our relationship more fully here in Wonderland." He looked pained, pathetic. "If you leave, I don't know what I will do. You have become a very special person to me in this short time."

Karae held back—skeptical, distant. "I'm sorry, Mr. Zadock, but my decision is firm." She studied the path, the flowers, the trees—anything to avoid having to look in his eyes.

"Just what is the draw at home?" Zadock pursued. "What is there in Pasadena that could possibly be greater than what I have offered you?"

Karae's skepticism now became anger. "You know all about me. Don't play games." She turned abruptly in his direction to reinforce her demand. "You told me about my infirm mother. You know about my profession, my other family members, my Southern California roots. It is my home, Zadock! It is my home. Is it so unusual for a person to want to return to her birthplace, her family, her community?"

Zadock was silent for a few moments as they walked along the path. They were the only two within sight or sound now. A couple of times he made expressions as though he was about to speak, but each time he hesitated.

Finally he responded. "I don't know how to say this, Karae, but I think you must know."

"Know what?" She looked him in the eye, studied him for clues as to what he was leading to.

"I'm afraid I have bad news for you."

"What kind of bad news?"

"I think I'd rather show you than tell you." Zadock had a funereal look on his face.

"Show me what, Zadock?" Her tone was irritated.

"Close your eyes, Karae." Karae struggled with this one. Her level of trust was not such that she wanted to be in Zadock's presence with her eyes open, much less with them closed. She balked.

"Please, Karae, it's all right. This is no trick." He sounded reassuring.

Karae closed her eyes and immediately entered a trance. She could see Zadock by her side, and the two of them were far above the earth, looking down as if from a plane. Below she could see what was obviously a Southern California suburb. The view of the earth was coming closer each moment. As the span of view narrowed, Karae could see a chapel, or something like a chapel, with cars parked around it, probably a hundred or so. As they drew closer to the ground, Karae began to get a sick feeling, a sense of foreboding, of something ominous.

It was as if they were Peter Pan and Wendy flying down and into the chapel together. Zadock did not say a word, but Karae could sense him at her side as they entered the door of the sanctuary. She could hear organ music playing.

It was a funeral. The sick feeling grew inside her as her view took her into the chapel. There were mostly Black people in attendance. Although the view was from the backs of their heads, Karae thought she could recognize some of the people in the pews. She did! There were her boss from the mortgage company, the neighbor lady and her husband, her cousin Louella, her uncle George, more and more of her relatives. But whose funeral was it, she wondered, now afraid of the answer.

Her line of sight now moved past the sprays of flowers to the open casket.

"No, no, no! Zadock, no, it isn't true!" She broke into repeated sobs, violent bursts of tears mixed with angry expressions of denial.

Zadock was as silent as a pallbearer.

"It can't be Mom!" She strained for a closer look into the casket. Indeed, it was her beloved mother.

Hysterical now, Karae turned toward Zadock and pounded on his chest with her fists. "*You* did this, you beast! This is *your* fault! If you had let me go home, she would not have died. I hate you! I *hate* you! I HATE YOU!"

Suddenly the trance was broken, and she was standing on the garden path beating on Zadock and shrieking "I HATE YOU!" at him.

He placed his hand on her shoulder in consolation. "Now, now, Karae, calm down." His words dripped—comforting, soothing, saccharine.

She collapsed on the path and lay there, sobbing uncontrollably, no longer forming words—just the wracking expressions of unbelieving sorrow. After a few minutes the intensity of her anguish subsided and, tearfully, she began to regain her composure.

"I'm sorry, Karae." Zadock attempted to put his arm around her, but she pulled away. "Please do not blame your mother's death on me. Your mother died before you came to Wonderland. She had a heart seizure the first day you were gone. Even if I had let you return home immediately, it would have been too late.

"You'll have to blame this one on The King, Karae. *He* was the one who took you away from her in the first place. *He* was the one whose 'divine experiment' prohibited your return in time to save your mom. *He* has to answer for this one, not me." Zadock was very convincing.

He helped her up off the path and walked her, still weeping, back to the gazebo where Mac was waiting.

When Mac saw Karae crying, he burst out of the structure and down the path to meet the two of them. "What have you done to Karae?" he demanded of Zadock.

"Hold your fire, Mr. McNeal. Karae has just had a very traumatic experience which has nothing whatever to do with me."

"She was all I had in life . . . " Karae whispered through her grief. "We have been like sisters since my dad ran off and left us when I was six. She has always been my best friend!"

"Karae is talking about her mother," Zadock explained to Mac. "She just learned of her passing."

"Without Mom I have no one—nothing." Karae spoke with chilling emptiness as another wave of grief swept over her.

"I'm sorry, Karae." Mac put his arms around her and held her. She did not resist his embrace as she had Zadock's. She dropped her head on his shoulder and, once more, let the tears flow. He held her for several minutes until she calmed down, then released her.

"Maybe you would like to go to your room, Karae," Zadock suggested. "Does that sound good to you?"

She nodded.

"Fine. I'll have food service send up some food and drinks. That way you can be alone through the dinner hour."

She checked her pockets for her room key, found it, and dismissed herself.

"If you're composed and rested enough by ten,"

Zadock suggested, "try to make it to the induction ceremony just off the main hall. I know you will enjoy it. I hope you will be part of it."

Karae said nothing as she disappeared into the building.

The two men held their gaze on the door as it closed behind her, then slowly turned to face each other.

"Want to take a little walk through the garden?" Zadock asked.

Mac was apprehensive, for the inner turbulence which had prohibited his earlier decision had returned. It was like a war in his abdominal cavity linked to a war between his ears—his gut and his reason each facing off with enemies they couldn't handle. The two headed down the path, retracing the steps Zadock and Karae had taken earlier.

"Mac," Zadock began in a comfortable, reasoned manner. He was playing the Great Counselor, the Father Confessor. "I know this is a weighty decision I have asked you to make. I also realize that I have given you an unreasonably short time in which to weigh the options and make your decision."

"I buy that," Mac said in a tone of flat irony.

"Let me help you with your decision. You see, I know more about you than you realize."

Mac looked in Zadock's eyes, hoping to read the meaning of this statement. But Zadock was inscrutable.

"I know all about your domineering, highly success-ful father, the captain of industry, the go-getter, the hard driver, the Type-A workaholic. I know the frustration you have had relating to him, the burden of never being able to please him, of getting notice and response only when you *didn't* meet his standards, never when you did. I know of the many times over the years when you would have done anything to get his approval—just once to hear that he loved you, that he was proud of you, that he thought you were terrific."

Mac was hanging on every word now. Was Zadock psychic or something? Did he ever have his dad pegged!

"I know the quiet desperation which results from never being hugged and never being told you are loved by the most important parent in your life, your parent of the same sex. I understand the point at which a person finally loses all hope of ever getting that parental approval and finally says 'Why bother?' and turns to other ways of getting attention and affirmation. I know that's what you have done."

Mac's head drooped a bit as he thought of the violent argument he and his dad had had that night when he was seventeen, a high school senior. He once again felt the frustration, the rejection, the futility, the anger, the bitterness, the *hatred* for his dad that had swept over him that night. Like it was yesterday, he saw himself storm out of the house, smash in the window of his car with his fist, get in, lay rubber backing out of the driveway, and head out to the bar to get smashed on the beer his older buddies bought him. As Zadock spoke, Mac felt once again the burning, empty hole inside him which a man never gets filled until he makes peace with his dad, gains the acceptance of his own father.

"I know of your contempt for your dad's money and grownup toys. They were symbols of being a son for hire, of prostituting yourself to fit your dad's mold to get the new Corvette or the stereo system."

Mac was stunned that this stranger knew so much about him, his life, his inner struggles, his feelings. Zadock really seemed to *care* about all this.

"That's why you went wild at Otterbein College. There were plenty of other miserable rich kids there, kids whose dads and moms had bought them off with stuff rather than giving them love, attention, support and time. That's why you were so desperate for attention that you sought it by being able to drink everybody else under the table, by taking every dare thrown at you by your fraternity brothers. You wanted to *be somebody*." Zadock was preaching now. His face was animated, his hands and arms waving in broad, graphic gestures. His only parishioner was in rapt attention, absorbing every word, reprocessing every feeling being stirred by Zadock's psychoanalysis.

They stopped walking. Zadock turned and looked at Mac square on.

"Mac, look at me." He lowered his voice and slowed his delivery. "For the first time in your life you are going to BE SOMEBODY! I am going to give you what your dad never would. I am going to give you immense wealth, wealth that will make your dad look like a street bum. I am going to give you international fame. Your name will be a household word in all of the western world. You will be given a high government position, a position so powerful that people from all over the world will come to you for decisions, for benefit. No longer will you be millionaire Richard McNeal's son—black sheep son at that. Richard McNeal will become known as *Arthur 'Mac' McNeal's father!* He will live out his days in the shadow of *your* greatness, of *your* wealth, of *your* power!"

An irresistible urge was building inside Mac, an urge to see all these promises, all of his own personal private dreams, become reality. And before him stood a man with the power and the promise to do just that.

"What do you say, Mac? Will you come with me so we can pursue this great dream together?"

His fight was gone. It was an offer he couldn't refuse. Something in his psyche relaxed and rejoiced at the thought of *being somebody*.

"I guess so."

"Great! Mac, you will never regret it. You will look back on this day and thank yourself—and me—for this commitment. Give me your handshake to seal the decision." With his chest swelled, Zadock held out his hand. Mac grasped it.

The two reversed direction on the path. Zadock extended his arm around Mac's shoulders, and they headed back toward the gazebo.

"Mac, you're going to love the induction ceremony. It will be a thrilling and life-changing event for you. I can't wait. Aren't you excited?"

Mac didn't know enough about the event to be filled with either excitement or dread. "Well, I am looking forward to it, I guess. At least it feels good to have the decision resolved."

"Mac, mark my words." Zadock put his index finger on Mac's chest. "You will thank yourself ten thousand times for the decision you have just made. I swear you will!"

Flashes of reflected light ricocheted off Zadock's ring finger, light beams from the diamond-studded pentagram by which he swore.

9

Every Which Way
But Loose

Waiters cleared the dishes from the leisurely dinner.
It had been a delectable meal with all the trappings
of a five-star hotel. The shrimp cocktail was a marvelous
opener and the choice of entrees magnificent—everything from pheasant under glass to grilled mahi mahi.
The cooked vegetables were so fresh they were crisp, not
mushy like they are in ordinary restaurants. Dessert was
an experience all its own. The waiters filed by the table
with tray after tray of exotic delicacies from which the
diners could choose. Mac was in Honey Heaven over the
breathtaking array of sweets. He was particularly blown
away by the chocolate options—there must have been a
score of them including chocolate and banana cream pie,
bittersweet chocolate and cinnamon pie, double chocolate fudge cake, brownie delight with French vanilla *a la
mode*, chocolate mousse with whipped cream and cherry
topping, royal chocolate banana sundae, and super-rich
chocolate/chocolate chip ice cream.
   Quipping that his most recent physical had revealed
a serious "chocolate deficiency" in his diet, Mac selected

two of the magnificent chocolate delights from the passing trays. Moderation was not his prime virtue.

The other two men, Zadock and Won, had carried
on light conversation during the meal, Zadock making
scant reference to the evening's planned induction
ceremony. And since Karae had taken up Zadock's offer
to have dinner in her room, the dinner table conversation
had been an all-male affair.

"Well, gentlemen, did you enjoy your dinner?"
Zadock smiled, anticipating the only plausible answer.

"Shure deed," Mac mumbled through a final
mouthful of chocolate mousse with whipped cream and
cherry topping. "T'was a mahty fahn suppah," he
drawled in a limp imitation of a southern accent. One too
many glasses of fine wine had loosened up a guy who
didn't need any loosening.

"Excellent. Thank you," was Won's three-word
answer. He had spent some time between bites of his
chicken *cordon bleu* trying to figure out how you could tell
the difference between illusory food and real food, if
indeed the meal was another of Zadock's "perception
manipulations." It all tasted pretty much the same to him.
He was willing to have Zadock manipulate his perceptions in this direction anytime he wanted.

"Ya' know, Big Z, you haven't heard my John
Wayne imitation . . . and I also do a great Jerry Lewis."

"Mac, my friend, now that you have committed to
be part of the Wonderland experience, you won't have to
imitate John Wayne or Jerry Lewis. You can *be* them if
you wish."

"Mahhvelllous, Z Man. Can I also have a seventy-
five-foot yacht?"

"Anything you can conceive in your mind can be
yours, Mac."

"How about a different beauty queen or movie star
every day of the week?" He laughed coarsely.

"If you can handle it, try two a day!" Zadock knew that he and the wine had Mac under control.

Mac slurred to Won, "Won, baby, you're a married man."

"I am."

"Have you heard about the man who told his wife that when she turned forty he was gonna trade her in for two twenties?"

"Regretfully, I haven't." Won was sober and not really in a joking mood.

"Well, that ole lady looked him in the eyeballs and said, 'You'd never live through it! You're not wired for two-twenty!' Get it? Har, har, har, har . . . " Mac convulsed in laughter over his story and in the spasms spilled the last tablespoonful from his wine glass down the front of his shirt.

Zadock enjoyed the story. Won was unmoved.

"What's wrong with you, Chinaman? Did you just have *humor bypass* surgery?" Mac rollicked in laughter once more at his one-liner. Won gave Mac an "if-you-call-me-Chinaman-once-more-I'll-deck-you" stare. Mac cooled it and began dabbing at the spilled wine on his shirt.

Unlubricated by wine, Won was getting some strange, queasy feelings about the impending induction ceremony. Maybe it was just fear of the unknown . . . and maybe it wasn't. Earlier, he had been so sure of his decision to commit to Zadock and Wonderland, but now that the ceremony was nearing he was having his doubts. Like a true scientist, Won liked to keep his options open. The word *irrevocable* kept bouncing around in his brain. Irrevocable was for a long, long time.

"Gentlemen, are you ready to depart for the ceremony? My watch says it's 9:30." Zadock had drawn an unusual pocket watch out of the dark uniform pocket.

"As ready as I'll ever be," Mac shrugged.

"I guess so." Won dipped his head.

"Then let's excuse ourselves and head down to the chapel." Zadock rose to his feet and laid his napkin next to the flatware on the table.

The trio stepped out of the dining room into the dark, sword-and-shield-bedecked foyer again. The hollow eyes of the armor helmets lent an eerie feeling to the vestibule in the flickering lights of the wall lanterns. The three made a right turn and stepped toward a door which was almost completely hidden in the dark oak paneling of the foyer. Just as Zadock put his hand on the panel and opened it a crack, a woman's voice penetrated the darkness.

"May I join you?" They all turned at the sound of the sad, hollow voice.

It was Karae.

She looked haggard and drawn. Deep lines etched her face, and her eyes were red and swollen. Her shoulders drooped, and wrinkles marked the dress she'd worn since breakfast, a dress obviously not removed during the hours she had been on her bed grieving.

"Karae? I didn't expect you." Zadock looked at the two men as if to read their responses to her appearance.

"Am I too late for the induction ceremony?" She stood with her head lowered and didn't lift it to speak.

"No, of course not. We were just heading toward the chapel." Zadock looked pleased, but somehow not genuinely surprised, at her appearance. "Have you decided to commit to the Wonderland experience, and to me?"

Karae stared at the floor in front of Zadock. "I have."

Her words were barely audible. She seemed to have trouble even mustering sufficient energy to mouth them.

"With Mama gone, I have nothing to return to Pasadena for, nothing to live for."

"Wonderful." Zadock's manner betrayed an inner gloating. He ignored the reference to her mother's death, and he did not seem unduly concerned about her desperation. "That makes it unanimous. What a grand day for Wonderland citizens!" He put his hands together in a silent, clapping motion.

Won was struck by that line, *Wonderland citizens*. He hadn't really seen any people since they had arrived in this place except Zadock, the waiters, Miss Sensuality, and his Asian seductress. Who were the "citizens of Wonderland"? For that matter, *what* was Wonderland? Was this part of the Kingdom? No, it couldn't be—everything was so different. Did that incredible fall they took drop them into another world? Was Zadock able to manufacture this Wonderland anywhere he chose? It was all so confusing. How could they tell? For all he knew he could be on a movie set at Universal Studios. He had a feeling he was soon to get answers to these questions.

Zadock held open the foyer door and motioned to Karae to step through. She shuffled feebly through the portal and into a large, long hall that was as murky as the foyer. Those same wall-mounted brass lanterns, spaced about every ten feet on both sides, glimmered the length of the corridor. The ceiling was high, maybe fifteen to twenty feet, with vaulted stonework rounding toward the center. Since it had no windows, the passageway could have been subterranean, even though they had entered from the same floor level as the dining hall. About the only color in the hall was the amber glass in the lamps and the large, hand-painted wall hangings on both sides between the lanterns. The paintings were stylized pictographs of some type, a mix of symbols and strange druidic cryptographs.

The party traversed the length of the hall and ap-

proached two tall, hammered copper doors with representations of the ancient goddess Ishtar in deep relief in
the metal.

Zadock stopped the delegation in front of the doors.
"Silence now. We must wait here until we are granted
entry." He paused momentarily and assumed an almost
reverent affect. His hands were together in a praying
pose. After a few moments he knocked on the door six
times, then paused. Then six more knocks, and a pause,
followed by six final knocks.

Won was preoccupied. *Irrevocable. Irrevocable.* The
word kept running in circles in his mind and causing
bizarre, buzzing vibrations in his stomach. He wondered
at what point the irrevocability commenced. Had he
skidded past the stop sign? Had he passed the point of
no return? Had his entry into this long hall been the
equivalent of entering that horrific chute that had sucked
the three of them into this weird world and put the
Kingdom out of reach forever—was it forever? Without
realizing it he wrung his hands as he contemplated
whatever it was he was getting into.

Mac's line of thinking was quite different. He was,
after all, a salesman by trade, accustomed to collecting
awards for his efforts. The trips to Hawaii, the Caribbean
cruises, and the dazzling weekends in Vegas were all part
of the game. He was about to collect. Zadock had sold
him on the payoffs. He envisioned the international fame
and the perks that would come with it. He pictured
himself on his new yacht off the Gulf coast of Florida with
one arm around a bikinied blonde and the other on the
ship's wheel. Mac could see the look on his dad's face, the
green hues around his dad's eyes, the guy who had called
him "stupid," called him the kid who "couldn't do anything right," the kid who would "grow up to be a worthless, good-for-nothing slob."

Open that door, Zadock, he thought. *It's time to collect the winnings.*

Karae knew her decision was wrong, flat-out wrong. She had had a glimpse into the soul of Zadock. This was not an Eve decision for her, not the unwitting result of some serpent's beguilement. This was an Adam decision. She knew full well what she was doing, that it was lethal, that it was worse than a dead end, that it was the entry into bondage. But, as is often the case in decisions, the price of the right choice seemed so high. It was so far out of reach given her strength, her resources, her will to resist. With no husband, no children, no really close friends and no blood-bound companion, Karae had been cut off from life with the demise of her mother. With her mother's passing her own will to live perished, along with her will to resist—even the devil.

She thought again about the glories of the Kingdom. How wonderful if that could be included as an option in this decision—the innocent people, the heavenly beauty, the warm and affectionate Jireh Ben-David. But no, thanks to these guys and their genius plan to escape from the Kingdom, it was gone. It was somewhere else, on the other end of that long and terrorizing fall, somewhere unreachable. She stood by the giant copper-clad doors holding an imaginary white flag. Surrender, that's what it was—unwanted, unconditional surrender at the hands of forces and enemies that were too overwhelming to fight anymore. Life she had handled rather nicely, but death and Hell had now defeated her.

S uddenly the large doors flung open and a burst of multicolored light struck the waiting contingent. Their eyes had grown so accustomed to the dimness of the long hall that the light was blinding. The three instinctively thrust their hands in front of their eyes for protection.

Zadock led them across the threshold of the chapel, where they stopped as the doors swung shut behind them.

As their eyes adjusted, they saw that it was indeed a church-like structure, a miniature Gothic cathedral complete with altar, stained glass windows and icons. The strong scent of incense was overpowering, its heavy fragrance wafting from hanging gold censers suspended from the ornate ceiling in a line down the center of the room. Lining each side of the center aisle, and facing them, were people in flowing silk robes in blood red and black. About fifty men were on the right side of the aisle, about fifty women on the left. The room was silent. It was the kind of silence that follows a tornado or a fatal auto crash or an atomic blast. It was the noise of death.

Zadock slowly raised his arms above his head with his palms straight and stiff. As his hands reached a vertical position, the somber hundred began to chant, in a low monotone, words unknown to the three. It sounded like the base pedal on a great pipe organ being played *pianissimo*. The robed people voiced the syllables in swells which rose and fell in volume like waves of the sea.

Won was totally overcome. The striking beauty of the chapel, the vivid colors of the robes, the glint of colored light from the stained glass, and the hum of the chanting voices created an aura of reverence that was incomprehensible. Mac, too, was visibly impressed.

Karae felt suddenly energized by the surroundings—*energy* was the right word. There was a dynamism, a force field in the room that was unmistakable. But it was an energy which created frenzy and tension rather than tranquility and peace like the energy she had felt in the Kingdom.

She began to survey the people who were gazing at them. They were *absolutely beautiful* people with perfectly formed faces and bodies. Their beauty was physical, even sensual. The assembly had all the marks of a Ken and Barbie production line . . . but with the same lifeless eyes . . . and wearing the same cheap glitz. It was a room of male and female prostitutes, bedecked with cheap attempts at beautification in an effort to hide inner, spiritual despair. A hollowness, a void, a vapid appearance marked the countenances of these citizens of Wonderland. *Slaves* seemed a better word. They were the very antithesis of the innocent freshness and transparent authenticity she had seen in Kingdom beauty.

As the low chanting continued, Karae's eyes began to roam around the room. They paused at an object at the front and center of the chapel, and she gasped when she realized what she was seeing. In the place where a cross or crucifix might hang above the altar in a church was the head of a goat—a large, horned creature cast in silver and polished to a glassy finish. The icons along the walls were not saints or apostles, but images of frightening creatures, composites of animals with the features of human beings. A slow chill began to descend over her body.

"Presenting three inductees to the glories of Wonderland," Zadock declared in a firm, loud monotone. "Karae Johnson, Won Kim, and Arthur McNeal." The chanting came to an abrupt stop and there was a momentary pause. Then the hundred suddenly came to life, as if someone had flipped a switch to empower them, had energized one hundred bionic creatures with a hidden *Applause* sign. The congregation burst into raucous praise with cheers and waves to the trio. The expressionless faces transformed to smiles and toothy grins until, as if on precise cue, the applause stopped and the one hundred faces went blank again, eyes sinking deep back into eye sockets as before.

Zadock led the initiates to the front of the auditorium, where a single shaft of light came from a hidden source in the ceiling and illuminated a circle about three feet in diameter on the altar. Lying on the sacrificial desk in the center of the light beam was a piece of parchment, an ink bottle and a quill pen.

He stepped behind the altar and knelt, facing the image of the goat. He spoke in an ecstatic prayer language for a few moments as the audience stood in rapt attention. Prayers finished, he turned and faced the three. The citizens chanted a benediction in the language of their earlier hymns.

Zadock spoke. "Aliens from another time and place, the Prince welcomes you to Wonderland. He is delighted to accept you into the citizenry of the realm. You will be asked to repeat a simple declaration of your loyalty to the Prince and to his priest, Lord Zadock the Third. After that, your induction will be sealed by placing your signature in the Book of the Blood Covenant. Is that clear?"

There was no visible or audible response. Won was overwhelmed by the whole ceremony, so overwhelmed that his rationality had been completely suspended. His spiritual and emotional dimensions were now in full control of his system.

Mac had a gleeful but nervous grin, like an adolescent about to ring the doorbell to commence his first date. He didn't seem to know what was happening, but he didn't seem to care, either.

Karae's spirit, however, had grown increasingly restless. Something from deep within was crying out for release, a voice that would not be silenced, a scream that could not be contained. Like a balloon being inflated to the breaking point, she felt she was about to explode.

"Please repeat after me." Zadock directed the triumvirate with very deliberate pacing. "Oh Lord Zadock . . . "

"*Oh, Lord Zadock . . .* " repeated the entire assemblage in a unison roar.

"We humble ourselves before you . . . " Zadock's voice was firm and clear.

"We humble ourselves before you . . . " Won was expressionless, Mac barely mouthing the words, Karae tight-lipped and pale.

" . . . and before the Prince, the Ruler of this World." Zadock watched the eyes and lips of the three.

" . . . and before the Prince, the Ruler of this World." If the initiates were speaking at all, their voices were being drowned by the hundred witnesses.

Zadock droned out the remainder of the pledge to the faithful responses of the attendees and the disengaged responses of the trio.

"Amen," closed Zadock.

"Amen," followed the congregation.

"And now for the signing of the Covenant of Blood. This signing will seal the three here gathered for time and eternity in loyalty and service to the Prince and to his Wonderland." Zadock paused and looked at Karae. "Karae Johnson, will you step forward and take the pen and dip it . . . "

Haltingly, Karae stepped to the ceremonial table and took the pen. As she did so, the pressure in her spirit tore asunder her composure and fragmented all her restraint systems. She swooned a bit as she dipped the quill in the bottle and retracted it. She bore the pen to the parchment and, as she did, saw a drop fall from the quill.

She froze.

It was not ink. It was blood.

She let out a desperate sigh and cried out, "Jesus . . . " She gasped and crumbled into a faint, her knees buckling under her.

At that moment the foundations of the chapel shook, the censers swung violently, and the concrete floor cracked and pitched in seismic rolls. The parishioners toppled over each other like domino chains. Screams of panic destroyed the aura of the ceremony. The bottle on the altar spilled blood across the parchment as the room pitched and yawed. Pieces of ceiling plaster dropped on the heads of the assembly. Icons fell from the walls.

Karae, alert now, looked at Zadock. It was happening again. His handsome features were distorted, his flesh gnarled and seeping, his fangs bared. He was the demon again! Lucifer's Serpent General closed his eyes slowly. His knees buckled. He fell to the floor in a swoon. The gold ring on his finger glowed weakly, and the diamonds on it radiated blood red.

In another moment the room became still and silent. A blinding shaft of light broke through the roof as if there were no roof at all. Every being in the wreckage of the chapel tucked his head under his arm to shield himself from the painful brilliance.

Karae looked above her to see the silver goat's head come hurtling to the floor, as though dashed by an invisible hand. It exploded into ten thousand tiny pieces upon impact on the cold stone. From a place high above the altar, the blazing brightness of a white-robed person shone.

Her heart lept. Her spirit soared. Strength surged within her. It was he. It was he! It was The Man! The glorious seven-footer had his arms outstretched in welcome. There was a seraphic smile on his face, a warm and innocent glow on his countenance. You could see the visage of The King shining through him, the embodiment of his Master reflected in his image. He raised his arms slowly, and as he did, Karae felt herself become light and lift off the floor. A few feet into the air she saw that she was eye-level with Won and Mac, who also were being drawn upward by the same supernatural power.

In a fleeting thought Karae remembered that she had uttered only one word: *Jesus.* Was that it—the name *Jesus?* What was it about that name?

As she ascended, she looked below her at the prostrate form of Zadock, at the rubble strewn about the chapel, and at the parchment on the altar. The spilled blood from the ink bottle rolling and pitching in the earthquake had formed a perfect cross.

10

The Tie That Binds

The soaring contingent hovered in over the grand metropolis. There was no mistaking its identity—Karae would now recognize it forever.

The spectacular, thousand-foot silver arches which marked the four entrances to the city were coming closer. The glistening wide boulevards, spectacular gardens, dancing fountains, terraced waterfalls and objects of art announced that they were back in the Kingdom, back in The Province of Divine Provision, back in Jehovah Jireh.

The flight crew descended in front of the provincial palace and came to rest at the magnificent incline which led to the seat of government and to the governor's mansion. The rich glow from the heavens which lighted the Kingdom was warm and inviting after the dank dimness of the Wonderland atmosphere. The Indian Hawthorns and Jacaranda trees were just as much ablaze with color and just as finely manicured as they had been on the previous visit. The three-hundred-foot quartzite ramp over the ponds and moats was just as breathtaking in its beauty as before. The exotic birds sang even more sweetly. Karae could smell the fragrance of the honeysuckle—so much more pure, more natural, more *right* than Wonderland's seductive incense or its illusory Pasadena-orange-blossom scents.

The members of the delegation looked at each other and breathed great sighs of relief at escaping Zadock and the chaos of the Wonderland chapel. Before anyone else could speak, The Man seized the opportunity.

"Welcome home, voyagers," he smiled at them. "Welcome back to Jehovah Jireh. I guess it goes without saying that I was dispatched to intercept you and bring you back here upon Karae's desperate call to The King. I know these traumatic transports are a shock to the system, but I had to do it. Not only was I under orders to do so, but you three were about to make a very serious mistake.

"You men need to thank Karae for calling the name of King Jesus. Without that you would have sealed the sale of your souls to the Dark Side! But more about that later. The governor has prepared guest rooms for each of you. You must be exhausted from your ordeal."

"Exhausted is an understatement," Karae agreed. "My bones ache, I feel tired and sick, I am emotionally rung out, my head aches . . . "

"Spare us the organ recital, Karae." Mac raised his hand like a traffic cop. "Next thing we know you will be showing us your scars from past operations." He was more playful than vicious. "Face it, we're all exhausted."

"I was standing here wondering how I was going to make it up the ramp to the palace." Won spoke weakly but cheerfully—as if relieved to be where he was.

"Walking up the ramp is about all you'll have to do, friends." The Man supported Karae with his arm. "I will show you to your rooms where you will find some refreshments and a warm bath waiting. The attendants have folded down your bed clothes, and the wardrobe is stocked with fresh robes, gowns and pajamas. No 'business' until the morning when you will have ample time to share your experiences and reflect on the state of your lives—and your souls."

"Will we have a chance to see . . . " Karae spoke, then hesitated.

"The governor will have breakfast with you at 9 A.M."

Karae blushed, and The Man looked away as a slight smile formed on his face. Karae hadn't wanted to be so obvious. How could she have forgotten so soon that she was back in the Kingdom—where both angel hosts and citizens could read the human spirit!

The contingent walked up the splendid incline toward the majestic portal of the palace. Nearing the entrance, they turned to the right, crossed a low bridge across a flower-ringed pond, and threaded the tall pillars of the governor's mansion. Inside, a spectacular crystal— no, it was more like diamonds—chandelier twenty-five or thirty feet in diameter hung in the center of the entrance foyer.

What a wonderful contrast to the vestibule in Wonderland, Karae thought. Everything here was so bright, so cheery, so relaxed . . . so at peace.

The guest rooms were located down a wide, pastel-painted hall. Small gold-and-crystal light fixtures set with large lavender amethysts formed a brilliant stream of light down the center of the corridor. Lovely original oils of pastoral scenes transformed the passageway into more of a gallery than a mere route to the guest rooms.

"Mr. Kim, this is your room. I trust you will enjoy the Korean-style decorating and original art by one of Seoul's most talented painters from your era. He is now a resident of the Kingdom." Won thanked The Man and stepped inside. You could hear him emit a great sigh as the door to the room closed behind him.

With a giant step across the corridor The Man announced, "Miss Johnson, the Garden Room is yours for the night. The governor thought you would enjoy the fresh cut flowers, the adjoining atrium filled with tropical plants, and the morning view of the formal gardens."

"How thoughtful!" Karae stepped into the spacious room and saw her favorite Monet watercolor prominently displayed on a wall in front of her. "Please express my deep gratitude to the governor."

She touched the silk bedcover and traced the lines of the roses in its pattern with her finger. Joy flooded her weary body, her spent emotions, her famished spirit. Once again she felt that strange *Kingdom peace* as the door closed behind her. Thankfully, she sank onto the plush bed.

That left Mac and The Man in the hallway, Mac wrapped in a look of anticipation as to the kind of room he had drawn.

"And Mr. McNeal." The Man looked superficially concerned. "We wanted to provide a room for you that would suit your tastes. But, frankly, we had a little difficulty deciding what that decor would be. We ruled out the Kit Kat Lounge, your room at the frat house at Otterbein, and your bachelor pad. Somehow the decorating in all three seemed . . . *incompatible* with the cultural values of the Kingdom."

The Man was grinning now. "Then we weren't quite clear how to capture the aesthetic ambiance of Euclid Street in Cleveland, either."

Mac knew he was being teased, but somehow he didn't mind. He had dished out a few to The Man, and now the angel was balancing the books. A broad but off-center smile crept across his face.

"So I trust you'll enjoy the Safari Room. Consider it symbolic of the wild, untamed nature of one Arthur 'Mac' McNeal, Ohio Buckeye."

Mac laughed aloud now, fully enjoying the banter. "And where's my room key, Mr. Clean? I wouldn't want you to slip in during the middle of the night and steal my boar's head off the wall."

"Not to worry, Mac. We have no one in the Kingdom who steals—unless you brought a stowaway clone along with you." Even the edge on that remark didn't sting. It was clear this was light-hearted fun.

"Well, okay, White Knight, but if I catch you in the room before morning, you'll find your pretty head mounted next to the rhino's."

"Get to bed; you need the beauty rest." The Man gave a sharp motion with his hand and ordered Mac with mock authority. He partially closed the door behind Mac. Then, sticking his head back in the room, he asked, "But one last question: Isn't a buckeye a *slick-surfaced but worthless nut?*" He shut the door quickly to avoid any flying objects.

The tower chimes in the palace garden struck 12 o'clock. It was the start of their fourth day.

T here was a gentle knock on the door and a soft, female voice announced, "Breakfast in the governor's private dining room in one hour."

Karae awakened with a start, emerging quickly from a considerable amount of time spent in that No-Man's Land between deep sleep and semi-consciousness. It's the place where dreams occur in rapid-fire succession, punctuated by quick flashes of awareness of what's going on in the real world. But it's not where the quick flashes make any real sense like they'll have to before you can say you're awake.

The snapshots of real life in Karae's mind had now reached motion-picture speed. She was able to activate various parts of her body. She rose a few inches from the down pillow to symbolize that she did have intentions of floating off this cloud shortly.

She sighed and flopped back on the pillow. She had been hit with a blow from her grief center. She pictured her dear mother cold in that casket and longed to see her alive again. She longed to hug her, to tell her she loved her, to ask her forgiveness for a slight unkindness that seemed insignificant a week ago when she had uttered it—but which now felt like a piece of eternally unfinished business. A tear trickled down her cheek and she dried it on the bed sheet.

The trio's adventure in Wonderland had been a crazy-quilt of feelings, experiences, motivations and struggles. That day and a half was the longest month she had ever spent.

She checked her watch: fifteen after. Her thoughts turned to breakfast and to the governor. It was silly how he kept coming to her mind. She realized she didn't even know whether he was married. The thought was a bit depressing, but she brushed it off with a *Get yourself together, Karae, you hopeless romantic! You have no business even thinking such a thought.* A match between a Kingdom governor and a Pasadena mortgage broker would be a little ludicrous. Besides, he might turn into a monster at their first kiss, like the last guy for which she had had these feelings.

She smiled. It felt good to smile about that horrific experience. "May Lord Zadock the Third rest in peace . . . or pieces . . . whatever," she declared out loud.

Now Karae's watch read half past. She catapulted out of bed and hustled to the washroom—it was spectacular. A sunken bath the size of a hot tub at many California spas. Extravagant marble fixtures artfully designed and masterfully crafted. Cabinets fully stocked with all the items she might desire for her personal hygiene, comfort and luxury.

She hated to think of parting with the gorgeous pure-silk gown she had selected the night before from the guest room closet, and, even more, she dreaded putting on the dress which had been her "uniform" for the last couple of days. It looked like it had been to Hell and back. Come to think of it . . .

She dashed to the wardrobe to see if, by any chance, there was day wear in it. Was there ever! She grabbed a peach-colored number that was not too dressy, not too casual, and slipped it on. It was stunning! The shade was just right with her skin color, the fit was as if custom-tailored, and the style—well, it was Kingdom chic.

She selected what looked like very expensive jewelry—simple, but of the purest gold—from the jewelry box on the dresser and took one last look in the massive mirror which decorated one wall of the room.

"Not bad, if I say so myself!"

Five minutes to nine. Karae stepped through the door backwards to make sure it was closed and backed into someone in the hall. "Oh, excuse me," she stammered. She had just collided with a very nice-looking man in a dashing white uniform with gold trim, like a dress uniform for a Navy man or Marine—she could never remember which was which.

"You're excused." He gave a little bow and smiled. "I was just waiting here to escort you to the private dining room . . . at the governor's request."

"Well, isn't that *class?*" Karae observed, obviously impressed. She took his arm and they strolled down the pastel corridor.

A left turn at the end of the corridor brought Karae and her escort to the open doors of a magnificent small dining room. It was round, paneled in exotic dark hardwood and overlaid with gold patterns which looked three-dimensional against the dark background. Tall, narrow windows separated heavy wooden columns which arched toward the center of the room as they headed upward. The columns met in the center of the room, turned downward, and burst into an enormous, circular chandelier, a giant ring of crystalline lights. The overall impact of the room was that of a royal crown. The room could have served as a coronation room for some Renaissance king or queen.

A large round table identified the geometric center of the room, and attendants in emerald-green uniforms put the finishing details on the place settings, complete with intriguing folds in the mauve-colored napkins, and returned to their stations to await the guests.

"Am I the first one here?" Karae asked.

"Yes, ma'am—by design."

"Oh, I see." Karae wondered what design, by whom and for what purpose. She didn't have to wait long for the answer.

"The governor has a marvelous grasp of details and likes everything just so."

"I understand," Karae said, then wondered if she really did.

"A blessed good morning to you, Karae!" The voice was unmistakable. She turned in the direction from which it came. The escort, knowing his job was finished, left the room.

"A blessed good morning to you, Governor Ben-David." Karae wasn't accustomed to "blessing" people, but it seemed like the natural thing to say, especially this morning when she was so happy to see Jireh Ben-David's kindly face again.

The governor was nearing the table. "Welcome back to the Kingdom and to Jehovah Jireh. I understand you have had some unusual experiences since I saw you last." He grasped her hand and leaned forward to give her a proper kiss on the cheek.

"*Unusual* is hardly a sufficient adjective to describe it all."

Karae gazed intently into his eyes. He was even

more attractive than she had remembered. She hadn't noticed before the distinguishing touch of gray on his temples, put there neither by age nor by stress but by wisdom.

Attendants seated the two. "Well, you have been in my prayers." The governor was just as intent on Karae as she was on him.

"I think I must have been, considering some of the revelations I had."

The governor smiled knowingly. "Did you rest well? You look wonderful."

"I rested like I don't know when. I feel like I got a month's sleep in one night."

"Terrific."

"Are Won and Mac delaying our breakfast?" Karae wanted to cover for them if they had overslept.

"No, Karae. They are eating in another dining area. In view of what I know you must have been through, I wanted the chance to chat with you without the others present. Is that all right?" He was so sensitive.

"Oh, yes, fine—an honor, to be sure."

"Not an honor, Karae, just the natural way of doing things among friends."

The attendants set a beautiful fresh fruit creation in front of them with luscious items Karae had never seen nor tasted before. She nibbled on the delectables and observed as Jireh gave soft-spoken direction to one of the attendants.

She hadn't been able to identify what exactly made him so attractive. He was definitely robust and good looking with the fine features of all the Kingdom citizens. But somehow his attractiveness was, well, more *spiritual.* He was a wonderful mix of usually incompatible traits— strength and tenderness, innocence and wisdom, graciousness and candor, vulnerability and control, tranquility and drive, affection and power. She definitely liked the man and found it hard to imagine anyone who wouldn't.

"Tell me, did you like Zion?"

"It was spectacular, Jireh." She hoped it was okay to call a provincial governor in the Kingdom by his first name. "The grandeur of the city, the beauty of the Holy Highway, the splendor of the River of Life, the light-hearted dancing, the procession of the nations—it was unforgettable!"

"I was disappointed that you and the men left without notice or permission."

He really knows how to cut directly to the chase, Karae thought. "I'm sorry about that. It was a very foolish thing to do."

"Not so foolish as trying to escape into a snare from the Dark Side."

"You mean 'His Majesty's Department of Repatriation'?"

Jireh nodded. "I can't believe you bought that ruse. But I felt badly about all you suffered because, you see, I gave permission to them to set the trap."

"You what?" Karae was incredulous.

"I gave permission to Zadock to set up the phony 'repatriation' scheme."

Karae was stunned. She had trusted the governor, but now she felt hurt and anger deep inside. "I am incensed that you would do that. It's—it's a betrayal."

"No, no, dear Karae. Not a betrayal, but an act of love."

"You consider it an act of love to permit an evil person like Zadock to set a trap and close it on your friends?" Her eyes were ablaze and her words radiated the heat.

"I consider it an act of love to let my friends experience the consequences of their own folly so they can learn never to fall again. That was done in the same spirit as a parent who allows a child to touch a very warm stove to learn the horrors of touching a hot one.

"Karae, please understand. Nothing happens even in the Kingdom of Darkness without allowance by The King, and He gave me orders to permit Zadock to pursue his folly.[53] You and Won and Mac never left the protective care of The King and the Kingdom. But it was clear that you were determined to test the limits of The King's grace—and of mine. So we loved you enough to allow you to learn who is trustworthy—with no lasting harm."

"But, Jireh, I didn't want to go, to leave the Kingdom. You must know that."

"You did go, Karae. The best test of our true desires is our actions. Many a mortal has gone to Hell protesting that he did not *want* to go there. But his willful choice of false evidence and his disobedient actions finally proved him to be a liar. If you had wanted to stay in the Kingdom strongly enough, you would have. It's that simple."

"I guess it was my desire to go home that seduced me. I thought the escape would achieve that desire."

"Karae, I'm not being hard on you, please understand. But unfounded desire must always be given second place to well-founded fact. There was nothing in the character of Mac or Won, nothing in their proven knowledge of the nature of the Kingdom, and nothing in their plan to return you home that deserved your confidence. You gave them the most precious gift you have to give: your good faith. They didn't even earn it! You tossed it to them like so many pearls before swine."

This was a painful conversation, not the kind Karae wanted to be having with this man she admired and could love. Never mind that he was 100 percent accurate in his observations. This was painful. Her throat restricted and tight lines in her face reflected the cramp she felt in her heart.

"And dear lady," Jireh lowered his voice and spoke

more tenderly, "you gave your trust to another who didn't earn it."

"Say no more, Jireh. I know what's coming. Zadock."

"Yes, Zadock. I am profoundly angry at him. If The King would permit me, I would personally send him to the Lake of Fire before his time. That snake tortured someone I love." Jireh flinched, as if shocked by the word slipping out of his mouth with such passion.

Karae studied Jireh's eyes. They were aswirl with both anger and affection. Moisture formed around his lids as he continued.

"He is a monster. First he endeavored to seduce you with his sound and light show—the lights of Pasadena, ha! If I hadn't beamed that glimpse of the true Zadock to you, you may have bought his come-on. Then when he saw that you were slipping out of his clutches, he had the damnable audacity to throw a pack of lies at you about your mother."

Karae's eyes froze into a disbelieving stare. "A pack of lies? What are you saying?"

"Karae, you have no basis for anything but trust in me and in The King. Your mother is fine! The King would not have taken you away from her for a minute without making provision for her care. A simple touch from Him and her heart condition went into recovery. She's stronger today than she has been in years. She will be fully recovered within the month. The physicians will find no trace of heart disease. You'll have her to love and enjoy for years to come regardless of where you are. The King has a plan which includes that. It is part of the reward for your participation in this experiment."

"But I saw her in the casket with my own eyes!"

"You saw an *illusion* of her in the casket with your own eyes. Sight isn't the test of truth, Karae—*reliable witness* is. Zadock had to find a way to break you down.

Knowing your love for your mother, he broke your will with his fraudulent funeral-home vision. Phony visions are as old as false prophets, lying fortune tellers and snake oil salesmen. Believe me, your mother is fine and in good hands."

Karae's heart pounded at the joyful news. She broke down and cried, and laughed, and laughed and cried at the same time. Dropping her napkin, she bolted to her feet and flung her arms around Jireh, embracing him with all her strength. "Oh, Jireh, Jireh, how could I have been so blind? I owe everything to you."

"You owe everything to The King! This whole plan is His. I am merely the one designated to carry it out."

"But you love me like The King does. I've never met and can't see The King. I can see you, touch you. I can see and feel your love!"

"That's the divine plan, Karae. Every citizen of the Kingdom is to be a channel for experiencing the infinite, unconditional love of The King."

Jireh held her tightly as she wept pure, cleansing tears—sobs of relief, of gratitude, of grief suddenly ended. Finally she relaxed and stepped back from him, still holding his hands in hers. "I'll never be able to show the magnitude of my thanks to you."

"Karae, you were angry with me a few minutes ago. I think you used the word *betrayal*. I didn't do what I did for either curses or thanks. I do what I do because it is right, because it is loving, and because it is the righteous will of The King. Living by that Law got me here from my earth life. Continuing to live by that Law will keep me in my position as governor. I would hope that it will enable me to keep you as my beloved friend . . . forever."

"Consider it sealed, Jireh." Karae put her arms around his neck and kissed him gently on the cheek, then leaned closer as she felt his arms tighten around her. After a long moment of floating warmth they pulled apart.

Jireh surveyed the uneaten breakfast and, with a pleasant smile, addressed the company of attendants still at their stations. "I guess you got in on quite a melodrama today, didn't you?"

They smiled graciously, and the head attendant replied, "We took the opportunity to pray for you and Miss Johnson as you talked. And be assured, sir, that what we see and hear in this room stays in this room. The King has decreed it."

Jireh looked pleased. "May His rich blessing rest upon you for your faithful service." He turned to Karae. "Feel free to go to your room, wander the grounds or walk the streets of Jehovah Jireh, Karae. I am going to be late for brunch with your two companions."

She smiled warmly. "I'm sure I'll be able to stay occupied in such a beautiful place. Especially with such a marvelous new outlook!"

"I trust you will. The four of us will meet in my office at noon. Much of The King's experiment still lies ahead of us."

That sounded a little ominous to Karae, but she was learning to trust Jireh, something she had not achieved with any other man—or even desired to achieve.

11

Two for the Show

The radiance of celestial glow brightened the patio where Won and Mac were seated. An ornate stone railing surrounded the patio overlooking the peaceful ponds, streams and gardens of the palace park. Swan-like birds glided across the mirrored pond at the base of a long, grassy slope which separated the patio from the water.

In the distance the two could see a magnificent fountain playing a hundred varied patterns of water spray. Children and maidens splashed and waded in the outer circumference of the fountain, and couples circum-navigated the winding paths which disappeared and reappeared among the flora. To their amazement, they saw bear and lion cubs, Husky-like pups, and small Saint Bernards roaming the park, providing delightful—and perfectly safe—company for adults and children alike who stopped to pet or play with them.

A light breeze wafted across the table where Won and Mac had been seated by the uniformed attendants. They were each sipping a cup of rich coffee as they looked over the menu.

"Not bad for brunch, eh, Won?" Mac stretched as if preparing for a great athletic challenge—eating.

"Not bad at all." Won held his coffee cup in a salute.

"Even a better selection than in Wonderland. Hope they let you have seconds."

" . . . and thirds and fourths and fifths and . . . " Won added with a knowing grin. He had watched his companion eat before.

"Knock it off, Kim." Mac feigned insult. "I just like good food."

" . . . or hot food or cold food or mediocre food or bad food . . . " Won had him on the run.

"Gimme a break! I don't like bad food," Mac protested.

"C'mon, Mac, you're the Will Rogers of food. Your motto has to be, 'I never met a meal I didn't like.'"

"I'm sure . . . the Will Rogers of food . . . " Mac paused to order "two of everything" from the attendant.

"A blessed good morning, gentlemen! Sorry I am a few minutes late for brunch." It was the governor, smiling broadly and checking his watch. It read 10 A.M.

"Good morning, sir."

"Good morning, gov."

"I hope you both had a good rest. I didn't think you would mind sleeping late, so I scheduled brunch instead of breakfast."

"Glaaaad to sleep in, especially with the boa constrictor." Mac's grin reflected the Irish Leprechaun in him.

"Boa constrictor?" The governor looked puzzled.

"Yeah, the Man from Glad put me in the jungle room last night. You didn't know it came furnished with a live boa?"

Jireh smiled, understanding. "No, I didn't. You liked the Safari Room?"

"Yeah, it was fine. I slept like a rock."

"I had a wonderful night in my Korean Room, sir. It

brought back fond memories—actually, it made me more homesick."

Mac interrupted. "You, Mr. Won Kim, have just said the secret word: *home*." He turned to the governor. "And when *are* we going home?"

Jireh hesitated a moment, as if weighing exactly how much to tell them. "I have just received word from The King that the experiment is to end at six tomorrow evening. But there is still much for you to see before then."

"May I ask where Karae is, sir?" Won asked.

"Karae and I had breakfast together earlier. I knew she had had a traumatic day yesterday and thought I might improve her outlook on life a bit over a good meal."

"Were you successful?" Won inquired.

"Highly. The key was giving her the news that her mother is not dead but in better health than she has been for years." The governor sipped his coffee casually, as if there should be no shocked response.

"What did you say?" Mac almost shouted. "Karae's mother isn't dead?"

"Never been more alive." Jireh's face beamed confidence.

"Waaait a minute!" Mac argued. "I saw Karae in shambles over the journey Zadock gave her to her mother's funeral! She saw it with her own eyes."

"Mac, you've never been to Hollywood, have you?"

"No. Why?"

"Then you don't even know what can be done with mirrors, strings and pulleys—much less what can be done spiritually to manipulate the human imagination."

"Doc, are you telling me the funeral scene wasn't real?"

"As fake as a seven dollar bill, Mac. As fake as the promises you bought about becoming a rich, famous, international leader with a yacht and hot-and-cold running damsels. I can't believe you fell for Zadock's pack of lies." Jireh Ben-David hadn't wasted much time getting to the bottom line.

"What makes you so sure those promises weren't genuine?" Mac said defensively. "They were better than any offers I've heard from you."

The governor paused a moment before answering. "Would you rather have fraudulent offers or none at all?"

That was a tough question for a guy who had made a good living in sales by making quasi-fraudulent promises. Mac squirmed and stewed a bit before answering. "Well, I can handle a little fraudulence." His mind spun in a circle of rationalizations. The foundation of his logic was crumbling and he knew it.

"And I suppose you would like to have a little poison with that juice you're drinking and a little infidelity from the woman you would marry and a little skimming of interest by the bank off your savings account. Mac, the world you come from has conditioned you to accept that damnable lie—a *little* playing with the truth doesn't make you a liar and a *little* filth is simply 'adult' entertainment and a *little* juggling of the numbers is shrewd business. But in your heart, you know you've been fed lies."

Mac was cornered. "But what Zadock offered was what I've always wanted."

"Of course it was. He's no fool. He knows that we are most vulnerable to the lies we want to believe. 'Buy this lottery ticket and become a millionaire' is an example. Check the probabilities, Mac, or have your scientist buddy here do it for you. You have a much better chance of being hit by lightning *twice* than of becoming a millionaire in the lottery. The truth is that millions in their earth lives enter poverty believing the lottery millionaire lie. It has *Made in Wonderland by Zadock* written all over it."

"But . . . " Mac feebly attempted to argue, but couldn't find the words.

"Another thing you missed, Mac, was the way Zadock played on the bitterness you hold toward your father. The overlay on his grandiose promises was that you were going to be able to stick it to your dad. He was playing dirty, because your inner scars from your relationship with your father scream so loudly you can't hear either what is reasonable or what is right."

"Now I'm dealing with the Kingdom shrink."

Jireh Ben-David didn't back off. "If you had put your signature to that parchment, you would have become an inductee all right. You would have been inducted into membership in Zadock's chain gang. They were the hollow-eyed, soul-less zombies that filled his blasphemous 'chapel.' You're right; I've made you no offers. You're in the Kingdom. You won't get offers here. You'll get only promises. This benevolent monarchy is built on total and absolute Truth. If even one promise turned phony, The King's throne would topple and the whole system would collapse."

Mac looked at Won and announced sarcastically, "Won, baby, it sounds like this trip really will end at six tomorrow evening! But for my money, I'll believe it when I see it."

"You'll see it, Mac," the governor assured him. "And believe me, everything you have seen, and everything you *will* see between now and then, will all come together for you. You will understand why The King has selected you for this experiment. And, hopefully, you will thank Him for doing so."

Mac slapped his hand on the table. "I just want this limbo to be over. You can have my signature right here and now. Where do I sign the dotted line?"

Jireh lowered his volume and tone. "We have no written contracts, no signed agreements in the Kingdom.

They are totally unnecessary. The most we have is informal notes of our conversations to refresh our memories of verbal agreements. Our word is our signature. Written contracts backed by binding collateral are symbols of the ethical degeneracy of your world system—they are not needed here."

Won frowned his skeptical frown. "But what if someone gets slighted in the verbal agreement, intentionally or unintentionally?"

The governor shifted his attention to Won and replied, "It couldn't happen intentionally. We have all received a new, righteous, heart motivation. It couldn't happen unintentionally, either, because The King providentially prohibits calamity."

"But if somehow it did . . . " Won wanted an answer.

"If somehow it did, the Kingdom citizen would accept the wrong with grace and rejoice that the other person received benefit even at his personal expense."

"Oh, bruth-ther!" This was too much for Mac. "Don't tell me you're one of those 'turn the other cheek' people . . . "

"Yes, I am, Mac. We all are." Jireh paused, dropped his head, raised it again, and continued. "By order of The King. He knows it's the key to genuinely loving one another, to living together in harmony."

"I bet *he* doesn't turn the other cheek," Mac huffed.

Jireh paused again, a contemplative look in his eyes. "Indeed, He did, many times, twenty-one centuries ago . . . "

Mac didn't pick up on Jireh's reference to human history. "Well, I'm not one to turn the other cheek myself. If that's the code here, then I'm outta here."

"You'll have the opportunity to make that choice in about thirty-one hours."

Jireh Ben-David shifted his chair toward Won to

indicate that the discussion was closed. Mac dived into his eggs Benedict.

"Won, you were duped also," the governor said.

Won wasn't willing to square off with the governor as Mac had done. "That sounds a bit harsh."

"I'm sorry if it sounds harsh to you."

"I mean the content of what you said, not the manner in which you said it. You must realize that I was fascinated by the whole world of Wonderland—Zadock's abilities to manipulate reality and create illusions, and the promise of learning the secrets of the universe. I've always been intrigued by the world of parapsychology."

"Spirits," Jireh Ben-David corrected him. "Parapsychology is a term made up to describe spirit phenomena by people who don't believe in—or don't want to admit they believe in—the spirit world. Whether you realize it or not, you were making a spiritual decision when you opted to commit to Zadock."

"On the contrary, governor, I was making a very rational decision. As a scientist I wanted to explore a fresh area of inquiry, an area which promised to bear great rewards. Legitimate research always bears great rewards."

"Research is not all rewarding, Won. Research into evil is both destructive and enslaving."

"If I were to commit to that premise, I would have to resign my position in the research lab. I would be surrendering to the idea that some areas of research are off-limits for legitimate, scientific investigation, subject to censorship by some arbitrary authority."

"Won, The King does not fit your definition of an 'arbitrary authority,' but He does extend limits, laws, prohibitions. They are motivated not by a capricious desire to spoil people's fun—what you call 'censorship'—but by the extravagant love He has for His subjects. In the same way that parents do not allow four-year-olds to 'pursue investigations' into toxic household chemicals, The King eschews research into areas that are destructive to the soul."

"I respectfully have to reject that notion, governor. It is essential for every true scientist to keep an open mind."

"I'm with Won." Mac took his stand between mouthfuls.

"Won, many an open mind like yours has been devastated by the wrong kinds of inquiry—to the point that it has had to be 'closed for repairs.' If you doubt it, I will give you a tour of drug rehabilitation centers, AIDS hospices, satanic covens, and the Holocaust memorial at Auschwitz. The mind of man was never intended to operate without the control of his spirit. And the spirit of man was never intended to operate against the guidelines of the One who created it, The King."

"That may be fine for you, Governor Ben-David, but at some point you chose to make a religious decision which brought you here and enables you to feel comfortable in this environment. As a scientist, I view religion as a biasing factor in my ability to do objective research. Frankly, I couldn't operate in this Kingdom environment."

"Won, look me in the eye. Do you really think there is any such thing as objective research? Honestly, now, have you really ever known a researcher who did not take tons of biasing baggage with him into his inquiry? Can you even postulate a person's being able to set aside *all* the lessons from his life experience, *all* of the blind socialization he has received from his culture, and *all* of his instinctive or learned predispositions? You're not looking me in the eye!"

Indeed, Won had looked away. He had begun to

perspire a bit. He mopped at his brow with his linen napkin.

"Won, at some level every decision you make is a spiritual decision. Every thought you generate, every choice you make, flows out of your human spirit, out of who you are at the deepest level of your being, out of your character. You chose to go with Zadock out of *spiritual* motivations—your intellectual pride, your selfish desire to have it all, your secret passion to have both wife and mistress."

"Yeah, and Won's little number was a beaut," Mac smirked. Jireh gave him a stern look.

"There was nothing rational or objective about your choice, Won. In fact, it was your denial of spiritual realities which made you oblivious to the powers Zadock was using to beguile you. Remember, you—the proud Ph.D., the great intellect, the rational scientist—were suckered by Zadock first, long before Mac or Karae."

Won knew he was beaten, but he couldn't admit it. He folded his arms in body language which said *I won't give up,* and retreated into a shell of silent, prideful stubbornness.

The governor, reading Won's spirit, realized it was useless to continue the conversation. He reached his hand across the table for a handshake. Won reluctantly extended his hand. They shook, and Jireh held on. "Won, this may be hard for you to accept, but I came on strong because I love you. I am desperate to protect you from a course which will destroy your soul in Hell."

Won accepted the gentle expression of caring. He knew it was an earnest expression, even if he didn't agree with the governor's thinking.

Mac had rolled his eyes up in his head upon hearing *destroy your soul in Hell,* but Jireh noticed that Mac did so with less conviction than he had before his trip to Wonderland.

The table dialogue was over. Jireh stood. "Well, Mac, did you get enough food to tide you over until lunch?"

Mac looked embarrassed. "I think I can make it for an hour or two," he said, patting the incipient pot which was forming just above his belt line.

"Good. You two and Karae may be eating on the run the next day and a half. Your schedule will be very full. The King has ordered two more tours for you before tomorrow evening."

Mac looked skeptical. "No bottomless pits inside phony government buildings this time, okay?"

The governor shot back, "No stupid attempts to escape to Homeland with the rest of the band, okay?" His smile let Mac know his reply was in good humor.

"*Touché*," Mac admitted with a smile as the three left the table. He felt good with a great meal in him, but that one phrase, *two more tours,* rattled him. What could it be this time? Was Zadock going to re-enter the picture? Would this roller coaster ever end? He could last until 6 P.M. tomorrow if that really was the end. He would make *sure* he lasted.

12

The Anti-Kingdom

The ornate skylights of the great corridor were just as splendid as Karae had remembered them. Today, however, the stained glass images of fruits and vegetables on the ceiling seemed more vivid, more alive. As she approached the governor's office she stopped to study the massive hardwood doors overlaid with gold leaf.

She stepped inside the cavernous room which served as the governor's office. The rich oak paneling was finely polished, the tall bookcases of ancient volumes in perfect order, and the French antiques perfectly positioned. A striking, fifteen-foot-square oil of Christ feeding the five thousand hung on the back wall of the room. Governor Ben-David was ensconced behind his impressive silver desk, busily scribbling on a pad.

"Am I the first one here?" she asked.

"Oh, Karae," Jireh stood quickly to greet her. "Yes, you are. I expect the others will be here directly." He stepped around the desk and gave her a short but warm embrace. "Please have a seat."

Karae sat in one of the three chairs which faced his desk. "Jireh, I hope Mac behaves more properly today than he did the last time he was in this room."

He laughed. "Oh, you can never tell about Mac. Mac is pretty well going to do what Mac feels like doing, whether it fits anyone's definition of 'proper' or not." He chuckled as he flashed back to the statue routine he had put Mac through to get his attention. "But you know, Karae, I love that young man. He has some wonderful qualities and a kind of infectious charm about him. Why, if he were around more, I might even suggest that others call me 'gov'!" He laughed enthusiastically. "But I doubt if 'Gyro' would catch on . . . " He chuckled again. When he laughed, a wonderful, merry light came from his visage.

"You are so gracious. You must love almost everybody." There was a touch of envy in Karae's voice.

The governor leaned back in his chair and fiddled with his pen. "Loving almost everybody isn't sufficient, I have found. The King set forth the standard of loving *everyone*, including the unlovely—even enemies. I've learned that this ethic was not for the benefit of our enemies so much as it was for us. I can't live with myself anymore if I'm harboring the tiniest hint of hatred. I used to struggle to love the Zadocks of the world, even though I hated their evil. I could only conquer my destructive motives by allowing The King's Spirit to operate through me, being carried on the back of His love. But in the Kingdom that kind of love has become second nature." He thought about what he'd just said for a moment, then added, "No, I guess I'd have to say *first* nature."

"You sound like my Sunday school teacher, Mrs. Washington."

"You went to Sunday school?"

"Oh, yes, in my culture it was pretty much expected that mamas would take their children to church. In the ghettos it was storefront churches."

"Did you go to a storefront church?" He seemed especially interested in this subject.

"No, I grew up middle class. We went to First Presbyterian. It was largely attended by whites, but Mrs. Washington was Black. As you would probably say, she 'loved The King'—she also loved us kids. She had a powerful effect on my young life."

Jireh leaned across the desk. "That's wonderful, Karae. You know, unconditional love from The King is the only offense for which there is no adequate defense. How can you keep someone from loving you if they are empowered to do it supernaturally and unconditionally?"

"If that's the offense you're using on me," Karae said shyly, with a glint in her eye, "it's working."

A slight hue of red crept onto Jireh's cheeks. For the first time he appeared just a bit nervous. "I'm glad."

The footsteps in the hall announced that Won and Mac were coming, as if Mac's recognizable voice weren't sufficient notice. Jireh rose to greet them before they came into view in the archway. They appeared in all their splendor.

"Greetings, men!"

"Greetings, gov."

"Good afternoon," Won added, precise as usual. It was afternoon by only a few minutes.

"Have a seat," Jireh suggested.

They sat. Mac looked impish. You could tell he was thinking something bizarre. You also knew he would be out with it soon, as Mac seemed to carry few unexpressed thoughts. "Say, gov, ever play Statue of Liberty?"

"Can't say as I have, why?" The governor looked cautious, much as a friend who knows he's being set up for a joke.

"Oh, never mind. We had a pretty good game of it the last time I was in this room, and I thought you might give me a rematch. You won the last one!"

Karae and Won laughed out loud. The childhood

game in which one calls out "Statue of Liberty" and everybody freezes in position was evidently unknown to Jireh. But he was getting Mac's drift.

"As I recall, that game was preceded by your launching a round of Hide and Seek." The laughter grew louder as all joined in. The governor was a great sport.

Mac looked at Won and Karae. "Sharp. The man is sharp." It was a relief to Karae that Mac, for once, was not acting like a jerk with Jireh Ben-David. Maybe Jireh's love was breaking Mac down.

After the merriment subsided, Jireh cleared his throat. "Friends, the next day and a half will probably be the most critical time of your life. You are going to witness things that no other mortal has witnessed on your side of death's door. These experiences will be the heart of the experiment for which The King took you out of your time and place and brought you here."

The trio looked at each other. Their countenances had suddenly become serious.

"This part of your test will run for thirty-six hours straight. You will not sleep, and you will not eat during that time. I will make sure, however, that you are supernaturally strengthened and nourished. By six tomorrow you will be asked to swear your allegiance to The King and His Kingdom."

"Here we go again," Mac sighed.

"I think you will find this quite different from your Wonderland experience, Mac." Jireh's suggestion seemed pregnant with implications.

Mac perked up. Jireh continued. "You will be told no lies or shown no deceiving visions. The King has done everything possible to make sure that you are able to make your decision as free from extraneous forces as possible, even though the things you see will be powerful—sometimes overwhelming."

"And I suppose if we come up with the wrong

decision, it's back to Purgatory." Mac never gave anyone a break for long.

Jireh studied Mac for a long moment. "The end result of either choice will soon be very clear to you, Mac. I cannot emphasize enough how important it is that you observe carefully what you are about to see. And that, when the time comes, you choose wisely."

"You gonna have women for us like the guy did at the last place we visited?" Mac winked at Won, and Won dropped his head in chagrin.

"Mac!" Karae looked at Jireh as if to apologize for the rogue.

The governor leveled his gaze on him. "Mac, you know the answer to that question."

"Sorry, gov," Mac replied, actually sounding a little sorry for displaying his chronic foot-in-mouth syndrome once again. "Do we get the White Tornado to conduct this tour? I'm kinda getting to like that guy."

"You took the words right out of my mouth, Mac. Yes, the one you call The Man will be your host. I'll even give you his real name. His name is Seraph Lightning.[54] He specializes in tasks for The King that require phenomenal speed and energy.[55] His ability to transport you so rapidly anywhere in the universe is proof of his qualification to bear this name."

Seraph Lightning. The three were mulling over the new name. "If there are no questions, I will summon Seraph Lightning now."

"Apprehensions, yes—but no questions, sir," Won replied. The looks on Karae's and Mac's faces indicated that Won was speaking for them as well. They seemed to understand that whatever was planned was inevitable, regardless of their questions.

"Very well." Governor Ben-David snapped his fingers and The Man, Seraph Lightning, stood in their midst.

What a powerful image Seraph Lightning created—the build of a seven-foot decathlete, the good looks of a leading man, the warmth of a counselor, and the innocence of, well, an angel! Then his immaculate white suit . . . you couldn't help feeling both attracted and comforted when he was near.

"Good afternoon, friends!" His voice was deep, rich, resonant.

"Good afternoon," the trio responded.

"It is a pleasure to receive yet another assignment from The King and Governor Ben-David involving you. We are becoming fast friends."

"The pleasure is all ours," Karae batted her eyelashes at him and grinned.

"Well, well, I guess you finished the run on your laundry truck and decided to come escort us peons around for a while." Mac picked up where he and The Man had left off the night before. "I still haven't forgiven you for the insult to my Ohio Buckeyes."

"Well, you're fortunate. Forgiveness can be found in the Kingdom." Seraph smiled.

"Here are your orders from The King, Seraph Lightning." Jireh held out a piece of paper pulled from a gold-foil diplomatic pouch. Seraph stepped around the desk and read the document slowly, carefully. His face grew serious as he read.

"Quite a challenge," Seraph observed to Jireh.

"Quite a challenge, indeed." Jireh agreed, glancing at the three who were exchanging nervous glances. Then he turned and saluted Seraph Lightning. "The King be with you!"

"And with you, His faithful servant," Seraph responded, returning the salute and handing the document back to Jireh. Seraph did an about-face and addressed the threesome. "Ready to head out?"

"As if we had a choice," Mac mumbled.

"Very well," Seraph said, "follow me and listen carefully. I want to prepare you as thoroughly as possible for what you will experience." He headed out the door of the office and into the long corridor.

As the three left the room, Jireh said his goodbyes to the group and exchanged an extended gaze with Karae. He stepped to the portal after them and watched as the quartet traversed the lengthy passageway. Seraph had begun his orientation as they walked, and the aliens were giving full attention. As the governor turned back into his office, an involuntary tear slipped from his eye and streamed down his cheek.

Have a seat on one of these benches," Seraph directed as the group left the palace and started down the glistening ramp of inlaid jade. Flowering shrubs hugged both sides of the delicate railing, their perfect spherical shapes adding complementary round lines to the square ones of the structure. Reflection off the ponds and moats below lighted the translucent inlays of the overpass with a rainbow of flickering back lighting.

The angel leaned against the railing and propped one foot up on a bench. "The King has directed that I take you first to His galactic prison. I know it may seem contradictory, in view of what you have seen of the Kingdom, to learn that there is a massive prison in Kingdom realms. But, as is the case in your society, evil must be dealt with and evil doers must be restrained. The converse of a free and righteous populace is the binding and incarceration of those whose evil would destroy it. The enjoyment of the peace and tranquility of a just community is to be realized only in the removal and restraint of those who would do violence or make war. Kingdom citizens are able to savor such joyful wonders only because those who would undermine their system have been purged."

"Here come the Fascists," Mac whispered to Won.

Seraph read Mac's spirit-to-spirit communication. "I understand your perception, Mac. I know you have contempt for totalitarianism. But that is because your world has never seen a totalitarian state which is perfectly righteous, one with a loving, benevolent, perfectly pure and completely just dictator.[56] The Kingdom is such a wonderful state *only because* of its total control. Total control enables total efficiency, total freedom, total justice, total provision, total love. Total control also permits the ultimate elimination of evil, of exploitation, and of the perpetrators of evil."

"That's what Adolf Hitler thought," Won protested.

"And Adolf Hitler was correct in his thinking. He was just hellish in his motivations, totally misguided in his judgments, and viciously cruel in his execution. One cannot create a perfect tyranny without a perfect tyrant, or a flawless kingdom without a flawless monarch."

Won assumed a professional stance. "The critical issue then seems to be who the dictator determines is evil. In Hitler's case it was non-Aryans, Jews, or anybody who disagreed with him or threatened his hold on power. Who does The King think is evil? Who is righteous?"

"That, my friends, is the object of this phase of The King's experiment, to help you determine who is evil and who is righteous. The King, the governor and I have all observed that you three have a fatally distorted view of evil and righteousness. A condition which, by the way, is not uncommon in the world you come from."

"Aw, c'mon," Mac put his fists on his hips and tilted his head to the side in a gimme-a-break stance.

Karae, too, spoke up. "I've always considered myself a good person. I've never deliberately harmed anyone."

"And that evaluation, Miss Johnson, could cost you your soul."

"Gimme a break, angel!" Mac tossed his hands in the air in frustration.

"Like everyone else who is confronted by The King, Mac, you will indeed receive *every possible* break. The real question is whether you will act appropriately on the breaks you are given. I trust that Part One of this experiment will motivate you to choose rightly."

Seraph lowered his foot from the bench to the ground. "Now please stand. It is time to go."

The three obeyed and suddenly that special, now-familiar lightness came over them as they found themselves rising into the air with their angel-guide.

In just a split second or two, the atmosphere grew darker and darker as they soared into space and away from the earth. Galaxies sped past, and nebulae whirled and disappeared behind them. Shortly, a desolate-looking planet came into view. It was somewhat like the earth's moon in size and configuration, but also very different. It was considerably darker, less reflective, and more rugged in its topography. As they approached the spheroid, Karae sensed a strange feeling gripping her, a mix of hot blast and cold chill, the kind of feeling one gets with the nightmarish malaise of a high fever.

There was something foreboding, ominous, about this place. The team settled onto a barren desert plain in a deep valley between two stark mountain ranges. This dismal satellite of some distant star lacked the features which made the earth a jewel—no shining oceans, no lush greenery, no snow-capped peaks, no flowing rivers, no rainbows of flora and fauna. It had none of the marks of an environment designed for habitation. This place was dim. Dull. Dry.

No one spoke as Seraph led the delegation a few hundred yards across the desolate, dusty plain. Each was hushed, as at a wake. The oppressive climate seemed to wring the life, the vitality, the joy out of them with every step they took. Even Mac was silent, almost sullen.

"Where are you taking us?" Karae ventured, a quiver in her voice.

"To the Anti-Kingdom, Karae," their guide replied, without turning in her direction. He was focused, as if possessed, on a spot straight ahead.

"The Anti-Kingdom?"

"Please, Karae, I will explain in due time." Seraph was kind but firm.

She caught a sudden whiff of sulfurous odor. Another more acrid odor, like that of singed hair, came next. A hideous, noxious stench, like burning flesh, followed. She put her hand over her nose to protect against the terrible sensations—to no avail. As they progressed, the odors turned to fumes, then steam, but no visible change could be seen in the desert ahead of them. Still, Seraph kept leading in a straight line toward an unseen destination. As he did, a creeping, growing sense of horror tightened its grip on each of them. Karae stayed close to Seraph. Close behind, Mac and Won seemed more tenuous, more apprehensive, than she had ever seen them.

"Stop!" Seraph stretched out his arms, and eight legs instantly locked into rigid positions.

All of Karae's senses were being challenged. Even as her sense of smell was adapting to the odors, her pupils dilated to take in whatever lay in the murky dimness. Her ears picked up sounds, distant sounds, noises like a far-off carnival with its shouts, screams, raucous music, barking ringmasters and blaring bull horns—all blended into one roaring cacophony.

Still, no one spoke. Mac, Won and Karae were now clinging to each other while staring straight ahead in the direction of the angel's gaze.

Then, all at once, Karae's vision cleared. As if a giant veil had been pulled aside, all the sensations which had been so dull and distant now became acute and near. The ghastly odors intensified even more, and the cacophony increased to decibel levels which seared the eardrums. All three of them now tried to hold their noses and plug their ears as well, but still the horrid smells and screeching sounds came through.

And then came the sights. Just across a great gulf, Karae could see hideous creatures writhing in pits of slime. Demon-like monsters slashed and tortured themselves in pagan rituals. Bizarre, misshapen specimens of humanity strutted and flashed themselves as if on parade—millions of them. More normal-looking humans, if they could be called that, engaged in sick perversities with each other and screamed lewd obscenities. Mobs of frenzied revelers mocked the God of Heaven and openly urinated and defecated on symbols of The King's realm. Some tore apart and feasted on human flesh around open fires. Refuse of every conceivable kind was strewn across the landscape, forming one gargantuan, rotting trash heap. Hovels and shacks served as shelters from a rain which never came. Desperate, thirst-crazed mortals cried out for a drop of water for their tongues. Cracks and crevasses in the earth spewed molten lava in and around the populated areas, making liquid with no moisture, rivers with no water, and seaways with no escape.[57]

It was more horrible than anything Karae had ever seen—or imagined. A nauseous terror overwhelmed her and she could only cry out, "No! No! Seraph, please! No more!" She turned away from the scene, but the odors and sounds continued to pummel her.

Won had collapsed to his knees in horror. "Yes, please," he gasped. "Please take us away from here."

Even Mac—braggadocious, macho Mac—was terror-stricken. "Seraph! Get us out of here! Now!" he pleaded.

Facing the horrible abyss, Seraph lifted his tear-filled eyes to Heaven and shouted with authority, "ENOUGH! In the name of King Jesus, ENOUGH!"

The translucent curtain closed slowly over the horrific landscape, leaving only a hazy outline of the ghastly scenes behind it. The abominable noises began to fade, as if someone had touched a galactic volume knob and turned it downward to the point of its original, distant roar. The air cleared sufficiently to make the atmosphere tolerable to the nostrils and a gradual, quiet, spiritual calm began to settle over the desert plain surrounding the quartet of tortured spirits.

Seraph, Karae and Mac all dropped to the earth, exhausted and shocked, their mouths parched with planetary dust.

Seraph spoke to a rock in their midst, "Spring forth!" and fresh, clear water bubbled out and flowed around them, cooling their feet and hands and providing a miniature oasis of satisfaction for their thirst.[58]

No one spoke. Several minutes of silence and many swallows of the cooling flow were required before the stunned visitors could regain any semblance of normal response. Perceiving their terror, Seraph gave them the time they needed to recover.

Karae was the first to break the morgue-like silence. She looked pathetically into the eyes of Seraph and ventured, "The Anti-Kingdom?"

Kindly, compassionately, he nodded. "The Anti-Kingdom of the planet Hades."[59]

"Looks like Hell to me." For once, Mac was serious.

"Hell it is, Mac. We call it the Anti-Kingdom because that's what it is, the obverse of the Kingdom. If the Kingdom values Truth, Hell is the consequence of lies. If the Kingdom expresses love and forgiveness, Hell spews forth hatred and vengeance. If the Kingdom honors altruistic self-sacrifice, Hell is the reward for selfish exploitation. If the Kingdom exalts the humble and the gracious, Hell houses the arrogant and the vicious. If the Kingdom prizes purity and wholesomeness, Hell exalts debauchery and obscenity. In these and a thousand other dimensions, Hell is the Anti-Kingdom."[60]

"How did those poor people, those poor creatures, get there?" Won asked.

"There are only two routes to Hell, Won. Making the wrong choice and making no choice at all."

Won frowned. "I don't understand."

"You will, Won . . . and Mac and Karae. By six o'clock tomorrow, I promise you, you will understand."

13

Wrong Choice, No Choice

The terrible, distant din of the Anti-Kingdom wore heavily on the senses of Mac, Won and Karae, still seated on the desert floor of the God-forsaken planet. The repulsive scenes of agony could still be seen faintly through the atmospheric veil. The repugnant odors still vaguely tormented their senses of smell.

"Please, Seraph, do we have to stay here in this terrible place?" Karae spoke for all of them.

"For a short time longer, my precious friends. You must stay aware, however superficially, of the realities of the Anti-Kingdom for a while longer."

"But, Seraph, why torture us?" Won covered his eyes with his hand. "We have seen enough in a few brief moments to give us nightmares for time and eternity."

"Not so, Won." Seraph shook his head. "The minute even hideous realities like these are out of mind they begin to sink into unreality. Truth changes into fiction, horror into discomfort, and discomfort into mild unpleasantness. The resolutions we make to do right fade quickly after the terrible pangs of guilt from doing evil subside. The pledges we make to prepare for death wane the minute we leave the graveside of a loved one. In the same way, these realities will begin to pale the instant they are out of range of your senses. Therefore, it is important that I apply The King's lesson while you can still experience the reality."

"Get on with it then," Mac shrugged in disgust.

"Get on with it we will," Seraph nodded. "What you have just seen is Zadock's homeland."

"No way!" Mac protested. "Wonderland was a beautiful place, not like this toxic waste dump you call the Anti-Kingdom." He slammed his fist into the sand for emphasis.

"Just how much of 'Wonderland' did you see?" Seraph asked.

"Oh, the palace or hotel—whatever it was—the grounds around it, the chapel."

"Exactly. Not more than a few acres of the place—and all part of a movie-like set Zadock put in place to seduce you into his make-believe world. All of that was done by manipulating your minds. About the only truthful thing he told you while you were there was that it was all an illusion of his making. Illusion it was!

"My friends, the vicious world beyond that haze over there is Zadock's reality, his homeland, his turf. He is a high-ranking demon commander, the Serpent General, of the Anti-Kingdom."

"Uh-oh. And I suppose you're about to tell us Zadock works for the guy with the red longjohns and the pitchfork."

"He doesn't wear longjohns or carry a pitchfork, Mac. But you've identified Zadock's boss all right— Lucifer himself."

Won's eyes widened. "You can't be serious! You don't believe in a devil!"

Karae stayed silent, taking it all in.

"I'm afraid I couldn't be more serious." Seraph's lowered eyebrows and intense blue eyes revealed that he was serious indeed.

"To deny a devil—a personal devil—and his horde of demonic cohorts not only denies the hard evidence of the centuries, but it also pays no compliment to humanity. It simply would mean that human beings have created all the heinous evil of history with no outside help. If you are a true humanist, I would hope you would give the human race more benefit than that."

"Yeah, I know. *The devil made me do it!*" Mac's lip curled in a sneer.

"If you believe there's no Prince of Darkness to influence mankind, you have to abandon completely all the humanist palaver about the 'goodness of man.' Man is either good and influenced to do evil or he is inherently evil and needs no outside help. He certainly couldn't be *good* and come up with all the awful atrocities which have marked his behavior since time began *with no outside influence*. Take your choice."

A new, sudden wave of acrid odors forced them to hold their noses for a few moments until the overpowering stench subsided. Won coughed and gasped for a breath of air. "If the Anti-Kingdom is Zadock's home, how did he get there? You really didn't answer that question before."

"He, his boss, and all the other characters like him have been incarcerated there for many years now. They're serving a thousand-year sentence."[61]

"But that's crazy—Zadock wasn't incarcerated," Mac argued. "He was free as a bird, a ruler in Wonderland."

"Only on temporary leave from the Anti-Kingdom, Mac. By special permission of The King. He was allowed to leave this planet—even step into the Kingdom—to approach you three, to try to seduce you, to cast his spells on you. It appears that he did a pretty good job with his assignment. Now he's back there on the shores of the Lake of Fire where he deserves to be."[62]

"But that's so cruel, Seraph." Karae said. "Surely no one could deserve to live in that Hell-hole, no one. Not even Zadock could be evil enough to deserve that."

"Not even if he chose to live there?" Seraph asked.

"You can't tell me anybody in the universe would choose to live in a place like that!" Karae stood to her feet in a burst of indignant energy, folded her arms, and turned toward the torture-filled chasm which lay before them. As if punctuating her point, the screams and tumult of the abyss rose in volume and then subsided again.

Seraph dropped his head in sadness. "I wish what you say were true, Karae. But, unfortunately, it isn't. Millions upon millions over the ages of man have chosen to live there.[63] You saw a sampling of those miserable masses with your own eyes."

"I agree with Karae," Won put his hand on her shoulder. "Under no circumstances can I believe that anyone would choose to go there." He glanced at the hazy image of the gruesome sights in the gorge. "I, for one, never would."

"I surely hope you would not, Won. Before this experiment is over, you will have a chance to prove the truth or falsehood of that declaration."

"What I want to know is, how did the place get so horrible?" Mac put one hand on his hip and gestured with the other. "It surely didn't start out that way, did it?"

"In the answer to that question, Mac, lies the lesson of this phase of The King's experiment. I will tell you all exactly how it got that way. Remember the unspoiled, Edenic beauty and tranquility which you experienced at the start of your adventure in the Kingdom?"

The three nodded. Karae's mind turned to visions of the tall forest jungles with their lush beauty, crystal-clear streams, verdant orchards, and blazing flora. She remembered fondly hugging and playing with the gigantic, lovable tiger Won had named Garfield.

"The Anti-Kingdom started out just like that," Seraph said.

"Impossible!"

"I speak the truth, Mac. In fact, the Kingdom earth was renovated after the model of what the Anti-Kingdom was in the days when it was not the Anti-Kingdom, in the days before the Wrong Choice."

"What's that?" Won assumed his researcher stance, one foot forward, hand stroking his chin. "The Wrong Choice?"

"In order to give the residents of Planet Earth an opportunity to demonstrate their love and appreciation for the idyllic wonderland they had been given, The King gave the inhabitants a free choice. It was a kind of referendum in which His creatures could affirm their gratitude for His creative genius, benevolent provision and loving friendship. However, in a stunning upset, the earthlings rejected The King's rule, showed contempt for His great gifts, and dashed the loving relationship to pieces—the Wrong Choice."

The trio hung on every word.

"As if the Wrong Choice were not a sufficient offense against The King, the earthlings then refused to admit the error of their stupid decision. They arrogantly distorted the facts about the Wrong Choice to make it appear to their progeny as a Right Choice. They made up elaborate and absurd rationalizations to defend their folly—nonsense like "the universe occurred by chance without The King's creative hand," or "man is King," or "nature is King," or "absolute guidelines for life do not exist." Seraph swept his arms out in a broad gesture. "For the millennia which followed, The King pursued extravagant methods of convincing His erring creatures to return to His rule, to His gracious provision, to His loving fellowship. He tried strict discipline—once destroying all but one family of the race in a global inundation with water—but after a short time they rebelled again and returned to their old ways. He tried reaching them through righteous patriarchs whom they ignored, through an elaborate system of guidelines which they systematically violated, through awesome demonstrations of power which they promptly explained away or forgot, and through a series of supernaturally endowed prophets whom they ridiculed and murdered. Finally, in a determined attempt to win them back, The King came to earth personally to live with them and to show His love for them."

Seraph dropped his head in anticipation of the next part of his story.

"So what happened?" Won patted his pockets, feeling for his note pad and pencil. This answer might be worth recording.

"Incredibly, some of the earthlings couldn't stand The King." Seraph stared at the ground and shook his head. "His pure words, His perfect love and quality of life, and His challenge to the existing social structures were more than they could handle. So they ran Him through a mockery of due process—even His judge declared he couldn't find any fault in Him—and they murdered Him. Murdered The King!"

Seraph's voice broke, his shoulders sagged. His heart had broken again as he related the story.

Karae looked at Won and Mac in stunned disbelief, then leaned toward their guide, straining to hear his words over the continuing clamor of the distant Anti-Kingdom.

Mac broke the silence. "Gang, we've just been conned. The Littlest Angel here just fed us the classic fundamentalist Christian propaganda line, only in different words." He fixed Seraph with a look of self-praise. "Caught you in the act, didn't I?" Won clamped his hand over Mac's mouth, annoyed with his arrogance, but Mac quickly pulled Won's hand away and thrust his chin at Seraph in defiance. "Well?"

Seraph studied Mac with empathy.

"Caught me in the act of exposing *your* Wrong Choice, Mac. That's exactly the kind of disbelief and contempt for The King which resulted in the Anti-Kingdom."

"That's ridiculous!" Mac maneuvered to square off with Seraph, fists on his hips. "That freak show over there isn't the result of people like me!"

"I'm sorry, Mac, but you're wrong again. The people of the Anti-Kingdom are all like Arthur McNeal . . . spiritually."

"What gives you the right . . . " Mac strutted around the small circle, flushed with anger, searching in vain for words to express his contempt. How dare this guy judge *him!*

"It's only a matter of degrees, Mac." The angel's eyes penetrated Mac's defenses. "Your little mix of 'lust with love' is just a lesser degree of the loathsome debauchery you saw over there. Your wild unruliness is the root of the anarchist violence on the other side of that veil. Your rationalized lack of self-discipline is the embryo from which all that Anti-Kingdom disorder and chaos grows. Your biting sarcasm and cruel put-downs are incipient verbal forms of the vicious sadism which rules that underworld. And your thinly disguised contempt for religious—especially Christian—answers is the prevailing ethos of Hades. Mac, the truth is that *self-made men like you inevitably reveal the full depravity of their creators.*"

Mac raged now, paced among the three, pounded

his right fist into his left palm and muttered expletives. He pivoted toward Seraph and barked, "I don't have to take this garbage!"

Seraph paused, looked down at the ground, then peered out through the mist at the nether world before them. He was silent for a few moments, then turned slowly toward Mac. "You're right, Mac," he said softly, tenderly. "You don't have to accept what I am saying, but not to accept it *is* the Wrong Choice. It is choosing to live first with a little bit of Hell . . . and ultimately with all of it."

He raised his arm and pointed across the gulf to the abhorrent scene through the distant haze. "It is the same Wrong Choice all of those tormented people made at some point in their spiritual journeys. For some, the decision came easier than for others. Their election was to make no choice—and for them, that, too, became the Wrong Choice. Not to choose *for* The King brings the same consequence as choosing *against* Him."

Seraph rested his case. Mac had no response to this blow to his worldview. Won and Karae sat motionless, each buried deep in thought.

Karae wept quietly, a collage of dramatic, emotional images flowing through her mind. Mrs. Washington lovingly telling her Jesus stories at First Presbyterian. Scenes of impurity from her past thought life. The hunger for love which had nearly made her another teenage pregnancy statistic. The arrogant, Ayn-Rand self-sufficiency which had driven much of her adult life. The upside-down priorities which had made money and possessions her personal god. The glory of the tall forest jungle and the warm embrace of her own personal pet tiger. The gullibility which had nearly cost her her soul in Zadock's ersatz "Wonderland." The tearing realization, at the scene of her mother's "funeral," of what her relationship with her mother meant to her. And the abominable sights, sounds and smells of the Anti-Kingdom still within range of her senses. She struggled to make sense of it all.

Beside her, Won carried on a running debate in his mind over Seraph's arguments—statements of philosophy and fact which ran cross-grain to all Won had been taught at the university, all he had internalized as his own belief system. He felt unsettled, disturbed, frightened. Was it possible that his philosophy of life and knowledge comprised a house of cards which could come tumbling down on him in an instant with one slight breath from a higher power? Amid the faint, sensate reminders of the Anti-Kingdom, Won battled against Seraph's revelation.

Mac continued to pace angrily. Words which were not in his vocabulary—probably because they were not in his dad's—now invaded his mind. *"I've been wrong."* Could it be? *"I've been wrong."* He fought to push the thought out of his mind. To admit he was wrong would require a radical new approach to life for him. It would bring an unwelcome revolution in this thoughts, motivations, business dealings, sales techniques, drinking habits, relationships, priorities—even his love life. Would Wanda have to go? He missed Wanda—he thought. But what if Wanda, like Miss Sensuality, were one more barb on the hook that would pull him into the Anti-Kingdom, drag him to Hell?

Slowly, Seraph studied the deep contemplation going on in the three as he walked away from them to pray. He prayed to The King about this painful mission, sought His counsel as to how to carry out the next and most crucial phase of it, and asked for The King's assistance and strength. He prayed for these three—aliens from another time and place—for the capture of their souls and allegiances for The King and His Kingdom.

Seraph pictured in his spirit the document from the

gold-foil diplomatic pouch which bore the words of The King to Governor Ben-David:

> ... I recommend an extravagant effort to convince the three of the glories of the Kingdom and of life with The King. You have My permission to use any resources you need to achieve this objective, including granting them entrance to the global worship in Zion or discharging them—within My limits—to the agents of the Kingdom of Darkness ...

He reflected on the mission. So far, he had discharged it faithfully. If only he knew the state of its success ... something only The King could know at this stage.

"Oh King," he prayed, "don't let Zadock get to them again. I can't stand to watch his vile attacks on those I have come to love ... "

Hours passed. Into the night each of the four continued in self-imposed solitary contemplation. As time passed, each wrestled at different levels of their beings with the events, messages, impressions and feelings of the past four days. They had no idea what the fifth day would bring.

14

Highway to Holiness

The long night in the desert on the forsaken planet was like Hell itself for Karae, Won and Mac. Never able to close out the nearby reminders of the Anti-Kingdom's reality, they wrestled within their minds, within their spirits.

As they had been promised, they were sustained by the supernatural—they did not tire, did not hunger, did not sleep. Any of these states would have been welcome relief from the continual wrangling within them over issues bigger than life itself. As the dimness of the planet turned to pitch, and then to dimness again, they grappled with the Wrong Choice/No Choice counsel of their angelic tutor.

"Mac! Karae! Won!" Seraph Lightning broke into their deep concentration.

They roused, as if sobering from strong drink, and gathered themselves and their wits into the small circle from which they had spun off many hours before.

There was no greeting or introduction to the new day. Seraph simply announced in a businesslike manner, "It is six A.M. There are twelve hours remaining of your test, twelve hours before you must give your decision to Governor Ben-David."

Each member of the trio surveyed the other two closely, looking for some clue to their state of mind and heart. If any member of the delegation had come to a decision about allegiance to The King and His Kingdom, he was hiding it nicely. Seraph likewise reviewed the countenances, even attempted to read their spirits to divine their intent. No success at either level.

"It is time to depart." Seraph summoned them with his hands.

At once the four became light and lifted off the desolate surface of Hades. Banking over the great gulf and through the putrid mist on their way back to earth, the quartet's senses were scored once again by the scenes, signs, sounds, screams, smells, scabs, scum, and slime of the satanic scourge. Gasping and groaning as they passed through the murky haze, the squadron broke away from both the gravitational pull and the spiritual bondage of the Anti-Kingdom.

"What a relief to be out of that place!" Karae said to Won beside her. She felt as if great iron chains had fallen off her spirit.

Once again the stellar features, milky ways and galactic glories disappeared beside and behind them at mind-blurring speeds. In moments the silent darkness of the universe was broken by a glimpse of the crown jewel of all planets—the object of The King's affection, the Kingdom Earth.

It was far more dazzling than the photos they had seen from the manned space flights during the 1970s and '80s. Oceans sparkled like prisms with the kaleidoscope stuff of the River of Life. Great tributaries shimmered like quicksilver as they cascaded down to the seas. Karae could see the emerald isles which paraded along the shorelines of the great continents. The parched brown deserts were no more. The vegetation was a richer green, and the deep blue seas, lakes and lagoons more plentiful than ever before. Lofty mountain peaks glistened with the gold and silver ore which had replaced the granitic slabs and igneous residue of the previous earth's ranges.

As they soared, Seraph apparently noticed the sense of awe with which Karae was viewing Planet Earth.

"This is the renovated Kingdom Earth," he explained to the three. "This is not the earth you have choked with fluorocarbons, polluted with waste from massive machines, and sterilized by the fallout from nuclear wars. This is the Kingdom Earth, not the one raped by the greed of mammon worshippers, littered with the instruments of destruction and stained with the blood of its fallen. This is Eden, recreated as a gift from The King to those of past millennia who have made the Right Choice—those who have become His bride, His lover, His family."

The now-familiar topography of The King's homeland came into view. Once again they could see the great shining sea on the west receiving the crystalline liquid flowing into it from its source in Zion. The Sea of Life received the healing waters of the River of Life which wound its way east and south into it.

The countenances of the homecomers brightened as they approached the Kingdom Earth and Zion. They touched down just outside the north gate of the city, the Judah Gate, near the place where they had made their infamous escape attempt a few days before.

"Welcome home, fellow travelers." Seraph Lightning swung his arm wide, like a tour guide, displaying the panorama of one of the wonders of the world.

"Welcome, indeed!" Karae released a deep breath. "What a relief to be away from Hades."

"Agreed." Won drank in the now-familiar sights.

"Ditto," Mac nodded.

Karae felt more like she had "come home" than she had felt since leaving Pasadena. The astronomical beauty of the Holy Highway lay before them, a feast for the eyes. As she gazed up the golden boulevard with its blossoming trees and central aqueduct for the River of Life, she was dazzled once again by the grandeur of the City of The King. She sensed once again the tranquility of the land. The joyful families, the radiant countenances, the gracious interactions, and the luxurious surroundings all declared that something was very *right* about everything. And Jireh . . . she wondered about him, longed to see him, checked herself to see how she looked after the ordeal she had been through.

Could it really be, Mac wondered, *that this radically different environment is the result of a whole population's having made the Right Choice?*

In a similar vein, Won asked himself, *Is it possible that something spiritual, something beyond the dimensions weighed and quantified by the scientific method, has created this true Wonderland?* It was an attractive thought to him, but one which fought against his rational side.

The contingent ambled northward along the great golden way a half mile or so, greeting residents and other visitors to the city and kitchy-cooing the beautiful babies being carried in the arms of their parents. As they strolled, they chatted amiably.

"Hey, gang," Mac shouted, "I just saw His Majesty's Department of Repatriation! Let's make a break for it!" He pretended as if he were taking off to the south and waved for them to come along.

"Not me, glorious leader," Karae called back with a laugh. "The last time I followed you I lost my mother and almost lost my heart and soul."

The others burst out laughing. Even Seraph enjoyed the joke. He, like the governor, had come to love Mac. Somehow, despite Mac's crude, untamed nature, he was attractively authentic. With Mac there were no hidden agendas, no pretense. What you saw was what you got! If you didn't like it, that was your problem.

Won wasn't that way. Beneath his more closed Asian manner you never quite knew what was going on. It wasn't that he engendered distrust. He was just one of those people with whom you wouldn't want to play card games—always thinking, always calculating, always unreadable. One who will beat you every time.

After having walked about a mile and a half up the highway, the quartet stopped at one of the many fountains along the aqueduct. Creative design had deployed the natural forces of the rushing water to power artful wheels which were stacked on a tall, central axis. Water splashed out of a fount about twenty-five feet in the air into beautiful silver bushel-basket-sized containers at the end of spokes on revolving wheels. Gravity drove the wheels around, and trip arms tipped the containers into similar receptacles on the next, slightly larger wheels below them. The overall effect was of a magnificent revolving cone of sparkling, dancing, splashing water. Two hundred tiny waterfalls revolved as they spilled their contents ultimately into a large basin which drained back into the aqueduct for the next leg of the journey from the Temple toward Zion.

The group, naturally intrigued by the wonderful water machine, perched on one of the stone benches around its base and studied it.

"Isn't it beautiful?" exclaimed an awestruck Karae. "I could never imagine anything like it. I wish I could take it back to Pasadena."

"I wonder how they calculated the ratio of weight to volume to velocity to get the mechanism to work?" Won marveled aloud, not caring whether anyone heard the question. "The Kingdom must have some good engineers."

Seraph appreciated Won's curiosity. "Won, until the Kingdom the world had never really seen craftsmen, artists, engineers, scientists, designers, or builders. In their previous earth lives even those with innate talent were bound by restrictive internal and external problems; debilitating physical, psychological and emotional handicaps; enslaving personal habits and attitudes; interpersonal conflict and contention; and severe limitations on resources. They could achieve only a fraction of a percent of their capabilities. In the Kingdom— with all of these restraints gone and the incredible extension of life—there is an infinitely greater level of achievement."

"Makes sense." Won nodded, confirming mentally the list of limitations.

"This fountain is only a tiny example of what is possible where The King rules," Seraph Lightning exulted.

Mac had on his sideways smile. "I guess that makes this fountain a royal flush!"

Karae and Won groaned in unison.

Seraph looked mildly displeased at Mac's taking the group from the sublime to the ridiculous with his one-liner. He shifted into an all-business mode. "Well, friends, it's mid-morning and you still have more to experience. Let's pick up the pace."

"Where are we going? What's the experience? What do we have to do?"

"Just stay with me, Mac. You'll find out soon."

"They don't tell you anything around here," Mac said. "I hate when that happens."

"The truth is, you hate to trust, Mac." Seraph didn't miss a chance to make a point. "One of the things everybody had to do to get to the Kingdom, and has to do to live happily here, is trust."

"Yeah, well, I don't have to like it. You don't like it either, do you, Won?"

"Don't drag me into your battles, Mac."

"I'll tell you this much," Seraph addressed Mac. "We are going to the Temple, and we will be met there by Governor Ben-David. He's going to accompany us on this last phase of the test."

Karae looked pleased.

"We've only about a half mile to go, but we need to meet him soon."

The group strode with more deliberation until Karae stopped suddenly. "Incredible! How incredible!"

The whole troop stopped and looked in the direction of Karae's gaze. The highway had been climbing very gradually in elevation for the entire distance, but the marvelous trees which lined the boulevard had obscured the terminal point of the highway. Now the highway had peaked as it reached a small plateau. Fully visible on a hill straight ahead of them was the Temple, the glorious gem, the setting for which the Holy City was the mounting.

"Breathtaking!" Won stood motionless, transfixed by the scene.

Karae surveyed the grandeur of the Temple's walls of deep, purple marble. Rising high above the outer walls and partly obscured by them was the sanctuary—a pure, white, alabaster cube with a wide band of gold overlay running like a border around the top. Red precious stones studded the gold in patterns designed to reflect the rays of light from the heavens and project them downward. The edifice itself was like a red-white-and-gold coronation throne draped in royal purple.

"I can't believe it." Even Mac was impressed. He stood motionless, blinking. "I have never seen anything more awesome."

As if hypnotized, they stood at attention among

hundreds of other visitors who stood on this natural lookout point to enjoy the ravishing beauty of this, the worship center of the Kingdom Earth.

A joyful commotion could be heard on their right. With no warning, a team of six beautiful white horses—delicately sculpted like show horses but half again as tall—swung into view off the vehicle highway which lay outside the tree-lined pedestrian boulevard. With manes flying and the gold and silver of their trappings glistening, the team drew closer. Behind them was a wonderful open carriage driven by white-uniformed attendants and capable of seating six. The carriage was beautifully hand carved with the shapes of various fruits and vegetables and was inscribed in Hebrew, and in gold leaf, *Jehovah Jireh*. Only one rider sat in the center of the second seat.

Governor Jireh Ben-David!

The magnificent carriage stopped in front of the four travelers and Jireh alighted from the coach. "Greetings and The King's blessings, my dear friends!" He greeted each one cheerily and gave each a warm embrace. They exchanged pleasantries. "I've been looking forward to seeing you again and accompanying you on your last adventure. Please do get into the carriage." He extended his hand to the lady to help her up into the coach.

"Guests of royalty, indeed!" Karae, deeply impressed, examined the lush upholstery and turned toward the governor who had seated her by his side.

"In the Kingdom everybody is royalty," Jireh replied. "I just have more responsibility to serve than do some others."

He ordered the attendants to take the coach to the east gate of the Temple. It began its journey on the winding roads which led through a slight valley and then up the Temple Hill. Hundreds of pilgrims, worshippers from all over the globe, trekked the roads through the forests and orchards to the Temple gates. The governor's carriage sped past them to the stationing area at the foot of the steps by the gate.

"Magnificent!" Mac leapt from the carriage, and when all had disembarked, the attendants drove the team away to await the governor's return. "Absolutely magnificent!"

The governor stopped on the steps and drew his four friends into a small huddle around him. Pilgrims moved patiently around the small group on their way in and out of this main gate to the Temple.

Jireh regarded the angel with gratitude. "Thank you, Seraph Lightning, for your faithful service to our guests. The King has suggested that I accompany our friends on this final leg of their spiritual journey. You may take your leave."

"Will we see him again?" Karae drew near their guide and took his arm.

"Probably not for a long time."

"Then let me give you a parting hug." She threw her arms around Seraph Lightning. "You have been a terrific guide and tutor and friend. Thank you for being so wonderful." She kissed his cheek, having to stretch tiptoe to manage it with the rugged seven-footer.

"You are very kind, Karae, but I was merely doing my duty."

Mac flashed his sideways smile, shook Seraph's hand vigorously, and gave him a half hug with one arm. "No more Buckeye jokes."

"And no more crazy escapes through phony facades into bottomless pits." The angel's smile was infectious.

"Many, many thanks for your care and protection." Won gave Seraph a slight bow and a warm handshake. "We will never forget you."

The four gathered in a huddle with arms entwined. Then, the group hug completed, Seraph's countenance took on an almost pleading look. He had difficulty getting out his parting request.

"One more thing . . . please, each of you. Make the Right Choice." He turned away quickly to keep them from seeing the tears in his eyes, and took the steps two at a time down to the paved road.

Sadness came over the three as The Man—the one with powers like lightning—disappeared among the pilgrims on his way back toward Zion. A momentary hush fell on the group, much like those awkward times in group conversation when the room suddenly goes silent and no one has anything to say.

"He's a wonderful man," Karae whispered to Jireh as she brushed a tear from her eye.

"He's a wonderful *angel*." Jireh's correction was gracious and reinforced an important Kingdom distinction. He turned away toward the Temple, leaving Karae with her thoughts.

There was so much good and wonderful about this place. In some ways she knew she would be a fool not to choose to live here forever. If she could be sure it would be with Mom, that would help. Her mother would surely like Jireh—but who wouldn't? Besides Zadock, that is?

Zadock and Jireh. The Kingdom and the Anti-Kingdom. The apparent death of her mom and the promise of seeing her again. The authentic goodness of Seraph and the sickening emptiness of Wonderland citizens. The Right Choice and the Wrong Choice. Somehow she had to sort this all out.

Her thoughts trailed off as she hastened to Jireh's side.

15

The Great
White Throne

Sometime Beyond the Year 3010

R*everence.*

That word best describes the sense which surrounded the governor and his charges as they entered the
east gate of the Temple area. The entry through the
marble-faced walls was packed with reverent pilgrims.
Temple attendants stood in alcoves on each side of the
entrance hall, giving a joyous greeting, providing information and helping manage the multitude of worshippers who filed quietly though the portico into the vast
outer court.

Light from the heavens bounced off the gold of the
sanctuary border and reflected through its brilliant red
gems, sprinkling the courts and columns with circles of
red and white reflection. Worshipping individuals and
groups knelt to pray in locations throughout the outer
court. The people's appearance reflected their diverse

historical, racial and national origins, yet all had the same joyful spirit, that same clear-eyed radiance. Some sang hymns to The King. Others repeated memorized passages, in unison, from The King's sayings. The peaceful mixture of quiet prayers, joyful hymns and unison readings created an organ-like hum, filling the courts more melodically than the hum created by a swarm of bees in a blossoming tree.

"How do you like it?" Governor Ben-David turned to his friends.

"It defies description." Won's breathless response spoke for them all.

"No, I mean the *spirit* here. You've sensed the spirit in Zadock's so-called Wonderland, you've sensed the spirit of the Anti-Kingdom on Hades, and you've sensed the spirit in the Kingdom's forests, mountains and cities. How does the spirit here compare?" The three looked back and forth at each other, groping for the answer for which Jireh might be searching.

Karae assumed her now-expected role of spokesperson for spiritual insights. "For me, governor, it is a spirit of love and peace . . . and of joy."

"I am glad you sense that, Karae. That is the spirit of The King. When He visited earth, His followers observed that His was a spirit of love, of joy, of peace, and of patience.[64] While His Spirit indwells all the citizens of the Kingdom and, thus, the whole Kingdom realm, I always sense His Spirit here in a much stronger dimension."[65]

Jireh's observations seemed to go over the heads of Won and Mac. Still, they were so affected by what they might have called the "ambiance" of the Temple that they were restrained, respectful—even reverent.

The group hastened toward a second entrance which would carry them even deeper into the heart of the Temple compound. Up a few steps was a second gateway. Before entering, Jireh turned to them. "Please remember that you are being afforded privileges never before extended to those who are not citizens of the Kingdom. No one who is not a subject of the monarchy could have come as far as you have come already. You are being granted further access only by direct permission of The King." His manner was deadly serious, as if some harm might come to him if his guests did not fully comprehend the significance of their privilege, or if they in some way profaned it.

Karae looked at Mac as if to say, *I hope you understood that*.

They entered the inner court. Before them stood a great pyramidal altar nearly twenty feet high, made of gleaming, polished black marble. The top rim was covered on the outside with gold overlay. On each of the four corners a large horn protruded upward and inward. Karae watched the priests who wore intricately designed, ornately tailored robes as they said their prayers and ministered to those granted entrance to this inner court. The aura was hushed. Those in the inner court whispered or did not speak at all.

Directly behind the gleaming onyx altar Karae could see the sanctuary. This glorious white edifice rose like an alabaster tower what seemed like 150 feet into the air. It had massive cylindrical pillars on each side of the entrance door made of the same polished black marble as the altar. Ornate carvings in the stone had been decorated with hammered metals. Spectacular cedar doors displayed their deep grain through the carvings of a great vine which twisted and curled its way from the threshold to the keystone over the arched doorway.

A powerful Presence fell across the foursome as they stood outside the towering doors. Karae could hear a shrill, quiet tone coming from somewhere atop the sanctuary tower. The sound rose in volume but not in pitch until it became an ear-splitting trumpet blast. Then the sound ended abruptly and the colossal doors slowly opened.

The sweet fragrance of incense wafted out of the sanctuary, and the four stepped quietly inside. Across the threshold, they were simultaneously driven to their knees by some unseen force from within them, some inner messenger which seemed to order them, *Bow! You are in the presence of THE KING!*

The doors closed behind them. Karae wanted to sigh in ecstatic relief, but she couldn't manage even the slightest motion or sound. The simple beauty of the sanctuary shone faintly in the light which came in through narrow vertical slits in the side walls. About two thirds of the way toward the far end she could see a curtain which extended from the floor to an arch about seventy-five feet in the air. The veil appeared to have been one piece at one time to prevent entrance to the most distant third of the sanctuary. Now it was divided, opened wide with ragged inner edges which looked as if they had been ripped and singed at the same time.[66]

All was silent.

The perfect silence prevailed for some time.

Then it was broken . . . gently.

"Blessings on you, My precious friends," came words spoken by a warm, gentle, affectionate voice—not frightening, not coarse, not affected.

The four raised their heads slowly, eyes searching for the one who was speaking. No one was visible.

"In a few hours now I will ask you to give Me a decision as to whether you choose to give your life, your future, your allegiance, to Me.

"By now I trust the contrast between the two competing kingdoms is quite clear. But I have planned one last experience which I trust will further clarify, further dramatize the choice you are being asked to make. Remember three things: First, no one else can and no one else will make this choice for you.

Second, you will live with the consequences of your choice forever. It is irrevocable. And third, I truly love you and want the very best for you. I genuinely desire that you place your trust in Me and join My Kingdom."

Silence again. Not a sound.

One minute.

Two minutes.

Finally, the kneeling mortals stirred. As they did, the great doors behind them slowly opened. They rose, turned, and faced outward.

Karae let out a gasp as she was struck by the view outside the Temple doors. Won, Mac and Jireh also uttered ecstatic sighs. The view was more than one could contain.

Framed by the sanctuary doorway was the golden-horned altar. Behind the altar were the purple columns and blocks of the inner and outer walls of the Temple. Above and beyond that—stretching off into the distance in a perfectly straight line—was the tree-lined golden highway with the life-giving stream flowing down its center. Nearer the top of the archway's framing were the walls of distant Zion and, above the city, beams of light coming from the heavens . . . forming a luminescent cross above Zion's Hill.

The four, still gasping for breath at the sight, stood transfixed, unmoving, for a number of minutes. Finally they regained their composure and stepped through the vast portal. As they did, the doors closed behind them without a squeak or a sound.

On the top landing at the entrance to the sanctuary, each looked at the other in dazed unbelief at the Presence they had felt. The three looked inquisitively at Jireh Ben-David. Mac verbalized the question they all had in mind.

"Governor, was this the beginning of the final experience?"

"The very beginning, my friends. Any moment now we will embark on the final leg of our journey. It will be a journey still farther forward in time than you are now, past the year 3010. I will take you to a place I am not permitted to reveal."

"But when . . . " Mac couldn't form the remaining words. Jireh raised a hand to still him. He hesitated for a moment, looked to the heavens and back at the trio. He waited, perfectly still, as if listening for a voice, a command.

"NOW!" he shouted at the top of his lungs.

A powerful updraft, like a tornado's funnel, sucked the four heavenward past the horns of the great altar, over the top of the sanctuary's colossal tower and into the crystal clear atmosphere of the Kingdom. The troupe soared one more time through the moisture canopy which perfectly balanced the moisture of the Kingdom Earth. Below them, in the distance, Karae could see great masses of people—people covering hundreds of square miles—focused on a central point, a radiant something.

There must have been billions. As she drew closer, she could see that the great hordes were gathered on an enormous grassy plain. At the center of the multitude was one enormous mass which divided itself into two branches as it moved toward the central light. One of the two branches of people was great and wide and became compressed into a wide funnel, then disappeared over the horizon. The other branch of people dwindled to a very small, very narrow line which headed off in a different direction, its people dispersing, then disappearing.[67]

As the governor's Kingdom guests drew closer to the central brilliance, Karae saw an incredible sight. In the center of the brightness was an enormous, twenty-foot-high, pure-white throne—upon which sat The King, whose face and form were barely distinguishable in the blinding glare emanating from Him.[68] The throne sat atop a broad pyramidal platform which was probably one hundred feet square at its base and stair-stepped up to the top platform. The stairs of the platform were covered with blood-red cloth from bottom to top.

As they hovered above the sight, Karae drew close to Governor Ben-David and instinctively grabbed his hand and held on tight. He didn't pull away. Mac and Won also crowded close to the others.

Surrounding the throne was a rainbow-like aura which radiated its multi-colored rays of light outward to reveal twenty-four other official seats of authority on platforms behind it. Four indescribable creatures—unlike anything earth possessed—grouped themselves around the great throne's base. The creatures observed everything, and quietly and continually voiced praises to The King.[69]

On the left of The King was a mountain of books covering many hundreds of acres, attended by thousands of white-robed assistants who were close enough to communicate with The King. A large banner written in Hebrew hung over this group of attendants.

"What does that banner say, Jireh?" Karae wanted desperately to know the meaning of the words, but felt apprehensive asking. She was learning that this world was full of wonderful surprises—and horrible shocks. You never knew which you were going to get.

"It declares, *The Books of Deeds*. In those books are listed deeds, thoughts, motives, and words of every human being who has ever lived—especially those who fall short of the perfect standard of righteousness of The King."[70]

The thought of such a record was sobering. Mac rambled through irrelevant *what-about-the-right-to-*

privacy? thoughts before realizing that "right to privacy" was not something which bound God or could be claimed by His created offspring.

On the right of The King was a great table on which just one enormous book rested, attended by white-robed individuals. Over that book and the attending servants was another banner.

"And what is written above the other side, governor?" Won was driven more by his need to know than by his desire to know.

"That banner reads, *The Book of Life.* It is a record of the Right Choice of every man, woman, and child who has made it."[71]

Won reviewed in his mind the Right-Choice tutoring of Seraph Lightning, then turned his attention back to the scene before him.

There was an aura of deathly calm over the billions. No conversation, no loud sound of any kind. It was like the viewing line at a wake, the silence interrupted only by periodic sobs or wails, and occasionally by shouts of joy.

The mysteries of the scene grew greater for the three with each passing moment. They touched down to the ground, and Governor Ben-David drew his friends into a position near the front of the biggest, widest line. Karae could hear a crier asking the name of each person in line. While not close enough to hear the conversations between The King and the individuals, it was clear to her that there was some kind of "sorting" going on. After the lead attendant on the Book-of-Life side heard each name, he would confer with his attendants for a few moments and then cry out, "No name!" Further interaction would then take place between that person and The King.

Karae strained to hear the conversations. She couldn't. But she observed that after The King heard the "No name!" response from the Book-of-Life attendants,

He would summon attendants from the Books-of-Deeds side. These would begin reading entries from the books which had been fetched rapidly from the great field of volumes. In most cases not much reading occurred before the individual would burst into tears, wailing, or angry argument. At this point The King would quietly gesture with His hand toward the left, and the individual would move around the throne and disappear over the horizon.

Karae looked at her watch. It read 5:11 P.M. and the reading startled her. "Governor, it's eleven past five! Aren't we to render our decision to you by six o'clock?"

Mac and Won both checked their watches and, equally startled, watched the governor intently. Jireh never turned from viewing the scene. In a firm and deliberate manner he said, "Everything is on schedule." The statement seemed to terminate further questions.

The three exchanged anxious glances. Karae fought off a rush of questions in her mind: Was he not going to keep his promise? How could he hear each of their decisions in less than fifty minutes, even if he started now? What was his purpose in bringing them to witness this strange scene? She felt her heart pound faster as anxiety gripped her.

The troubled visitors pulled a distance from each other. Karae dropped Jireh's hand and folded her arms, turbulence raging inside her. Still, Jireh gazed silently at the interaction taking place between The King and the individuals at the front of the line. The others, still distracted, nonetheless redirected their attention on that interaction as well.

An attendant asked for the next name. This time the attendant on the Book-of-Life side shouted, "It is written!" At that word thousands of men, women and children—apparently out of sight over the horizon—burst into cheers and applause. The King gave a warm smile to the individual at the front of the line and motioned to the right. The released individual shouted The King's praises, wept for joy. He ran, jumping and skipping, out of sight across the horizon, the cheers and applause continuing until he was long out of view.

Karae's wristwatch read 5:20.

Beside her, Mac was feeling very uncomfortable. The pressure of time until 6 o'clock, this mysterious scene with no explanations, Jireh's stony silence, the culture shock of the Kingdom world, and the rush of questions in his mind all boiled over in one catalytic action inside him. The result was an explosion:

"Look, gov, I can't take it anymore! You promised us that in less than forty minutes we'd be through with this whole weird trip. You aren't even talking to us! You've got us out here on this overgrown football field with all the huddled masses lined up for free chest X-rays. For all I know you are a Zadock in sheep's clothing, a bigger cheat and liar than he is. I demand that you get us out of this mob scene! Do you hear me?"

Mac was red-faced, the veins on his neck bulging as he clenched his fists.

Jireh turned slowly, then looked each of them in the eye. Finally he set his gaze on Mac. "I hear you, Mac—and Karae and Won." He had read all their spirits and knew the volcanic eruption that was building inside each of them. He could have guessed that Mac would be the first to blow. "Please give your attention to this scene just fifteen more minutes, and I will wrap up our business, take your decisions, and send you on your way."

5:24 P.M.

Begrudgingly, the three returned their attention to the events happening around them. As they did, Jireh said something under his breath, and instantly the three found themselves next to the front person in line—a middle-aged white woman of apparently high social standing. Here they could hear every word of conversation. Karae leaned closer to Jireh and to the lady.

"Name please!"

"Lady Virginia Ward-Major." She was of retirement age, attractive, fair-skinned, handsomely attired, poised. There was a pause before the attendant under the *Book-of-Life* banner shouted, "No name!"

"Your name is not found in the Book of Life, Mrs. Major." The King was firm but kindly. "On what basis should you be admitted to the Kingdom?"

"I have been a good woman."

"The standard is perfection, Mrs. Major."

"Well, nobody's perfect!" She managed a weak smile.

"Yes, Somebody is."

"Well, I have tried to practice the Golden Rule."

"Are you willing to be evaluated on that principle?"

"Well . . . yes."

Mac was showing visible signs of anger. He fidgeted and rocked from foot to foot as he listened. Won was stoic but rapidly losing color in his face. Karae was intent on the scene as The King turned to the Books-of-Deeds side.

"Attendants! The deeds of Lady Ward-Major, please." An underling handed the lead attendant documents marked, *Virginia Beth Ward-Major, 1881 to 1945.*

The attendant read aloud, "In 1925 Mrs. Ward-Major began a secret, adulterous relationship with George Waterbury, a male friend she met while her husband was on a business trip. Over the next seven years . . . "

Lady Ward-Major paled. Apparently, no one had ever discovered the relationship.

"Does that fit your definition of the Golden Rule concerning your husband?" The King asked her. "Do you want the attendant to continue?"

Lady Ward-Major hung her head and uttered faintly, "No."

"Lady Ward-Major." The King leaned forward on His throne and gazed even more intently at the woman. "Why did you silence your maid when she tried to talk to you about Me?"

"I—never felt I needed religion."

"You never chose to seek Me, to trust Me, to follow Me, did you?" The King spoke very tenderly, as if each statement caused Him pain.

"But I never chose *not* to!"

"Lady Ward-Major, you knew of My love and forgiveness. You knew of My sacrifice for you so that you could enjoy eternal fellowship with Me. Yet you made the decision of No Choice. You may go to the home you have chosen." He waved His hand to the left. She broke out in quiet sobs as the attendants ushered her around the side of the throne.

"Where is she going, governor?" asked Won.

"She is going home."

The lady was just about to the horizon, soon to pass from view. Won looked at Mac with terror on his countenance.

Mac asked, "May we see her home?"

"Yes. Only for a moment," replied the governor.

In an instant the four ascended above the earth, just high enough to see Lady Ward-Major take one step beyond the horizon.

"Oh, no, not *that!*" cried Karae. She turned away and hid her face in Jireh's coat sleeve.

Lady Ward-Major stepped onto the very edge of a pitch-black pit which extended downward for what seemed like miles. At the brink of the pit was a hideous form, laughing repulsively—a creature with fiery eyes, gnarled flesh, rotting fangs. Lady Ward-Major tried desperately to steady herself as she felt herself being drawn in the direction of the gaping void. In a flash a powerful maelstrom, like the eye of a tornado, sucked her over the brink and into the swirling orifice. At the far end of the pit was the writhing agony and litter-strewn landscape of the planet Hades. A fiery sea flowed like molten lava over the helpless inhabitants but didn't destroy them or relieve them of their misery.

Mac grimaced. Won looked away in pain.

The three were returned to their earth-level view.

5:33 P.M.

Mac was dumbstruck. Won, paralyzed. Karae felt shredded by internal confusion. Was this what Jireh and The King meant by "going home"? Was this what the three travelers had been anticipating for the past five days?

"Name please," rang out the crier's voice. He motioned to the next person in line.

"Jose Pasquale Fernandez," came the answer from the front person. Jose was unkempt in appearance, poor but clean, with high cheek bones and olive skin. He had the hands of a laborer and the muscular build to confirm a lifetime of hard work.

The King turned to the Book-of-Life side. The attendants flipped through pages.

"Mr. Fernandez," spoke The King.

"*Si, Señor?*" He barely lifted his eyes, as if afraid to look at the radiance from the throne.

"We have met before." The King was intent.

"*Si, Señor.*"

"It was in a cell on death row in the Cuernavaca prison."

"*Si.*" Jose's head dropped in shame. He fidgeted and cleared his throat nervously.

"The murder of five men, if I am not mistaken?"

Humiliated, Jose could barely squeak out another "*Si, Señor.*"

The King paused, thinking, before He said, "On what basis should I grant you entry to The Kingdom?"

Jose fell to his knees with his head bowed, then looked up pleadingly at The King. *"Para Jesu Christo!"* he cried.

The King's eyes twinkled. The Book-of-Life attendant took a note from his assistant, whereupon he turned the pages of the gigantic volume once again. The attendant then stopped, double-checked the name and cried out, "It is written!"

The King smiled broadly and waved His hand to the right.

Jose bolted from his knees and let out a shout of triumph. *"Gloria a Dios! Gloria a Dios!"* he shouted. Dancing and cheering, he skipped toward the horizon. Great cheers and applause rang out from over the edge of the horizon. Music like that of great military bands played.

Once again the three were lifted up to see beyond the brink. As they rose, Karae was struck with the vision of a glorious city of gold on the eastern end of the panorama, a city which appeared to be more than one thousand miles square. Precious stones studded the city's foundations—emerald, topaz, amethyst. Gigantic glistening gates appeared to be made of pure pearl.[72]

It was breathtaking. Karae could see a vast multitude of laughing, cheering people lining both sides of the glassy streets—all there to greet Jose. Angelic creatures hovered above the gleeful spectators. His shouts of *"Gloria a Dios"* were echoed by the cherubim until the praises faded into the music and cheers.

Jose pranced into the open arms of generations of long-unseen loved ones and friends. His back-breaking common labor and poverty were ended. The agonizing years of separation from his murdered son were over; the two embraced. He lifted his son off the golden streets, kissed him repeatedly, and swung him around and around in his muscular arms. Jose's devout mother, who had left him at age twenty with the responsibilities for the other seven children, nearly leapt into his arms. He pressed his head to her breast and wept great tears of joyful ecstasy. The silver-haired prison chaplain, who had shared the Good News of The King through the bars of Jose's prison cell, stuck his arm through Jose's and danced with him down the great boulevard. Their heels clicked and clacked on the polished streets of his new homeland. Jose was a new citizen of THE ETERNAL CITY OF GOD!

5:40 P.M.

16

Now Is the Hour . . .

Mac was seething with rage. Watching what happened to Lady Ward-Major and Jose Fernandez had not been enjoyable, to say the least.

"All right, Ben-David, your cover is blown." Fists on his hips, Mac started out slowly and built in pitch and volume as he progressed. "Now I know *for sure* that this Kingdom is a hypocritical farce. If I have just seen a sample of a 'benevolent monarchy,' of The King's 'justice,' I want no part of it! If that good woman who has tried hard to keep the Golden Rule is sent to Blazes just because she had a little indiscretion with a secret lover, I've seen enough. Furthermore, if a murderer like Jose Whatsit gets a free ride to Heaven, I don't want to live there. I'd rather rot in Cleveland!"

Karae, too, was visibly shaken. "I have to agree with Mac. How could The King sit there and calmly wave that classy woman—or *any* woman or man, for that matter—into that hellish existence we witnessed? What kind of fiend could do that to a human being of *any* kind or character?" She trembled with unbelief and agitation as she spoke.

"And to allow a mass murderer to go free," Won's

face showed pain and his voice was high-pitched from strain, "is hardly my idea of fair play. Since when is murder—a multiple murder at that—a lesser offense than adultery? Besides, the lady's husband never found out about it, so it didn't hurt him."

The three pressed in close to Jireh Ben-David, each speaking closer and closer to his face.

"And what kind of sadist would depict going to the Anti-Kingdom as going home?" Karae was incensed, shaking her finger in Jireh's face as she spoke. "That woman never lived in a slime pit like Hades. What an unspeakable indignity to refer to it as her home—to say nothing of *sending* her there!" She folded her arms and turned away in anger and disgust.

Karae's words cut deep into Jireh. He had never been called a sadist before, and it cut even deeper coming from a woman for whom he had such deep affection.

"You really do not understand, do you?" Jireh replied, a tinge of sorrow in his voice. He knew that their present contempt for The King's values—as they understood them—would cause them to reject the Kingdom if they made their decisions now. He looked at the ground, breathed a silent prayer for wisdom, and faced the three troubled members of his jury.

"Friends, The King speaks to every living person in bold and varied languages. In order to win the human race, He reveals volumes about Himself in nature. He shows His power, His infinite intelligence, His genius planning and control, His mathematical perfection, His complete transcendence above and beyond anything man could ever be or do. Mankind is accountable for these disclosures.[73]

"Furthermore, The King reveals Himself to human beings in conscience. There has never been a person who has not had an inner voice proclaiming the difference between good and evil.[74] While that voice can be silenced by repeated shunning and trampling, it renders every person additionally responsible. It keeps a record of each word, thought and deed which does not conform to what that person knows—in his heart of hearts—is good or evil.

"As a further step, The King takes even the *slightest* human response in His direction as seeking Him, as knocking to have His spiritual Truth opened, as asking for answers to feed the hungry soul.[75] He watches constantly for these indicators of interest in Him and acts on them aggressively to provide more revelation.

"Then, to a significant percentage of the human race He reveals exponentially more of Himself through a faithfully recorded written record—His life, His words, His miracles, His way of salvation through making the Right Choice. Despite all these efforts, some of those to whom The King has given the most comprehensive data are the most hardened against the Right Choice."

Jireh spoke with such confident authority that his words burned deep with conviction. Karae found herself hanging on every syllable with an odd mix of skepticism and teachability. There was something special about Jireh's impact when he spoke—something more than the sum of the parts of his thoughts, words and expressions. She had the inexplicable feeling there was a powerful, unseen authority standing behind him with a bullhorn proclaiming, *This man is telling the truth! Listen to him!*

Jireh continued. "Once an individual begins to reject The King or takes the first tiny step away from Him in denial or rejection of His revelation, He begins confirming that person's ultimate choice of an eternal abode. He knows that a person's spiritual parentage is revealed by these responses or reactions.[76] He knows that those who trust Him are eager to live with Him and with His children. Those who choose against Him, or who make no choice at all, evidence that they desire to live with their spiritual ilk rather than with God. You've heard people say it: 'I'd rather go to Hell; that's where all my friends will be!' Those who choose to express—even moderately—the values of the Anti-Kingdom on earth are demonstrating that Hades is where they desire their ultimate spiritual home to be."

Won tracked Jireh's logic. The more it made sense to him, the more troubling it was. He tried to process every thought and extrapolate the implications with his usual computer-like efficiency, but even Won's mind had trouble weighing the ways of the infinite, eternal God versus the knowledge of finite, temporal man.

"What you have just witnessed," Jireh continued, "was not a case of The King making fresh judgments about these people. He was just confirming millions of minuscule decisions these two had already made—most of them over and over again—prior to their deaths. He was just making certain that these people got to spend eternity with the types of people they chose in life . . . the types of people with whom they shared a genuine spiritual affinity."

"But—a murderer!" Mac sputtered.

"The reason Jose's past crimes were discounted in his ultimate assignment was that he came to the point where he saw the error of his Anti-Kingdom ways. On his knees in a Mexican jail, he genuinely repented of his sin and surrendered his life to The King. For the rest of his short life, Jose validated the authenticity of his surrender by a radical desire to live both with The King and with His other children. It was clear that he would enjoy The King, His values, and His children for eternity. He had already demonstrated that.

"Lady Ward-Major, on the other hand, for all her social standing, couldn't run fast enough to get away from anything The King had to offer. She harbored persistent disdain for the King's followers, whom she labeled 'bloody fundamentalists' and worse."

Gradually, Mac's countenance relaxed from the anger and turbulence he had shown before Jireh's explanation. But could he really buy it? That was the question which agitated his spirit.

"And Won, regarding your comment about Lady Ward-Major's husband never finding out about her infidelity. Since when is the reality of an evil determined by its discovery? Is an embezzler any less a criminal for the years his theft goes undetected? Does a rapist or thief deserve any less punishment for crimes that go unsolved for a long time? You see, Won, Lady Ward-Major's offenses were noticed by the only One who counted, the One in a position to confirm her ultimate destiny. And since she never truly repented of her sinful lifestyle, never embraced The King's offer of love and forgiveness, her final home was her choice, not His."

Won's defenses had crumbled under the weight of Jireh's reasoning. As the blocks of his excuse structure fell, the crushing weight of his own the guilt—of his own adultery—pulverized him.

5:43 P.M.

"Dear friends, I gave my word that I would accept your decisions by 6 P.M. That leaves just about 15 minutes. While I have ventured a short explanation of The King's thinking, I know I cannot answer all your questions in the amount of time left. But may I emphasize that the decision you are being asked to make—while a reasonable decision—is not a *reason-based* one. It is a *will-based* decision. If I presented thousands of volumes of irrefutable evidence to support the claims of The King and to explain the glories of the Kingdom, you could still exercise your wills against the evidence. You do this very thing in smaller decisions every day. No one has ever been reasoned into the Kingdom, argued into a trust relationship with The King, debated into the Right Choice. While the Kingdom perspective is reasonable, arguable, and defensible, citizenship in it is not acquired through these channels. This decision is a matter of the heart, a decision based in the human spirit.

"Therefore, I will make only one last statement before leaving you each alone for the remaining fifteen minutes. It is the final statement made by The King while we were in the Temple sanctuary: *'I truly love you and want the very best for you. I genuinely desire that you place your trust in Me and join My Kingdom.'* "

As Jireh said these words, the echo of The King's voice seemed to ring behind his.

Jireh pulled three pens and three pieces of paper from a pocket. "Please slip away by yourself now. Take this paper and pen with you. When you are ready, put a cross on the paper if you desire to choose the Kingdom. Put a pentagram on the paper if you wish to choose the Anti-Kingdom. Initial the paper, fold it in half, and give it to me. Is that clear?"

Each nodded.

"I trust that the experiences you have had, the things you have seen, and the instruction you have received will guide you to the Right Choice."

5:45 P.M.

W ithout a word the three parted quietly and found spots on the ground away from the others—to think and to decide their fate.

As Jireh watched them, he felt a cold chill surround him. It was the same Arctic blast which had gripped him on his first encounter with Zadock the Third.

Around him, the breezes went still. Kingdom citizens were stirred in their spirits to pray. The Spirit of The King whispered messages to them so they could pray intelligently. The invisible heavenly witnesses gathered. Unseen eyes focused and unseen ears aimed like antennae on the four persons sitting close to the encompassing radiance of the Great White Throne.

The endless "Name please!" of the crier rang out with uncomfortable predictability. The anxious pauses until attendants called out "No name!" or "It is written!" created a morbid tension in the air. The distant billions continued to file one by one past The King for review. Single-file lines still passed on one side or the other of the throne. Screams muffled by the distance came from the plunging persons who had been waved to the left. Faraway cheers and applause rang from the right in welcome of each new Kingdom arrival.

Jireh knelt to pray. As he did, the atmosphere around him darkened. Though a good distance away from the three, he suddenly felt surrounded, pressed as if in a crowded elevator. There was a sound, like the report of a distant artillery piece, and then a thud like a giant boulder hitting the ground near him, then two more.

Jireh looked up from his kneeling position.

It was Zadock. This time, his masquerade was that of a military officer. But this time he was not alone. With him were two other creatures in uniform, each with a strange-looking weapon strapped to his waist. Each had the fiery pupils, the dark circles around the deep-set eyes, the steely gaze, the rugged physiques, the sinister half-smiles. By The King's permission they were on their last free time before beginning their eternal sentence in the Lake of Fire.[77]

"Well, well, well, *governor!*" Zadock bowed and scraped in mock respect for Jireh Ben-David's position. "We meet again! *Jehovah Jireh,* eh?" He laughed cynically. "God will provide! Utter a prayer of thanksgiving, Ben-David. Your God just provided a welcoming party for the three new recruits for the Army of the Prince. I am confident they can be disciplined into valiant warriors by the time of the Great War! After all, I have nine hundred years to whip them into shape—and I do mean *whip* them into shape!"

All three of the demon commanders laughed and jostled each other like football players after a big play . . . but their eyes didn't smile.

Jireh stood to his feet and faced the formidable triad of Dark Side officers. The innocence of his radiant visage contrasted with the three hellions like a gem on black velvet. "Dream on, Zadock! Consider yourself favored if you get one of the three!"

Zadock leaned forward and exhaled his hot breath in Jireh's face. "Oh, but Mr. Ben-David, you forget that we already *have* all three! I couldn't help overhearing your sweet sermonette to the unwilling parishioners. They have 'already taken repeated steps in the direction of the Anti-Kingdom.' You said it yourself—'The King is confirming their already-made decisions!' "

A vile sneer slithered across Zadock's face. He turned and threw a wink to one of his lieutenants, who returned it.

Jireh didn't back away. "No kingdom really owns a soul until physical death. You know that."

Zadock ignored the comment. "But forgive me for interrupting your little prayer meeting." He twisted the massive pentagram ring on his finger. "Fondle a few beads and light a few candles, too. You'll need all the divine reinforcement you can get for this one! But pray fast; you're about out of time!"

5:48 P.M.

Zadock turned away from Jireh and barked orders to his two comrades. "Captain Gormod, take the Asian. Lieutenant Modreb, the Irishman! *I* will handle the lady!"

Jireh felt a sick numbness move through his abdomen. The thought of Zadock "handling the lady" was more than he could stomach. He had seen this slippery lizard work on Karae before. Carefully, the three veteran seducers sneaked around their charges. Now positioned behind Mac, Karae and Won, the evil lords assumed trances, conjuring up Hell for the three decision makers.

Jireh returned to his knees. "Oh King, I pray for the souls of these three. I pray for Your power to overthrow the minions of Lucifer. I pray for the Spirit of Truth to penetrate the hearts of these three subjects. I pray for Karae . . . "

He broke down and wept. Little streams of salt water dripped from his cheeks onto the ground of the great plain. Billions still faced the glorious radiance of The King on the White Throne.

Won's face flushed. Small beads of perspiration formed on his forehead and on the bridge of his nose. He had his notes out and was flipping rapidly through the pages, speed-reading his scribbles from the past five days. He tried to think logically, but logic wasn't working. It didn't require a Ph.D. to discern that this decision had dimensions far beyond the realm of the scientific method.

Across the wide screen of his mind flashed rapid-fire images, like those in a music video. The rush of images first would support the Kingdom decision and then be countered by split-second collages of Anti-Kingdom impressions. There were scenes of purity and love and life and joy from the Kingdom. Then there were sensations of titillation and power and self-exaltation from the Dark Side.

In his visions, Won held Mary and Justin tenderly in his arms—walked the fabulous streets of Jehovah Jireh—splashed in the spectacular water fountain on the

Holy Highway—smelled the hideous stench of Hades. Then he touched the naked form of his Asian seductress—felt the glory of discovering the secrets of the universe—sensed the joy of discovering ways to control reality. He took the pen from his pocket and made a short, straight line on the paper Jireh had given him, then paused.

Mac's face was tense, his color pale. As he sat on the ground thinking about all he'd seen, he envisioned himself with Wanda walking down a church aisle together—gamboling on the lawn of one of the great parks in Zion with their small children—traveling through the galaxies exploring the universe—touring the palace of Jehovah Jireh—camping along crystal streams in the tall forest jungles of the Kingdom. He felt once again the horror of being sucked into the endless mine shaft to the Anti-Kingdom. But then he saw himself in the lap of material bounty—gloried in the autograph seekers and press photographers clamoring to get to him as an international celebrity—felt the wheel of his luxury yacht in his hands as he plied the waters of the Caribbean with a boatload of sensual beauties—watched his Rolls Royce Silver Cloud move up the driveway of his thousand-acre estate and park in front of his two-hundred-room mansion. Mac put the pen to the paper, then hesitated.

Karae hated hard decisions but knew this was one she had to make. She labored over the bombardment of vivid images which pounded her. She saw her now-healed mother witnessing an exchange of companionship vows in a lovely grove by a dancing waterfall just outside of the city limits of Jehovah Jireh—observed herself with her beloved, watching the glorious procession of the nations along the Holy Highway—felt the closeness to God she had felt in the Temple sanctuary—experienced the loving embrace of a handsome, dark-skinned man—recoiled at the sick perversion of the Anti-Kingdom.

Then she felt the gnawing questions of fairness which troubled her at the White Throne—wondered if one could really trust Jireh and The King—questioned whether her mother had really been healed or was dead as her Wonderland vision had indicated—suspected that Jireh's special attention to her might be merely part of a ploy to get her to choose his kingdom even as Zadock's romantic moves had been. Karae began a stroke with her pen on the paper.

The demon masters standing behind Mac and Won and Karae contorted their faces as they read the images being flashed on the minds of their victims. When the images were of The King and supported a decision for the Kingdom, the demon lords grimaced and choked and reached deeper into their occult powers for energy to combat the impact of those scenes. When the images supported a decision for the Kingdom of Darkness, they worked their faces into sinister smiles and projected as much seductive power into the visions as they could muster.

Jireh agonized in prayer for each of his new friends and pleaded with The King to secure the destiny of each for the Kingdom. But as he prayed, the dark atmosphere which had become a trademark of the agents of Lucifer settled around each of the struggling aliens, charging the air with the kind of ensnaring magnetism which had gotten them to the point of willing surrender in Wonderland.

5:55 P.M.

Mac finished drawing his symbol, initialed it, and

folded his paper in half. While it wasn't clear whether Won had drawn more than an initial line or two, his paper, too, was neatly folded in half in the palm of his hand.

Karae agonized more than ever now. She tapped her pen nervously with one hand against the palm of the other, then mopped her brow with her sleeve. Then, suddenly, she seemed to get a burst of insight. She finished drawing the symbol, signed her initials, and folded her paper in half.

5:58 P.M

"It appears that all three of you have made your decision." Jireh stood to receive the responses. "May I please have the papers?" As each person stepped forward to surrender his folded paper to Jireh, the demon chief behind him disappeared to avoid detection. But Jireh knew that, though invisible, the three warlords were still present. The spiritual atmosphere was still lead-heavy.

Jireh's heart stopped as he handled the papers. He breathed a prayer and unfolded the ballots.

He gasped, then dropped his head, heartbroken. And as he did, he heard uproarious laughter cackling from the dark cloud which hovered around him and his guests.

It was 6 P.M.

17

The Divine Seal

Miss Johnson, may I speak to you alone?" Jireh trembled as he spoke.

Won and Mac gave each other a *What's up?* look as Karae stepped toward the governor. Apprehension was written on her face in bold letters.

As she drew near, Jireh pivoted and fell into step beside her, his hand on her shoulder as they walked away from the other two. Won and Mac muttered to each other, annoyed that they would have to wait longer for the disclosure of the decisions.

"Karae," Jireh was hesitant, nervous, as he spoke. "I have not yet checked the initials on the slips of paper. I have just glanced at the symbols, and there *is* one pentagram. In case it is yours, I wanted to say something to you before you walk out of my life forever."

He stopped, faced her, reached out and held her hand in both of his.

"Karae, I love you. I love you as I have never loved anyone in life or in the Kingdom. I never married in my earth life. I am a Moor, and the only woman I ever loved abandoned me when she learned of my call by The King to go to North Africa as a missionary. She returned my

engagement ring and walked out of my life. It was because of my decision to suffer that heartache, remain
unmarried, and spend my life for The King in Morocco
that He rewarded me with the governorship."

Karae's head dropped to her chest—whether in embarrassment or regret was not clear.

"If I never see you again, if I never get to express the
love I have for you, remember one thing. I put that image
of your mother witnessing companionship vows . . . to
me . . . in your mind. I personally picked that spot in a
lovely grove, by a dancing waterfall, just outside the city
limits of Jehovah Jireh.[78]

"But . . . how could that be, if Mother is alive on the
old earth, in the time that I come from?"

"Time does not matter in eternity, Karae. You will
soon learn that. Remember that we have brought you and
Won and Mac forward in time. Your dear mother will join
millions of other believers who are raptured by The King,
prior to a Great Tribulation on earth. After that Tribulation, she and millions of other believers will return with
Him to set up a thousand-year reign on earth—the new
earth, the Kingdom Earth you have experienced in the
year 2084. If you have chosen the Kingdom, you will
indeed be together with her. And, if you consent, she will
witness our exchange of companionship vows."

Jireh smiled affectionately and squeezed her hand
more tightly. "As a love gift to you, I planned a lovely
suite in the palace . . . and a pet eight-foot tiger."

Karae looked up into the eyes of this magnificent,
righteous man. She understood him better now, saw him
in a new light. His look penetrated deep into her—eyes
overflowing with love, purity, strength and character.
She was speechless. Her eyes glistened. She looked away,
then turned from Jireh and walked thoughtfully back
toward Mac and Won.

Jireh followed, dabbing the moisture from his own

eyes with his sleeve. Silence reigned for a few moments until he regained his composure.

"Now the moment of truth, my friends." Jireh was sober. He knew one of his friends was lost. He faced the three and addressed them formally, like a judge reading a verdict. "Before I disclose the decisions you have made, I need to tell you why you were chosen for this experiment. Each of you was chosen because The King knew the fate of your earth life. He knew that each of you would be rendered comatose by injuries to your heads within seven minutes of each other."

The three looked at each other in unbelief. Mac strained to remember something beyond the last scene he could recall before ending up in the Kingdom. Nothing came.

Jireh proceeded.

"Karae, you entered a coma from a bullet to the head. It was a random shooting on the Foothill Freeway just as you turned onto the Lake Avenue exit ramp. Won, your coma was caused by an explosion in your laboratory which created massive brain damage. Mac, an aneurysm greatly impaired your brain cells. In each case the damage was so severe that no medical recovery was possible. Each of you would have been hooked to life support machines. You eventually would have starved to death or would have had the 'plugs pulled' on your machines. In each of your cases, your loved ones have not yet been notified.

"This trip to the Kingdom has occurred in compressed time—it has been five days to you, but only a matter of minutes of earth time. Going home to the earth you know has no meaning any more. You will never regain earth consciousness. In fact, the moment I read your decisions, your earth bodies will die."

The three were paralyzed, speechless. Before they could respond, Jireh continued.

"It was necessary that you not die before this experience, for physical death seals—finally and forever—the eternal fate of a mortal. But while your bodies are all fatally injured, your spirits are still very much alive. This is clear by the interaction you have enjoyed. In the ultimate sense, you are going home to the destination you have chosen on the papers I hold in my hand."

Jireh reached for the papers and started to unfold the first one. As he did, the demon warriors materialized, faintly visible, behind each of the three. Zadock hovered over Karae, as did his accomplices over Mac and Won. And in the heavens behind them Jireh's trained eyes could see that the eyes and ears which strained to see and hear belonged to legions of angels intently awaiting the outcome of The King's challenge.

Jireh had the paper unfolded now. "It is a cross." He turned it right-side up to read the initials. "The initials are *A. M.* Arthur McNeal, welcome to the Kingdom!"

Suddenly that strange but enrapturing music which Karae had heard in the jungle began to play—a fugue, a sonata, a hymn, a lullaby in whole notes and eighth notes and rests. As the music played, Commander Modreb let out a string of obscenities heard only by Jireh. He fumed and raged and made obscene gestures, like a head coach over a bad call from a referee. From the Dark Side it seemed that the grinding of teeth could be heard, but the demon commanders held their places.

Mac broke into an enormous smile, lunged for Jireh and gave him a bear hug which threatened to crush the governor's rib cage. "Sorry for the hassles I gave you, gov! I had to pick the Kingdom. I've had too much sales experience not to recognize Zadock's phony pitch. Besides, I'm not real eager to get freeze-dried again by my old friend Gyro here!" He whomped Jireh on the back with a teeth-rattling slap. Mac was ecstatic . . . and lovably out of control as usual.

Won was intent on the reading of the next slips of paper. Karae was quiet, expressionless. By calculation she now knew the symbols on both remaining slips.

Jireh fumbled with the next paper. "It is a pentagram." He paused, as if crushed once again by the reality of the disclosure. Zadock's gang exchanged high-fives with each other, then turned their attentions back to Jireh. "The initials are *W. K.*"

Won had chosen intellect over faith. In a nanosecond, Gormod grabbed Won with his boney appendage and swept him into his arms. A mild earthquake shook the ground on which they stood. Gleeful curses and shouts from the underworld filtered up through the sod as the hellion fled with his charge into the skies at warp speed back to 2084 and Hades. The delegation watched in horror as Gormod and Won Kim became tiny specks and finally were absorbed by the infinite darkness among the galaxies. A moment of stunned silence locked the setting in time and space, then dissipated.

Karae, her face neon with the ecstasy of having made the Right Choice, started for the open arms of Jireh. In a flash Zadock reached out and grabbed her, putting a strangle hold on her with one slimy arm and grabbing the weapon from his side with the other. His face had turned to gnarls, his teeth to fangs, and his flesh to sores and scales.

"This woman is MINE!" the Serpent General bellowed, aiming the weapon at her left temple. Modreb unsheathed his own weapon and aimed it at Jireh, crouching by Zadock's side.

"Ben-David, you damned goody-goody," screamed Zadock, "you're not taking Karae to your Jonestown heaven to feed her Kool-Aid laced with your king's own brand of moral arsenic! If the Prince and I can't have her, nobody can!"

He tightened his choke-hold on Karae and tightened

his finger on the trigger of the strange weapon. Karae's face began to flush. She clawed desperately at Zadock's arm with her nails, opening small wounds but making no impression on him whatever.

Jireh smiled confidently, unconcerned. "Really, Zadock, what a feeble threat. What happens to you demonic weaklings to make you think that you have any power whatever against the King of Kings? Over and over you suffer defeats in confrontations with Him—the plagues of Pharaoh, the Red Sea, the lions' den, the empty tomb. You have won a battle or two but *never a war!* What idiocy overtakes you in situations like this? Is this just more of your blind arrogance?"

He shifted to a softer voice. "Relax, Karae, and watch the omnipotence of The King at work."

Jireh raised his right arm and shouted at the top of his lungs, "IN THE NAME OF KING JESUS, BE GONE!"

Zadock dropped his weapon and raised his hand in a sign of defiance. Lethal rays beamed from the pentagram ring on his finger toward Jireh but bounced harmlessly off him.

Karae squinted and gasped for breath as the heavens seemed to flash with nuclear fission. A deafening roar, like that of ten million tracked vehicles rumbling across the plain, hammered her eardrums. A violent, tornadic wind swept in from a far galaxy and focused its power on the evil hellion. Karae opened her eyes enough to see that it was *70 legions of angels—led by Seraph Lightning!*

Seraph sped within a few feet of Zadock and repeated Jireh's words at a shout, "IN THE NAME OF KING JESUS, BE GONE!" And just as the word *GONE* shot off his tongue, a massive bolt of fire flared at Zadock from Seraph's mouth, blasting the demon from his death grip on Karae, blowing both Zadock and Modreb away. The blast shook the articles of clothing from their vile bodies. Their screams and curses could be heard fading into the distance as they were swept over the horizon and into the dark, swirling maelstrom which sucked the Wrong Choice/No Choice people into the fiery ocean of Hell.

Then quiet.

The sky grew calm. The breezes resumed their gentle, heavenly breaths; the atmosphere became clear and pure again.

Karae fell into the arms of Jireh. "I love you, too, Jireh," she sighed, exhausted from her struggle with the Serpent General. "Since I first met you, something within me has whispered repeatedly, *Finally, a man who can be trusted.*"

She laid her head on his chest and reached her arms around his waist. "I do trust you. I do love you. I want to spend eternity as your companion. I had to make the Right Choice—I saw The King in you. Once that became clear, nothing else in the universe held any attraction."

Jireh returned the embrace, and they kissed.

"Ahem." Mac slipped up beside them and tapped Jireh on the shoulder. "Excuuuse me for interrupting the love birds." His face was ear to ear with merriment. He flung his arms around the two and impersonated Karae's voice, "I want to spend eternity as your companion, too, gov!"

They all laughed light-hearted, heavenly laughs as the huddle broke and Jireh led them arm-in-arm across the vast plain, away from the masses and the Great White Throne. As they ascended a near rise they could see the distant horizon of the Kingdom again, the gleaming sanctuary and walls of Zion on one extremity and the shining arches of Jehovah Jireh on the other.

As they walked further, Karae grew quiet. After a few moments she asked, "Jireh, was there any way we could have saved Won?"

Jireh Ben-David exhaled, sadly resigned to what

had taken place. "I'm afraid not. Won Kim prided himself on basing his decisions on knowledge, on things he could see and feel and touch and measure. Yet—and it may seem contradictory—he was also enamored by ideas and grand, attractive theories. He never came to realize that human knowledge is superficial, totally unreliable, and that grand ideas are worthless unless they are Truth. He consistently shut down the illumination of the human spirit and the Revelation of The King. The King speaking to the human spirit—not reason—reveals things that no academic training can divine. Won had to prove everything by his own subjective reason. That motivation cannot co-exist with faith."

"I miss him—I really do." The word *irrevocable* flashed through Karae's mind.

The three walked on in silence for what might have been a few miles on earth but what really was more than 926 years of Heaven time—back to 2084, back toward the Kingdom, their new *home*, where Karae's mother would soon join her and witness the ceremony of loving companionship between her and Governor Ben-David and where Mac would find personal happiness and fulfillment that far transcended the yachts, Rolls Royces, and fame and fortune he had dreamed of—a happiness beyond anything he had ever imagined.

Jireh, Karae and Mac had glimpsed the future—the Great White Throne judgment that would follow the thousand-year Kingdom Earth reign—and all three reveled in the knowledge that their eternity was sealed and secure, that when that day actually came, The King would smile upon them and wave them to the right to be received into the Heavenly City.

As Karae watched the ground pass beneath them, she suddenly stopped short, knelt, and picked up a sparkling object nearly hidden in the grass.

"What is it?" Jireh asked.

"It's gold. It looks like it was once a ring." She turned the golden object around in her hand. It was no longer a circular band. It appeared as if it had been heated in a mighty flame until it had melted into an ellipse.

"I *know* it was a ring!" she exclaimed with a twinkle in her eye as she held it up for Mac and Jireh to see.

Before them, a medallion sparkled with diamonds which formed a perfect cross . . . where once there had been a pentagram.

Biblical References

1. Jesus declared the signs of the end of the age in Mark 13. In verses 32-34 He declares that no man, no angel, not even the Son (at that time) but only the Father knows the timing.

2. This is the place to which Jesus invited the thief on the cross next to Him in Luke 23:43.

3. This is the place to which the unbelieving rich man went at death in Jesus' parable in Luke 16:19-31 and the place which is forced to surrender its inhabitants for final judgment in Revelation 20:13.

4. The establishment of this kingdom is described in Revelation 20:4-6.

5. The White Throne Judgment is depicted in Revelation 20:11-15.

6. The return of Christ for the Church is described in 1 Thessalonians 4:13-18.

7. The thousand-year imprisonment of Satan and his demons is described in Revelation 20:1-3.

8. The great war of satanic forces against God after the Kingdom reign of Christ is described in Revelation 20:7-10.

9. The extraordinary peace of the Kingdom is described in Isaiah 60:17b-18.

10. The phenomenal fertility of the Kingdom land is described in Isaiah 32:15; 35:1-2.

11. The spectacular illumination of the earth with no sun or moon is described in Isaiah 60:19-20.

12. The luxuriant growth even on the mountains in the Kingdom is described in Ezekiel 36:4-11, especially verse 8, and in Psalm 72:16.

13. The tameness of Kingdom animals is described in Isaiah 11:6-7; 65:25.

14. The promise of angelic protection from harm is written in Psalm 91:10-13.

15. The promise of God's provision of unlimited food in the Kingdom is included in Ezekiel 34:29.

16. The transformation of carnivores to herbivores in the Kingdom is foretold in Isaiah 11:7; 65:25.

17. Jesus demonstrated this ability to project Himself through space in His resurrected body in Luke 24:13-31 and in John 20:19-20, as did departed prophets in the transfiguration event recorded in Mark 9:1-8.

18. Isaiah 61:4 describes the Kingdom renewal and renovation of everything old and ruined.

19. God's provision of a dependable watering system in the Kingdom is prophesied in Ezekiel 34:26.

20. The spectacular Kingdom provision of streams and springs in unlikely places is described in Isaiah 30:25; 35:6-7; 41:18.

21. In Matthew 14:22-36 Jesus demonstrated the ability to project Himself onto water without sinking and, after His resurrection, to enter locked doors (John 20:19-20), appear and disappear on the road to Emmaus (Luke 24:13-31), and ascend into the heavens (Acts 1:9).

22. The marvelous health and freedom from physical defects of Kingdom citizens is described in Isaiah 33:24; 35:5-6.

23. Isaiah 61:1-3, the "Kingdom manifesto," describes the marvelous character of life in the Kingdom.

24. The safety and security of Kingdom citizens is described in Ezekiel 34:25-28.

25. The devastating conflict is described in Revelation 4—19; the military victory establishing Jesus' rule on earth in Revelation 19:11—20:6.

26. Jesus demonstrated this ability with the woman at the well in John 4:16-18.

27. Exodus 20:7 states the commandment defining misuse of the divine name as sin.

28. The ability of an angel to render a person temporarily paralyzed is shown by Gabriel's striking Zechariah speechless in Luke 1:19-20.

29. Zechariah 8:20-23 and 14:16 describe the global Kingdom worship.

30. 1 Corinthians 15:42-44 describes the resurrection body and its features.

31. The longevity of Kingdom citizens is described in Isaiah 65:20.

32. Ezekiel 36:24-27 describes the new heart and spirit given to Kingdom citizens.

33. The promise that Kingdom children will all be taught by the Lord is stated in Isaiah 54:13.

34. The longevity of Kingdom citizens is described in Isaiah 65:20.

35. Zechariah 14:16 tells of the Kingdom's global worship center.

36. God challenged Satan to consider His servant Job in Job 1:8.

37. Annual Kingdom worship in Zion is described in Zechariah 14:16.

38. The Holy Land boundaries in the Kingdom are given in Ezekiel 47:15-20.

39. The dimensions of Zion are given in Ezekiel 48:20.

40. The river of living water flowing east and west is described in Zechariah 14:8.

41. Ezekiel 48:30-35 describes the gates of Kingdom Zion.

42. Isaiah 35:8 describes the Holy Highway linking Zion with the Temple.

43. Ezekiel 47:1-12 describes the River of Life flowing from the Temple.

44. Ezekiel 40:5,16-21 gives the dimensions of the Kingdom Temple.

45. Ezekiel 47:1-12 gives the depth, direction of flow, and other features of the Kingdom River of Life.

46. The Issachar gate is described in Ezekiel 48:33.

47. Christ's yielding of His position and right for mankind is described in Philippians 2:5-11.

48. The River of Life's flow by the Holy Highway is described in Ezekiel 47:1-9.

49. Ezekiel 47:7-10 tells how the River of Life transformed the Dead Sea.

50. Ezekiel 47:12 describes the effect of the River of Life on the trees.

51. Ezekiel 47:12 describes the monthly fruit-bearing of trees in the Kingdom.

52. Ezekiel 48:30-31 describes the Judah gate on the city's north side.

53. In 2 Chronicles 18:18-22 God allows a lying spirit to be His instrument.

54. A seraph is one of a number of classes of angelic creatures as indicated in Isaiah 6:1-3.

55. The speed of angelic beings is described in Daniel 9:20-23.

56. Zechariah 14:9 describes the totality of The King's rule over the world.

57. The gulf fixed between the righteous and those in torment and the agonizing thirst of that place for unbelieving spirits is portrayed by Christ and recorded in Luke 16:26. The hideous character of Hell is described by Christ in Mark 9:47-49.

58. Moses was directed by God to secure water for God's people by striking a rock in Numbers 20:2-8.

59. *Hades* is the Greek word Jesus used for the place of departed, unbelieving spirits in Matthew 16:18. It is the Greek equivalent of the Hebrew *Sheol*.

60. In John 8:42-47 Jesus contrasts the values of God and of Satan.

61. The imprisonment of Satan during the 1000-year reign of Christ is described in Revelation 20:1-3.

62. The Lake of Fire is a designation the apostle John used to describe the final destination and residence of departed, unbelieving spirits in Revelation 19:20 and 20:14.

63. The choice of the road to destruction by the masses is described by Christ in Matthew 7:13-14.

64. The attributes of His Spirit are delineated in Galatians 5:22.

65. The Spirit's indwelling of believers is declared in Romans 8:9-11 and the implication that has for Kingdom living in Luke 17:20-21.

66. The Temple curtain into the Holy of Holies was torn from top to bottom at the crucifixion of Christ symbolizing the free access to God now granted through the sacrifice of the Great High Priest. This tearing is described in Mark 15:38.

67. Jesus described the broad road leading to destruction and the narrow road leading to life in Matthew 7:13-14.

68. This Great White Throne is depicted in Revelation 20:11.

69. The heavenly throne of God, most likely different from this special, white throne judgment seat, is described in Revelation 4:1-11.

70. The description of the books of men's deeds is found in Revelation 20:12-15.

71. The description of the Book of Life is found in Revelation 20:12-15.

72. The New Jerusalem with its 1400-mile dimensions, its gem-studded foundations and its gates of pearl is described in Revelation 21.

73. The revelation of God in the created order as a basis for man's guilt is established in Romans 1:18*ff.*

74. The revelation of God in the created order as a basis for man's guilt before God is established in Romans 1:18*ff.*

75. The promise that "those who ask will receive, those who seek will find, and those who knock will have things opened" is found in Matthew 7:7-11.

76. In John 8:42-27 Jesus lays out the concept of "spiritual parentage."

77. That Satan and his demons are cast into the Lake of Fire after the end of the Kingdom reign is taught in Revelation 20:7-10.

78. Jesus taught that there is no marriage as we know it in the resurrection (Matthew 22:29-30), but surely there will be relationships of righteous love and commitment!

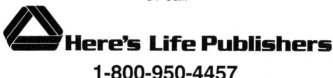